# The Reluctant Assassin

# A Valerie Stone Thriller

# R S Sutton

Published in February 2024 by emp3books Ltd
6 Silvester Way, Church Crookham, GU52 0TD

©R S Sutton 2024

# ISBN 9781910734995

**Disclaimer:**
This novel is a work of fiction and was completed before the conflict in the Middle East began towards the end of 2023. No connection is intended or should be presumed.

# CONTENTS

## About the author

Born in the midlands, R S Sutton has worked around the UK, Northern and Southern Ireland, South Africa and Mozambique. Although now living in the West Country in England, he has raced yachts on Lake Windermere, and taken part in clay pigeon competitions; much preferring an inanimate object to a live one.

When asked about Valerie, he will tell you that he is not sure whether he is in love with her or she is his alter-ego.

## Other books by R S Stton

### Stormfront ISBN 978-1913913137

Valerie Stone has two possessions, a vintage Jag and an old watch. She smokes too many French cigarettes, rents a houseboat on the Thames and keeps male admirers at arm's length. Investigating the lucrative and mostly legal, she's been a private detective for the last four years. And before that? Well, that's her business. Money has been tight of late, but a sizable pay-out from an insurance investigation could level things up, at least for a while. When a body is washed up on the south coast, it seems a straightforward case of death by misadventure. That is until she finds herself blackmailed by a covert organisation looking into the same incident. Silence mixed with misinformation leads Valerie, and those around her, into a very dirty storm.

# ONE

The sand turned crimson as the young girl lay behind the dune, exhausted after giving birth in isolation. Unaware she was dying; she gave the child a name no one would ever hear. Twenty minutes later, the pair were huddled together against the cold desert night, journeying either to the girl's believed paradise or dissolving into oblivion.

\*\*\*

Early morning sun warmed the faces of a short row of prisoners. Terrified and denied any chance of relieving themselves in a dignified manner, the embarrassing smell hung in the stillness. They stood with their backs to a freshly dug trench, some shivering, others staring blankly across the road. As it dried, yellow soil piled behind the ditch ran in tiny rivulets into the darkness. Seven shots rang out; seven figures fell. A breeze momentarily pulled at the scarf of one of the executioners as he walked along the ditch. A slight movement caught his attention; he drew a pistol. A single bullet returned the grotesque stillness.

One or two shovels of sand had landed when a call came from behind the dune.

'That bitch you lost last night...' With a red-check keffiyeh pulled across his face and an AK47 slung over his shoulder, the insurgent shouted again as he climbed the soft sand and waved, 'She's here.' The accent was thick Mancunian.

Wearing a white neckerchief, one of the men stopped; his spade in mid-air. 'Want a word with her.'

'You'll have a bleedin' job.' The man on the dune adjusted his rifle and signalled for help. 'Someone give us a hand, I ain't doing this on me own.'

Nothing was said as half a dozen "witnesses" were forced to watch the girl and infant as they were thrown on top of the pathetic bodies. There were no departing prayers as reluctant helpers were conscripted with the last acts of covering the murdered innocents.

With the last spade tossed into the back of a battered Toyota, the squad withdrew down the poorly surfaced road. Dirt spat from spinning wheels, sending pebbles towards the remains of the once white-washed houses to either side.

Returning to the remnants of his once neatly walled house, an old man shook his hanging head. 'There is no God. It's just one huge joke... only this time, no one's laughing.'

'Shush.' The woman by his side gave him a sharp dig with an elbow.

'You want us to end up like that lot?' She threw a glance over her shoulder as they stumbled across the rubble-strewn courtyard.

Once more, as most days, tears rolled down the man's face as they entered the kitchen. Baggy trousers, caught above his foot, were thick with dust, as was his calico jacket. Worn sandals, held together with twine, flapped at his ankles.

'You learn to keep your tongue still.' His wife took the last few pieces of fatty goat meat from the cupboard and mixed them into a meagre pile of couscous. Wood was not hard to find among the ruins; she pushed a few sticks into the stove's embers. 'If they don't issue anymore, we'll be catching rats.' She blew gently at the fire before dropping a little corn onto the meal.

'Rats?' The old man made an effort to laugh as he sat down. 'When did we last see one of them? They know when the end has come, when there is no point in remaining.'

His wife moved to his side, and kissing him tenderly, caressed his head. 'My husband, my husband. If you were just a few years younger. If you were just half the warrior you were, you would drive them from our lands.'

'In my mind, darling wife, only in my mind. I fear I am no use to you anymore.'

'Hush.' She looked around the home that once brought so much pride. At one time, there was electricity, a flick of a switch produced light and entertainment. Gathering layers of sand in a neglected corner, the dials of a radio were long extinguished. She took a worn brush to the floor. 'One day, they will be gone.' Leaning on the handle, she looked out on the dusty street where only a sleeping dog was at peace. 'One day.'

On the wall, a cracked mirror returned her reflection. A face once so vibrant was now lined beyond its years.

Her husband left his chair and removed the lid from the battered steamer. 'How long?'

'Be patient, beloved one.' She swept stray ashes from the hearth before taking the lid from her husband. 'Be patient,' she repeated, replacing the top.

The old woman rhythmically moved the brush's stubbled bristles across the floor, gathering tiny pebbles and grit as she went towards the door. She ushered the small pile of dirt into the yard and, putting the broom to one side, went out. In the corner, an apricot tree had a few remaining branches. Hidden towards the wall, four fruits remained. Smiling, she gently touched each swelling prize. Her husband had not noticed them. They would be ready in two or three days at most. She closed her eyes, imagining the look on his face as they appeared on top of the steaming couscous. The harvest had produced bulging baskets at one time; now, they were priceless jewels hanging under a constant sun.

2

She made her way over the broken stones and plasterwork towards the remains of a rusting gate. The dog was still asleep, flies exploring its nose and eyes going unnoticed, an occasional wag of a tail the only sign of a brain chasing better times. Laughing and playing, children were no more. Those left cowed behind their mothers' aprons, frightened to leave their, now, slum homes. Men that had sat in front of the café playing drafts had gone. Broken chairs and upturned tables had been piled to one side. As they passed teasing young men, laughing, chattering girls who had once shyly pushed each other along had vanished. The lively place had been replaced with desolation. A desolation the villagers had been told was the better life. The way life on earth should be…was going to be.

Shading still piercing eyes from the sun, the old woman guessed it was around noon and, with God's blessing, the men that had brought the horror would not return that day.

She sat by the fountain that no longer bubbled cooling water. Across the street, a piece of sacking moved to one side of a broken window. In the shadow, a woman mouthed with careful exaggeration, 'Are they gone?'

'They won't return today,' the old woman answered, leaning back on the wall. She produced a crumpled cigarette from a hidden pocket and waited. Looking both ways, her younger friend crossed the dusty road.

'Oh, evil one.' She struck a match, holding a steady hand as the old woman drew in the cherished nicotine. They passed the illicit bounty between them, smiling as they released the smoke in long streams.

'If only we could bottle this for another day,' said the old woman, waving a hand at the rising fumes.

While waiting for her turn, the younger one smiled. They both knew that punishment would be harsh if caught. Not stoning, nor flogging, but punishment wouldn't be a simple lecture.

When finished, the old woman pinched the stub between her fingers. She emptied the remaining tobacco into a square of paper. They both pushed their hijab back, letting the sun fall across their pale faces. The old woman's hair had long been grey, but her friend was young; a ravishing black silkiness cascaded around straight shoulders. They both looked down the street before closing their eyes, letting their heads rest against the arid pipework.

After a few minutes had passed, the younger one turned her head. 'How many?'

The old woman, with eyes closed, held onto the tranquil moment. 'Cigarettes?'

Although the old woman could not see her, the younger one nodded before adding, 'Yes, cigarettes.'

'Two. And you?'

'Five.' The old woman opened her eyes and sat up.

3

'You are truly fortunate.'

'And you don't think I will share them with my best friend?'

The old woman got to her feet and ran the back of her fingers down her young friend's cheek. 'I know you will, dear sister, I know you will. Maybe more will drop from heaven.' She laughed and turned to go. 'I must see to my husband.'

He was in the only place peace came to his mind, asleep by the stove. Measures from a wooden spoon divided the ration. 'Husband.' She shook him gently, placing the bowl on his lap.

The old man stirred. The start of a smile was wiped from his face as he looked up from the plate. 'In the name of God, woman, replace your hijab. Are you crazy? We'll both end up in the next pit.'

She did as she was bid and, sitting by his side, took long, elegant fingers to the couscous. She then tore a half piece of flatbread in two. 'Here, I saved it from yesterday.'

The scowl on his face returned once more to a loving smile. 'I would have perished long ago if you were not with me.'

She pushed out a gentle elbow. 'Shush,' she said quietly. 'I have not even begun to repay the debt of being your wife. It is me that is the fortunate one.'

A few minutes later, his wife carefully scraped the remains of the two meals back into the pan. The old man took a backgammon board from a drawer and laid it on a faded table that had once been rich with vivid colours. After laying the game out, he thoughtfully tossed the dice. When happy with his move, he revolved the board and repeated the process. He momentarily looked to his wife, receiving a slight smile, along with a gentle shake of the head.

'Try the café; someone might walk past.' Her encouragement went as far as opening the door. 'They won't be coming back today.'

'Yes…yes.' He got up and, closing the board, put it under his arm.

When her husband had left, she cleaned the solitary couscoussier and kettle. The few pieces of cutlery were cleaned several times, along with the few bits of furniture. In the past, it took two to three hours to keep her home in a condition she could be proud of. Now, with most possessions gone, it was finished in fifteen minutes.

\*\*\*

A frantic shout from outside summoned her to the doorway. Her friend from across the street came running into the courtyard. 'Come, quick, hurry!'

They both tumbled out into the street, the young woman pulling frantically at her elderly friend. 'At the café. Quickly!'

4

The old woman kept pace as best she could as they went down the street. Her husband, huddled in the dust, was trying to defend himself from a young man's heavy boots directed into his back. Several others looked on.

'Stop, stop!' She launched herself at the nearest one, catching him off guard they fell to the ground; feeble hands grasping at the muscular arm. 'Leave him! Leave my husband!'

Holding a hand up in defence, her friend dragged the old woman away. 'Please, please. What are you doing? They are both old. Please stop.'

Others jumped from the nearest vehicle and stood in the middle of the struggle. One of them pointed his AK towards the cloudless sky and let off three rounds.

'Enough.'

With her friend's help, the old woman struggled to put her husband on the only available chair. 'What's the matter?' she asked turning to the one that had fired the rifle. 'My husband is weak; you are strong; he cannot defend himself.'

'This old man,' said the one that had been dishing out the unnecessary punishment, 'he was disrespectful. Would not stand when asked about accommodation.'

They all were primarily dressed in black, but this one had a lime green shirt showing from beneath his jerkin. Dust clung to his beard and hair, perfect white teeth the only relief from a face fixed with menace.

'Please ask me.' She brushed debris from her husband's hair. 'What is it you wish to know?'

The old woman studied the one that had stopped the attack. He was different, detached, aloof. The side of his face was disfigured. He pushed up his sleeves, revealing a left arm peppered with poorly sewn-up gashes and burns as if he had held up a hand and arm in defence. The old woman thought it could have been from a hand-grenade blast. She silently wished the explosion had been nearer than it had. '*Maybe it would have sent you off to hell,*' she said under her breath. His hair was dirty, thick, and smelling of stale sweat; as they all did. He came from somewhere not too far away, but his accent had been diluted; it was hard to tie down.

They had come from northern, central and eastern Europe, all across the Middle East, and as far away as the Americas, all with one disgusting aim, as if thrown into a giant mixing bowl then poured into identical moulds. They dealt in death, destruction and a depraved outlook on her beautiful part of the world. Bow down or perish… and perish in hideous ways not dreamt of since the black waves of Nazism had swept any signs of non-conforming civilisation into the filthiest of sewers.

'These men here.' With a Kalashnikov propped on his hip, he waved towards half a dozen men in the back of the truck. 'They need somewhere to live until I can organise something permanent. Come.' He gestured them in front as he started to walk away from the café and a few remaining shops. The lorry ground on behind. 'Which houses are occupied?'

Helping her husband, she pointed to a gate hanging from a single hinge. Beyond was a small, single-story building. A shell-hole by the side undermining a collapsing wall. 'Through there. It's empty.'

The man stopped and confronted the old woman. 'My men are to be looked after. Which one is your house?'

The old man, limping with the help of his wife, held out a hand. 'We cannot look after anyone. Our house is damaged; there is no room.'

'I will decide.' The leader's righteous contempt frightened the old man. 'Which is your house?' he growled.

The old woman cowed at the intimidating menace in his voice. 'Here, it is here.' She pointed to the crumbling wall and the pitiful dwelling beyond.

'Quickly.' Receiving a surly response from his men, he raised his voice, 'We haven't got all day… you, in here.'

A man in his early twenties jumped from the back of the lorry. A tattoo on his forearm, of a dagger dripping blood through a Union Jack, differed him from his comrades. The old woman recognised him as one of the executioners from earlier.

'Look,' he said, passing the apricot tree. He plucked the meagre harvest, throwing three to his friends while eating the fourth.

Helping each other, the elderly couple shuffled towards their house. With the fruit stolen, the old woman had been broken. Violated.

'How can we look after him?' the old man appealed to the leader. 'We have no food.'

Entering the kitchen, the leader looked around. The young fighter finished the apricot, spat out the stone and dropped his backpack to the floor.

'Where can I sleep, Dad?' Cradling an AK-47, he kicked a stool towards the fireplace. 'I need a decent bed.'

The couple shrank back at the fighter's thick London accent. He was a Brit, full of righteousness; they were amongst the worst. An ancient empire mentality was etched deep, mixed in with building a warped caliphate.

Announcing his satisfaction, the leader stood in the doorway. 'You'll get extra food,' his voice was level… measured.

The young fighter took the old man's chair and put his feet on the stool. 'Anything to eat?' He pulled a two-hundred pack of Marlboro from his bag and broke them open.

'Only a little left-over couscous.'

'That'll do.'

'But we have nothing else. There will be nothing for my husband or me.'

He leaned back, lit a cigarette, and blew the smoke above his head. 'You'll get some this afternoon. There'll be a delivery.' He held up the cigarette, 'You tell no one.' He drew a finger across his throat with a smile, then laughed.

Ignoring the offer to have the couscous heated, he kept smoking while greedily scooping up the meagre ration. Not looking up, he asked where they had learned to speak English.

'BBC World Service.' Immediately regretting the volunteered information, the old woman put a hand to her mouth.

'Well, there'll be no more listening to that crap, will there! State-sponsored pig shit.'

Feeling her leg muscles losing strength, the old woman sat on one side of the table. 'How long do you think you'll be here?'

'Not long. We'll be on the move soon.' He scraped what little there was from the bottom of the bowl with a grubby finger. 'Nothing else?'

The woman shrugged her shoulders. 'We don't receive much.'

He threw the bowl on the table and got up. 'Where's my room? I need to sort through a few things.' He pointed to her husband, 'Hey you, old man. Bring my bag.' He slung the rifle over his shoulder, 'Which way?'

The old man pointed towards a door at the rear. Before he could lead the way, the young man pushed ahead. As the bag passed by on her husband's shoulder, the old woman deftly took a packet of cigarettes from the open top and threw it under the cupboard.

That afternoon, one of the trucks returned. Men demanded help as battered crates were dropped into the dust. As the old woman came out, one of the men kicked at a box. 'For you.'

She pulled it across the road, calling over the collapsed wall for her husband's help.

Struggling with the crate, the old man faltered, falling backwards. 'What have they given us, bricks?'

There was no sign of the fighter when they put the box on the table. 'Must be hiding with a cigarette.' The old woman tore a length of tape from the sealed flap.

They both gasped as she removed a large bag of rice, then couscous. There was mutton or goat, she was not sure which, in a plastic bucket. Oil, onions, dried fruit, eggs and spices were also turned out onto the table.

'How long has this to last?' Looking on, her husband raised his eyebrows. 'It would last us weeks.'

A rumble from outside took their attention. Looking from the yard, away to the south, a black column of smoke drew a scar across the sky. The old man sighed.

'I had hoped it was thunder, even at this time of the year.'

7

Grabbing his arm, she said quietly. 'That's why he's with us.'

'And the other fighters in the village,' her husband added. 'If it's a large attack, we may be lucky; they could run.'

She lifted her head to the sky and tutted. 'The idiots think they'll go to paradise if they die here.'

'Not so sure about the one in our house,' the old man said quietly.

\*\*\*

Just before four the following day, the elderly couple were shocked awake. 'Up! Get up!' The young fighter kicked at their door. 'Get me some food!'

Rubbing his eyes, the old man stumbled from his bed. Standing in his nightshirt, he steadied himself on the doorframe. 'What's happening?'

'I need food. Where's your wife?'

'She must dress. I will get you something.'

As he lit the oil lamp, heavy thumps of distant artillery shook the night air.

'What is happening?' Licking his fingers, he extinguished the match.

'The heretics are attacking.' With his rifle in one hand, he pushed the old man towards the stove. 'Quickly!'

Along with a little oil, the old man cracked eggs into a frying pan and then, encouraging a flame, blew at the glowing root of wood. The eggs were barely cooked when the fighter grabbed the pan and took a spoon to them. Demanding bread, he slumped into the fireside chair.

He was scraping around with a crust when the kitchen door crashed open, and two of his comrades tumbled in. 'Out! Come on. Quickly.' One of them grabbed the fighter, threw the pan to the floor and pushed him outside. Villagers, emptying onto the street, were joined by the dog. After sniffing the air, it dropped to the gutter, preferring to continue its sleep. From across the street, the old woman's friend came out, shrugging her shoulders.

'What happened? We were hiding behind the pantry door.' They looked up and down the now deserted street.

The villagers' speculation lasted around thirty minutes before six lorries kicked up a swirl of dust as they lumbered into the street. The old woman took a few steps back as an army major jumped from the first truck. He was around six-foot-tall and removing his cap revealed closely cropped, black hair. The moustache was accompanied by a couple of days stubble. The blood around a gash in his cheek was dry and discoloured.

With hands-on-hips, he looked around, then approached the two women. 'They will not return.' He replaced his cap and saluted. The accompanying modest bow was reassuring. 'Is everyone all right?'

'I think so.' The old woman's friend swept a hand around, 'There are not many of us left in the village; it won't take long to check.'

He held the younger woman with his chill, grey eyes. 'I will accompany you.'

The old woman left her bewildered husband in the street and went inside. She made her way to the young fighter's room. Sitting on the bed, she pulled his rucksack onto her lap, emptied it, and spread out the contents. The few clothes, a lighter, and a British passport in the name of John Bentley, she pushed back into the bag. The open carton of two hundred cigarettes, along with the two packs of twenty, she hid under a loose floorboard.

She went back to the convoy and handed the bag to the major.

The salute and bow did not change. 'Thank you, ma'am.'

# TWO

Beneath her breath, Valerie cursed as her mobile rang. She smiled at the few waiting patients. 'Sorry.' Without looking at who was calling, she switched it off.

The minor distraction faded, and the worry returned as she looked around. The usual posters of inoculation reminders and not asking for antibiotics for the common cold adorned the walls. Blue, pseudo-leather chairs placed around the room sat on a drab contract carpet.

\*\*\*

Jane had bundled her off to the doctors. They had been putting the final touches to a divorce report when a coughing fit resulted in blood staining Valerie's handkerchief.

'Holy cow,' Jane had said. 'Is that the first time or...'

Valerie had waved a dismissive hand. 'A couple of times. It's okay.'

'That's the last thing it is,' Jane had retorted. 'It certainly is not okay.'

She'd then closed the computer program and put up the Yellow Pages. It took pushing and bullying, but Jane had got her to the nearest clinic.

\*\*\*

And so now, after three lots of tests, Valerie sat transfixed in the chair, avoiding the explicit cancer poster opposite. The sinews in her arms tensed as the TV screen flashed the next appointment. A young girl, accompanied by her mother, got up and left the room. A slight cough brought pain to her throat as tiny beads of sweat formed on her back. The screen came to life again; a young man, dressed in a rather smart suit, left. *Got to be next*, she thought. Like the hours and days counting down to now, the horror returned: how was she going to tell her parents?

The screen glowed once more. "Miss Valerie Stone Room 4".

The shaking and sweating stopped as she left the room and turned down the corridor. Pushing her hair back, she knocked on the second last door.

'Valerie, come in.' A nurse stood to one side of the seated doctor. The shaking started again. A nurse could only mean one thing: she was there to comfort her when the bad news was delivered.

The usual doctor's surgery of beech table and straight-back chairs didn't register; they all blurred as the doctor asked her to sit down. She put a shaking hand on the side of the chair to steady herself.

With hands flat on the table, the doctor leaned forward, fixing her with his cold blue eyes. 'I should bloody well frighten you... frighten you to death.'

'What?' The flood of relief refused to descend. She heard him, but it wouldn't register. It refused to sink in. Coughing blood is only one thing.

The doctor pushed his face even closer, 'It's not cancer.'

'What?' Valerie could only stammer the single word. The information bounced around her frozen brain.

'How many of those ruddy things do you smoke in a day?'

The answer faltered as her senses struggled to reboot. 'I... It's not cancer?'

'No, you have a rupture in your throat.' He sat back, still refusing to smile. 'How many?' he repeated.

'Er, too many, I suppose.'

The doctor didn't let up the interrogation, 'How many? And no lying.' As the room returned to normal, chairs and tables, the doctor and nurse, came back into focus.

'Twenty.'

The doctor raised an eyebrow.

'Some days thirty... maybe.' The smile was weak.

'Dear God in heaven. How do you bloody afford it, for a start? Never mind banging nails into your coffin.'

On her lap, restless hands refused to calm.

'It stops,' he said.

Valerie managed to string a few coherent words together. 'Haven't had one since I... you know. It must be ten days.'

'Not climbing the walls, then?'

'No. Seemed to have something a bit more serious on my mind. What now?' Valerie put her elbows on the chair arms and rubbed at her forehead. 'What did you say the blood was?'

'Rupture in your throat. Small one. Nurse will hold your hand while I take a last look.'

The doctor took a laryngoscope and, with the occasional um and ah, confirmed himself satisfied.

'Can I go?' said Valerie. 'Do I have to do anything?'

'Besides never going near fags again?' He tore a prescription from the printer and handed it over. 'Get this filled at the chemist; it'll help with healing and ease the tickling.'

Gripping the green form, Valerie made trembling arms and legs push her from the chair. She tried to talk, but her voice had gone; a nod was all she could muster.

***

The most enormous raspberry doughnuts available were visible through the cellophane panel in the brown bag.

'Thanks, Jane.' Pushing her lips together, she threw her jacket onto a chair. Jane raised an eyebrow. 'Yes,' said Valerie, 'it's okay.' Then, raising a smile for the first time that day, added, 'It's chewing gum from now on. Or at least until I can forget the fags.'

While waiting for the kettle to boil, Jane put a teaspoon of Gold Blend into a couple of mugs. Reaching for a carton of semi-skimmed, she looked at the bag of doughnuts. 'We're on thin milk, and you bring a gazillion calories into the bloody office.'

Sitting down, she passed one of the coffees across and ripped open the bag. 'Gordon Bennett! What were these made in, a friggin' concrete mixer?'

'Asked for two of the largest,' said Valerie, 'felt like a celebration.'

'Don't go changing the fags for these.' With fingertips, she held a dripping doughnut. 'They're like homing pigeons, except instead of going to the birdhouse, these go straight to your bloody hips.'

'Yeah.' Jam dribbled down Valerie's wrist as she took a large bite. 'Right at this minute, I could eat half a dozen.' She wiped away the sticky red stream and turned her phone back on. Immediately, five misses chirped their arrival. 'For crying out loud.' The calls were from the same number. 'It's the colonel.'

'Thought he'd forgotten about us.'

'Thought, or hoped?' said Valerie. She put the half-finished pastry on the split bag and returned the call. She'd hardly had time to lick her fingers when he answered.

'Valerie, how are you?'

'Fine... now.'

'Why, what's the matter?'

'Nothing, Colonel. Just a little thing that's just been resolved. What can I do for you?'

'I'd like you to pop in. No great hurry, this afternoon will do.'

'Crikey, I'm up to my neck in-.'

'Around three would be convenient.' The call abruptly ended.

Valerie watched the screen fade to black. 'Bloody terrific.'

*** 

The only thing to have changed at the entrance was the temporary, modern doorknob. It had been replaced with brass; large, fluted, and highly polished. The small sign to the side still read "Art Records". The display of lilies on the reception table had been exchanged for blue iris, interspersed with spikes of green fern. The tight-fitting pink cardigan, worn by the woman behind the desk, was straining against the small buttons with extra effort as she rose from the swivel chair. The black hair pulled back in a tight bun, was flecked with white.

'Miss Stone.' The Aberdeen accent was soft. 'The colonel is in his office.'

To the right, carpeted stairs led down to a stone passageway. The recently painted green floor did little to reflect the mediocre lighting. The overlying smell was still of concrete. With three arrows pointing right and two left, B1, B2, B3, B4 and B5 were painted on naked walls. On the last steel door, B5 (C) was impressed on a plastic plaque.

The meeting with Dennis, the colonel's assistant, was always going to be awkward. The last time Valerie had been involved with this shadowy department; one disaster had followed another. She'd presumed Dennis had been involved, came close to killing him, and then had to watch him near fatally wounded as he was shot by someone she had trusted.

In a state of embarrassment, Valerie managed a modest smile. 'Hello, Dennis.' Wanting to get out of his presence as soon as possible, she skirted around an apology.

With a reddening face, Dennis got to his feet. 'The colonel is expecting you.' He opened the door and waved her through before scurrying back behind his desk.

'Valerie.' Colonel Thompson placed his cigar in the ashtray and put out a hand. 'At last, a companion from the last bastion of civilisation. Feel free to get your cigarettes out.' He pushed the desk lighter across. 'I always have to throw these away when I get a visitor.' He picked the Havana back up and ran it between thumb and forefinger.

'I'm okay at the moment.' After ten days without nicotine, the cigar smoke gripped her throat. 'Why the call?'

'That's what I like.' Leaning back, he started to swivel from side to side. 'Straight to the point.'

Valerie unravelled a piece of Airwaves Menthol and popped it into her mouth. The only plus about giving up smoking, at the moment, was the intense flavours and smells. She breathed in almost clean air amongst the clearing menthol. 'I'm back to working for myself. Dreary but safe. Almost.' The colonel kept up the gently rhythmic swaying in silence; Valerie thought she must say something, no matter how pathetic. 'So, I'll say thanks, but no thanks. If that's okay?'

The colonel's smile was disconcerting. 'I'm afraid it's not as simple as that.'

Defensively, Valerie folded her arms. 'Oh, and why would that be?'

'Since you last helped us out, a not-insignificant amount has been paid into your account every month.'

Valerie drew her response out slowly, 'Yes... thought that was a winding down payment. A kind of thanks.'

'Erm, not quite.' The colonel crushed the cigar into the ashtray. 'This isn't football. You don't get a parachute payment because you dropped out of the premiership. That money is a retainer. It's among the papers you signed. We have a contract.'

'I was afraid of that.' The vision of chasing bad debtors and unfaithful husbands started to fade.

'You still have the Glock.' He waved his hand as she was about to speak, 'I know, I know, it's locked up, not been used. But I do know you have been making use of the ID we provided.'

That was true. The security pass, and especially the chief inspector warrant card, had been most helpful when someone didn't want to part with information. Waving an automatic in the face of an uncooperative prat may have been tempting, but one she had so far resisted.

'Also,' the colonel continued, 'there is a certain amount of money that has not been accounted for.'

'I said that I'd taken some out for Jane and Dan. Help them along.'

'Yes.' Saving himself from saying that they both knew she had a decent amount secreted away, the colonel smiled. 'But,' he got up and touched the bottom of a picture that was perfectly straight, 'we'd like your help without twisting any arms.' He moved back a couple of feet, satisfied that the painting was as perfectly level as it had been before.

'Okay.' Valerie knew that the colonel could bring down onto her head just about anything he liked. 'What is it, then?'

The colonel went back to his desk and took out a slim file. 'John Bentley.' He handed the folder over and sat in one of the comfortable chairs, keeping quiet for the few minutes it took Valerie to read the little there was.

'Unsavoury character.' She threw the folder back onto the desk. 'But if you think I'm flying out to a Syrian prison camp-.'

'No, no. Nothing like that.'

'Glad to hear it.' Valerie satisfied herself with another piece of gum as the colonel selected a fresh cigar. 'I take it, then, he's not over the hills and far away?'

'No, not very far at all.' Clouds of rich blue smoke whisked up through the air-conditioning grid as he shook the life from a burning match. 'It's just that we can't find him.'

'So, with all your resources, you've run into a brick wall?'

'Nearly. He has somehow got back into this country. But now we can't find him.'

'This is stupid. How can I find him if you can't?'

'You have a friend.'

'What?' Valerie threw the gum wrapper she had been rolling between her fingers into the mesh bin. 'I have several, but none that would get mixed up with a piece of crap like that.'

'Not now, no. But before Bentley saw what passes for the light… as it were.'

'Well, go and see whoever it is. I'm not going to get any further than you.'

'Valerie, do we have to go through all this rigmarole whenever we ask for help? It gets a little tedious.' The colonel's tone took on its usual, patronizing friendliness.

'You stringing me up by those things I hold dear, you mean?'

'Valerie.' The colonel's voice took on a new firm tone, and she knew it was of no use carrying on with futile excuses.

'Okay, then who's our mutual friend?' Then she added quietly, 'If you'll excuse the literary reference.'

'Charles Francis.'

'What, Charlie? He wouldn't have anything to do with-'

'As I said before, Bentley was just an ordinary strong-arm before. He did it for money.'

'Now he's been called; he does it for God,' she said.

'Something like that.'

Valerie got up. 'I suppose that's all I get, is it?'

The colonel nodded and tapped his phone. 'You know where I am.'

The reply was inaudible. *'Yeah, comfortable and safe on your fat backside.'*

***

The colonel's office was adjacent to Trafalgar Square. Valerie walked across, leaned on the stonework supporting one of the lions, and pulled out her phone. The number went straight through to voicemail. She hung up and went across to Café Nero.

She was halfway through a black Americano and cinnamon Danish when her phone rang.

'Valerie.' Charlie's familiar voice was on the other end. 'What's up, how are you?'

'I'm fine, Charlie. You, okay? What about the girlfriend?'

'Getting married. Girlfriend's pregnant.'

'Good grief. Does that mean you're going to settle down and get an ordinary job?'

'No way, ain't no money in regular jobs. Kids can be expensive, I've been told.'

'Yeah, I suppose.' Valerie took a sip of her coffee. 'Any chance of a meeting?'

'For you, yes, of course. Where are you?'

'Trafalgar Square, having a coffee.'

'Okay, how about the National Gallery, half an hour?'
'A little bit of education? Suits me, Charlie.'

\*\*\*

Valerie was sitting on a marble bench, looking at a painting of a woman drying herself, when she felt a light tap on her arm.

'You like Degas?'

'Charlie.' She got up and felt his handlebar moustache brush her cheek as they momentarily greeted each other with a gentle embrace.

'I seem to remember *you* owe me a favour,' he said as they started walking along the hallway, 'not the other way around.'

'I've not forgotten.' Valerie stood to Charlie's side as he stopped, scrutinising another Degas. 'I've not forgotten.'

'Well?' He took a pair of spectacles and perched them on his nose. 'What is it this time?' With hands behind his back, Charlie stretched his chin towards the painting.

'John Bentley.'

Charlie removed the glasses and straightened up. 'Oh, yes.'

'We'd like to trace him.'

'We've gone round in a circle from last time, Valerie.' He spoke slowly, deliberately. 'Who are you working for? And don't tell me he hasn't paid his council tax.'

'I can't, Charlie, but it's official…. kind of.'

'And why you?' Charlie put his spectacles back on and looked at the last painting. 'Come on, there's some Turners in the next gallery.'

They moved casually, quietly, from painting to painting. 'Unbelievable, some of his work, the texture, lighting, subdued colouring.' Charlie removed his glasses once more and, sitting down, patted the space next to him. 'Like I said before, why you? I think it's like that last lot of scum you were tracking. Someone has you under a rather dirty thumb.'

'Well, not really, Charlie, but it could get a little messy if I-'

'It'll get more than a little messy if you catch up with this one, I can tell you that.'

'Come on, Charlie, don't leave me up in the air.'

They came face to face as he swivelled around. 'He's a psychotic womaniser.'

Valerie's eyes widened as she moved her head back. 'Bloody hell.'

'Yes, bloody hell.' Charlie pushed at his receding hair. 'Any idea why, whoever it is, has chosen you for this reckless errand?'

'Probably because he's a psychotic womaniser. I'm the only one properly equipped.'

Charlie's screwed-up face changed to one of exasperation. 'What?'

17

'I'm the one with the tits and lipstick.'

Charlie got to his feet. 'If that's all you've got, you're going to come off second best.'

Valerie looked down at her breasts.

'What do you mean, if that's all I've got?'

***

Valerie ran her hand down the iron rail as they left the gallery. 'Well, he's not going to be going by the name of John Bentley. Any ideas? And where to start looking? Will he even be in London?'

'Don't want much from a free consultation, do you.'

'Any ideas, Charlie, just send me the bill. I'll make sure you get some of the folding stuff.'

'He'll be in the city, that's for sure. It's the only place he has friends… as far as I know. Where to look? Fish market, abattoir. Anything to do with shifting food when I first came across him. Name? Now there you've got me. Mother's name, granny's name. I suppose your guys can run that one down better than me. One thing to remember, people changing their names usually keep the Christian name; less complicated when someone shouts to you. And a lot use the same first letters in a new name. You know, John Bentley, Jim Brown. Don't ask me why; it just comes automatically I suppose. My best bet, you're looking for a John Brown. You got a photo?'

'Yeah, got a good one.' She took it from her pocket and held it up.

'That's him. By the way, what's he done?'

'It goes no further, Charlie.'

Charlie shrugged his shoulders. 'Sure.'

'He was with Islamic State.'

'Must have been in the naughty branch if someone official wants him.'

'Yes, that did run across my mind.'

'I'm off this way, meeting the other half at Simpson's.' Charlie pointed towards the Strand.

Holding his hand, Valerie stood on tiptoe to kiss his cheek. 'Thanks, Charlie.'

'You take care.' He prodded her shoulder with a stiff finger. 'This is a whole pit of crap you're about to jump into.'

'Okay, Charlie.'

Leaving the square, he waved over his shoulder, 'I'll send you the bill.'

***

Perched on a high stool, Valerie had her elbows on the kitchen worktop as she trolled through the markets and slaughterhouses in the capital.

18

'Never knew there were that many,' she whispered under her breath.

She was scrolling the laptop, jotting entries on a notepad, when her mobile lit up. 'Charlie, how nice. Do you know how many ruddy markets and abattoirs there are in London?'

'Might have a shortcut.' Valerie poured the last of the coffee down the sink.

'Well, I can't say it wouldn't help.'

'His father's dead. His mother has moved abroad with another man. Not sure what she's called now. But...' He paused. 'There's a grandmother. Bad news is she's in a home and a little out-of-orbit with the rest of us. Don't know where, and she's maternal, so the name won't help.'

'Brothers, sisters?'

'Sister. My contact thinks she's married, but we have no name. You might be able to dig something up in the records. Any help?'

'Is that it, Charlie? Thought at least you'd have brought him round to my front door, bound hand and foot.'

'Dream on, Valerie. I've got a banana and tikka pizza to pick up for my girlfriend.'

'Well, that's your fault, isn't it?' Valerie laughed, 'Teach you to keep it in your trousers.'

'Bye-bye, Valerie.'

'Bye Charlie... And Charlie... Thanks.'

***

Valerie nibbled on a last piece of toast. While holding the phone to her ear, she jotted the grandmother's and sister's details onto the back of an EDF final demand.

'I'll need a car, Colonel. Can't go following anyone in the E-Type, might as well write Secret Agent across the bonnet. Anything small will do. Renault, Citroen, that sort of thing.'

'French?' She caught the quizzical tone in his voice.

'Sure, small and French. Feminine, sexy.'

An hour later, Enterprise delivered a metallic red Clio.
***

Next to a modern pub, the residential home was in the middle of a housing estate. On the large expanse of freshly laid tarmac, she parked next to the name board. The place was set over four floors, the odd piece of decorative brickwork breaking up the pebbledash finish. Looking at the sign, she vaguely wondered why it was called White Cliff, when there wasn't a cliff, white or otherwise, for miles.

The button for the double glass doors responded immediately; each

19

panel silently slid away. Dressed in a cream nurse-type uniform, the woman behind the desk produced a regulation smile. 'Yes, madam?'

'I've come to see Mrs Camberley. Old neighbour of my mother. I've meant to come and visit for a long time. Such a lovely lady; always used to give us kids a lemonade and biscuits.'

As the receptionist picked up the phone, Valerie took in the surroundings. Pale greens and pinks were predominant. Washed-out poster prints of flowers and birds decorated the walls. Although central heating kept up a steady twenty-two degrees, it was cold and desolate. She shrugged at the prickles rising up her spine.

'Nurse will show you up.' The woman pointed towards the back wall as another pair of glass doors parted.

The nurse, dressed in dark blue, could have been no more than five feet. Valerie guessed the young woman came from somewhere in the Far East, Malaysia, maybe.

'Hello.' She put a code into the adjacent lift. Giving the watch attached to her blouse a cursory glance, they ascended to the next floor. 'Please.' She held a guiding hand along a corridor decorated in the same bleak style as the reception.

Mrs Camberley was seated in a substantial high-back chair in the communal lounge, paying no attention to the daytime television. Although not underweight, she looked frail and drawn. A hairstyle that had once been one of pride was now a pathetic grey clamp.

The pitiful image was repeated around the room. The occasional male also bore the signs of scant attention to any styling. Thin hair was left in wisps, thick hair was clipped short. A life of functional co-operation in a close community was now in the final waiting room.

Valerie sat to one side and took her hand. 'Hello. Do you remember me? It's Valerie.' With a half-open mouth, the old woman turned her blank face. Valerie took a tissue from her pocket and removed a lump of unfinished potato from Mrs Camberley's lower lip.

'Er.'

'How have you been? I've meant to visit before now, but I've been so busy.'

For the next ten minutes, Mrs Camberley could only manage the odd 'Er' as Valerie wedged lies between the weather and any light news she could think of.

'Any joy?' The nurse returned with a mug of coffee for Valerie and a baby's drinking cup for Mrs Camberley. Holding the cup to the old woman's lips, Valerie shook her head.

'No, not really. Is she ever lucid, or-?'

The nurse returned a shake of the head. 'I'm afraid not. Speaks a little gibberish now and again. I've been here four years and not heard anything

I could understand.'

Four years. Christ. A surge of compassion, with more than a bit of apprehension, filtered into Valerie's brain. She got up and followed the nurse to her office. 'Anyone come and visit?' she asked, taking a sip of the coffee.

'Recently, a man comes along, doesn't stop long.'

'Do you know who he is?'

The nurse shook her head, 'He didn't say.'

'What? People can come and go as they please?'

'Sure. The residents here aren't prisoners; it's their home.'

'Sorry, I didn't mean, you know. Nice coffee this,' she said, slightly embarrassed.

The nurse leaned back in her chair and tapped the Tassimo machine, 'Our little luxury... There was another, a younger man who came in a few times. Not seen him recently, though.'

'What kind of time do these guys visit?'

'Oh, around this time, usually.'

Valerie finished her coffee and got up. 'Thanks, I'd better get going.'

'See you again?'

'Maybe,' said Valerie. 'Maybe.'

'The code for the lift,' said the nurse as Valerie left, 'two, four, six, eight.'

\*\*\*

The next day, Valerie arrived back at the home. Giving it an hour before she had come the previous day and up to two hours after leaving seemed a reasonable time to keep watch. From a corner, around the main entrance, the whole of the car park was visible.

Releasing the seat back a few notches, she unwrapped a piece of gum and tuned the stereo to Radio One. Two young men arrived but were dressed in nursing uniforms and looked nothing like Bentley's photo. Nonetheless, she photographed them and all other arrivals, and just for good measure, all departures.

After a week of surveillance, Valerie glanced at the back of the camera. Ninety-seven exposures, including delivery personnel and staff. Given the sixty-three residents, it worked out at one visit per person per month... maybe.

'We should have a small switch behind our ears,' Valerie whispered to herself. 'When there's no longer a point....'

\*\*\*

21

'Hello.' The nurse looking after the first floor was standing by the back wall, surveying her charges. 'Mrs Camberley's asleep,' she whispered.

Valerie held up a hand, 'No need to wake her. Let her sleep.'

'Okay. Hopefully having a peaceful dream. Better than reality.' The nurse pushed herself away from the wall, 'Coffee?'

After a few minutes small talk, Valerie asked if there had been any visitors and was surprised by the answer.

'The older one. He's been a couple of times.'

Yanked from the cosy chat, Valerie sat up. 'What?'

'Er, yesterday, and Tuesday, if I remember.' Valerie had left the camera in the car so couldn't, for the moment, shuffle through the memory card.

'What did he look like?'

'Like he comes from the Middle East.' Furrowing her brow, the nurse dropped another cube of sugar into her coffee. 'Why? Think you may know him?'

'Yes, might do. Would be nice to catch up with old friends.'

'No need for descriptions.' The nurse got up and swivelled a small monitor around. 'Let's see. About this time yesterday.' She took a remote control and scrolled back to the day before. Figures jumped and fluttered across the screen until the fast reverse was released. 'That's him.'

The man was definitely of Middle Eastern origin. Neatly dressed, he was somewhere around six feet tall. Jet black hair was styled into an even crew cut. A neat moustache divided his face, the nose large but not overly. A scar down the left cheek did not detract from the handsome looks. Valerie and the nurse looked at each other and smiled.

'Yes, he is, isn't he,' said Valerie.

The nurse flicked to another image. 'That's the other one,' she said, freezing Bentley in the middle of the screen. 'Do you know him?'

Seeing little to be gained by admitting to the truth, Valerie took another sip at her coffee and shook her head. 'No.'

The nurse pushed the monitor back and flicked the remote off. 'Dishy with a capital D... the first one, I mean. Know him?'

'Maybe,' Valerie lied. 'But it was years ago. We were only kids. What does he do when he's here?'

'Same as you.' The nurse once again looked at the watch pinned to her tunic as if timing the day's events. 'Sits with her for maybe ten minutes, then goes.'

'Does he talk to you, ask about her?'

'Just small talk. Asks if anyone else has been in.'

'Me?'

'Yes, I mentioned you'd looked in. Said you knew Mrs Camberley from when you were young.'

'Anything else?'

'Just asked what you looked like, age, etc. Suppose he's like you; thought he might have known you.'

'Suppose,' said Valerie.

'Oh, just a minute.' The nurse turned the monitor back on. 'Slipped my mind; there was another, came in a while back, just the once, made my flesh creep.' As if ridding herself of goosebumps, she rubbed her hands up both arms and shuddered. The scrolling menu stopped at the end of a list. 'Lucky, this would have been over-recorded in a few days.'

The time counter started again in the corner of the screen as another visitor appeared in the corridor. This man was also from the Middle East, but there the similarity ended. He was neither good-looking nor smartly dressed. An ugly scar disfigured a side of his face that had never been handsome. He was wearing a *Sex Pistols* T-shirt. Running up his left arm, healed gashes and burns were visible.

# THREE

On the third day of waiting for the good-looking visitor, it was raining. Valerie's coat was wet, her feet were wet, and so was her hair. Combined with body heat, she had to wipe mist from the Clio's glass every few minutes.

'Hell's teeth, where is this bloody man?' She took another tissue from the dwindling supply and again cleared the screen.

Whoever had laid the retirement home's car park had done a remarkable job. There was no camber; it was billiard table flat. Large pools lay inches deep on the surface as visitors navigated their way to the front door. Valerie watched a woman, supporting herself on the porch frame and mouthing easily discernible obscenities as she emptied one shoe and then the other.

'Think I'll put up with misty windows,' Valerie muttered. A blue VW Polo came through the entrance, aquaplaned across the tarmac, and pulled up just short of a row of bushes. 'Shouldn't come in so quick, should you.' Valerie smiled, then saw it was the man she'd been waiting for.

Supporting a coat above his head, he ran for the door. Valerie leaned over the seats and made use of the short time she had to take a handful of tissues to the murky glass. Starting the engine and turning the fan to maximum, keeping it clear.

'Bloody hell,' she said as he reappeared, 'he only had enough time to say "hello, goodbye".' She gave the screen one more wipe and lowered the window slightly. 'Okay, buster. Where to?'

Taking no notice of the warning signs, Valerie followed him towards the inner-city congestion zone; the charges would land on the colonel's desk, not hers.

Trusting he knew the one-way systems, she followed up and across the river. 'Careful, matey. I only come around here on a bus... or in the back of a taxi if I'm flush.'

As the rain eased, they came around the British Museum and down an affluent side street. The Polo drove straight into a residents-only bay, forcing Valerie to go past. 'Great. What now, put the bloody thing in my pocket?'

She cruised around the block while phoning the colonel. 'I need a resident's parking permit.' She gave him the details. 'How long?'

'I can get you something in a couple of hours. Visitor's permit.'

'Great, what do I do in the meantime? Go round and round the block until....' But just then, coming around for the third time, the Polo pulled out in front. 'Get it to me later. Better still,' she added quickly, 'get me a permit to park anywhere... and drive anywhere. We're on the move again.'

Trusting the guy not to go somewhere they would get pulled up, she followed. They travelled out of the city and into a rundown estate dominated by flats built in the fifties and sixties.

'Dreams of the bloody future,' said Valerie, looking up at the bleak apartments.

As the man left the Polo, Valerie grabbed her coat and pulled up the collar. 'Move over, Raymond Chandler.'

The pathway across the threadbare grass was slippy with mud. Pausing by a convenience store protected by metal doors and wired windows, she waited to see which block he would go to.

Getting to the second tower, he bypassed the lift and started up the concrete stairway. The council had begun painting over the vivid graffiti but had given up as new aerosols established prominence. Valerie followed, keeping one flight behind, checking each level as they went up, counting each landing. She was getting short of breath when he turned off. *'No more fags!'* she thought. Suppressing a cough, there was still the taste of stale tobacco.

Pressing herself into a shadowy corner, the rain dripped from a broken gutter, splashing the back of her neck. It was impossible to see who opened the door to the apartment or hear the few muttered words. Valerie took a chance that this would be the only place he would visit and returned to the car.

Flopping back in the seat, she tapped her mobile. 'Check the voters' list for me, Jane.'

Calling back a few minutes later, Jane said, 'Flat six, fifth floor, yes? Single adult... must be with kids... don't think you can take one of those places on your own. A Mrs Reynolds.'

'Thanks, Jane.' Valerie dropped the phone onto the passenger seat and looked longingly at two bottles of Pepsi. 'Better not. Don't know when this geezer's going to let me get to a loo.' She fell back against the headrest and took out another strip of Wrigley's. Deciding against the radio, she pushed a USB stick into the vacant port and scrolled through Bob Dylan.

She had begun wishing she'd bought some nicotine gum when he came back out. 'Where to now?'

Juggling the mobile, she swerved around a cyclist. 'Colonel...' putting the phone on speaker, she dropped it onto her lap, 'a Mrs Reynolds is living halfway up a block of flats.' She gave him details as the Polo dived ahead by a couple of cars. 'Can you dig up anything about her? Maiden name, relatives, where she comes from?'

As she dropped the call, the small VW changed lanes. Narrowly avoiding a van, Valerie stood on the brakes and had to watch the Polo disappear down a side road. 'Bollocks!'

Jammed between a Stobart truck and a Roller, she banged the steering wheel in frustration.

\*\*\*

'Jane.' Valerie pushed the office door open, dropping another two doughnuts and the mobile onto the desk. 'Get out to that car and pair it up with this, will you? Came close to creaming an eco-warrior.' Jane picked up the phone and then looked at the doughnuts.

'This is going to end in tears,' she said in a sing-song voice.

'It's okay,' said Valerie, plugging in the kettle, 'they're plain, and in any case, I crossed my fingers.'

'Ha.' Jane fiddled with the mobile and went out, just as the colonel called with the information.

Valerie took the call and then tossed the mobile back.

When Jane returned, Valerie pushed one of the coffees across. 'Where's that boyfriend of yours?'

'Not sure.'

'What? You two go around joined at the hip. He's not usually out of whistling distance.' She rubbed her thumb and fingers together while sarcastically mimicking Jane's voice, 'There's money in it.'

'Hello, sweetest one.' Jane ignored Valerie's teasing imitation of being sick as she phoned Winston. 'Are you busy…? Can you come around…? We're at the office... Love you, darling.'

Valerie swung her eyes to the ceiling as Jane ended the call. 'Oh, my great aunt Beatrice.'

'Fifteen minutes.'

With firm hands, Valerie smoothed down her hips, then looked at the doughnuts. 'Yeah, think I'll let you take them home.'

Nearly to the second, six feet-odd of an immaculately dressed West Indian entered the office. Giving Jane a quick kiss, he held out a hand to Valerie.

'Miss Stone. Hear you need a little help.'

'Please, Winston,' said Valerie, only imagining what the melting voice did to Jane.

'Now?' he said.

'May as well. Should get you back before Jane locks up.'

\*\*\*

Getting into the car, Winston ducked his head. 'What's to do?'

'Right, you're Sergeant Jones, and we're from the Met. You'd better call me ma'am or boss, or guvnor. Just remember not to call me Valerie or Miss Stone. Okay? Just take my lead.'

27

Returning to the apartments, Valerie had to call him back as he bounded up the steps two at a time. 'Steady on, I've not long given up fags.'

Getting to the fifth floor, Winston stood by as Valerie steadied her breathing. 'Jesus, didn't realise how much bloody cigarettes take it out of you.'

'You need an exercise bike, boss.' He winked and followed her along the balcony.

The door was opened by a woman. Her face was drawn and tired, but Valerie guessed her to be only in her late-twenties.

'Mrs Reynolds?' Holding up her warrant card, Valerie bustled her way into the hall. 'I'm Chief Inspector Stone.' She nodded over her shoulder, 'This is Sergeant Jones. Lounge through there?' She held a hand towards a door, 'Can we have a word?'

The woman's frown was deeply etched. 'What?'

'In here?' said Winston, holding the door.

Valerie moved a pushchair to one side and ushered the woman through. 'Sergeant, would you like to make us all a cup of coffee?'

Valerie sank into a discoloured settee opposite the iconic poster of Che Guevara. 'Mrs Reynolds, just an enquiry. We need to chase down a few loose ends.'

The woman dropped into the chair under the poster. 'What is it?' She rubbed at wet hair with an undersized towel.

'Mrs Reynolds, used to be Bentley, yes?' Valerie leaned forward, moving her knees to one side. Mrs Reynolds said nothing. 'Your brother is John. Is that right?' Still, Mrs Reynolds kept quiet, seemingly more interested in the tinkling of a spoon coming from the kitchen. 'We need to have a word with John, clear a few things up.'

Showing disdain for the police in general, and Valerie in particular, her answer was clipped. 'Chuck him in the bleedin' slammer, more like. Anyway, I don't know where he is these days. Okay?'

Winston returned with a tray and, after handing around the mugs, scrutinised a chair before sitting down. He smiled at Mrs Reynolds. 'It's Jasmin, isn't it? Lovely name. Where did that come from?' Demonstrating a friendly, no-hurry attitude, he leaned back and took a sip of his coffee.

'Er, mum. Our father was half Iranian; she thought it sounded exotic.'

Looking at her now, Valerie could see that what she thought was a light tan was natural. She took a breath, about to speak, but when Winston beat her to it, she sat back and let him carry on.

'Oh, I see,' said Winston. 'Don't you approve of your name, then?'

'No, it's fine,' said Mrs Reynolds. 'But it's a bit out of place in a dump like this.' Resigned to her surroundings, she looked around.

'Mrs Reynolds?' queried Winston, attempting to bring her back to talking about her brother. 'Can you tell us anything about where John might be?'

'Don't know, and what's more, I don't bloody care.'

'It's the way, isn't it?' Winston flashed a sympathetic smile. 'Life's full of people letting us down. I suppose he's a bit of a disappointment too?'

'What is this?' Jasmin put her coffee on a stained side table and reached for a cigarette packet. 'Suppose you ain't going to argue about me smoking in me own bleedin' home, are you?'

'No, no,' said Valerie. 'You carry on. Tell me about your other visitor. The guy that comes around from time to time.'

Jasmin blew out a stream of smoke before biting a fingernail. 'What do you know about Albert?' She pronounced the name as on the continent, with a silent "t". 'He's just a friend. Why? What's this all about?'

Valerie took a look at Winston, giving him the go-ahead to continue; he seemed to be more on Jasmin's wavelength.

'Have you heard from John?' Winston communicated with a slight smile. 'Bit of a worry for you, I'd have thought.'

'Don't know where he is. Still overseas. I've not heard from him in twelve months or more.'

'Did he ever send a letter? Cards?'

Valerie got up, thinking Winston might get on better alone. 'Left my phone in the car,' she said, patting her pockets. 'Just be a few minutes.'

Winston nodded.

Valerie could hear the small talk continuing as she closed the front door. Along the open corridor, a woman appeared at the top of the stairway.

'They say the lift will be working by tomorrow,' she puffed. 'And about bleedin' time, if you ask me.'

'Yes,' said Valerie, 'must be a right pain, going up and down this lot every day. Tell me… Mrs Reynolds in six.' She pointed a hand along the walkway. 'Does she have a male friend?'

Blowing her cheeks out, the woman dropped the bags to the floor. 'Why? What's it got to do with you?'

Valerie took out her wallet and removed a couple of twenty-pound notes. 'Oh, just idle chitchat,' she said, holding out the folded money.

'Idle chitchat, is it? I'm all for having a little idle chat.' She pushed the twenties into her pocket. 'No man as such, but she does have a visitor. Real good-looking guy, tallish and dark. Has a lovely moustache.'

'Bit of a scar on his left cheek?'

'That's 'im. Speaks with a foreign accent.'

'Where from, do you know?'

She shook her head, 'All that lot sounds the same to me.'

'What about her brother?'

The woman took a key from her bag and opened the door behind them.

'Come in.'

Helping with her bags, Valerie followed into the kitchen. The woman flicked on the lights and turned around. 'Tea, coffee?'

'Coffee... milk, no sugar.'

'Only got skimmed.' The woman tapped her bulging waist, 'Doctor says I've got to lose a bit.'

'Skimmed is fine, don't like it creamy.'

The middle-aged woman removed her coat and slung it over a stool. Her face was lined with resignation: she would be in this flat until the day they took her off to a retirement home. Perching herself on another stool, she wriggled a couple of times before a smile of satisfaction pronounced she was ready to tell all she knew. 'Yeah, she has a brother. Real nutter, gone off to one of them terrorist things.'

'Islamic State?'

'That's the one.' Taking two hands to her mug, she sipped gently. 'He disappeared. Oh, what would it be...? Got to be three years ago, maybe more. Stupid kid, he was barely ready to cross the road on his own, let alone go and join that mob.'

'What about the rest of the family?'

'Think their father is dead, cancer. Used to smoke something bloody chronic.'

Valerie squirmed uncomfortably. 'Mrs Reynolds,' she nodded towards the wall that separated them from the next flat, 'the mother. She's abroad, I understand?'

'That's right, dearie.' Warming to the conversation, the woman reached for a tin of Hobnobs and pushed it across. 'Married a West Indian. Gone to the Caribbean somewhere. I like them West Indies men.' She rubbed her hands and smiled. 'Could keep one of them happy, I could.'

'Mrs Reynolds.' Husband? Kids?'

'Yeah, couple of kids. Husband departed long since.'

'Have you seen John?'

'No, not for ages, or...' she hesitated, 'at least...'

'What?' Valerie took a biscuit and started nibbling.

'Could have been him, I thought. One night.'

'Recently?'

'About two weeks ago… maybe.'

Valerie looked around the small kitchen. Worn white cabinets with red trim ran along one wall. A window above a stainless sink overlooked the next tower block. A drop-down ironing board was attached to the wall, next to a door leading into the lounge.

'Here on your own?'

'Two grandkids,' she said. 'Father's run off with another woman, and me daughter's in hospital.'

'Oh, I'm sorry.' Valerie took a second biscuit. 'Serious?'

'She won't be coming out any time soon. Mental breakdown. All she did was stare at the TV and pour bleedin' vodka down her throat.'

Valerie got up and, placating her conscience, replaced half a biscuit on the tin lid.

'What are you?' The woman followed her to the door. 'Newspaper reporter or something?'

'Yes, that's right... or something.'

She descended the stairway and negotiated the muddy surround. Winston was already waiting by the car.

Fingering the car key, Valerie looked back up at the high-rise building. 'Any joy?'

'Maybe,' said Winston. 'Got photos of a few letters.' He tapped his phone as they got into the Clio.

\*\*\*

Back at the office, Jane plugged the kettle in. 'Not for me,' said Valerie.

'Sweetie?' Jane looked at Winston as he connected his phone to the computer. He shook his head as the information transfer started. 'No, thanks, petal.'

'Well done,' said Valerie as several copies came up on the screen. Sitting next to Winston, she rested her chin on clenched fists. 'Were there no emails?'

He stood back and put his arm around Jane. 'Not online. She's about as broke as you can get.'

Valerie scrolled through the few photographs of young, bearded men dressed in black, all of them armed with knives, AK-47s and sidearms.

'Bloody hell,' said Jane, looking over Valerie's shoulder, 'wouldn't want to meet any of them down a dark alley.'

'That's him.' Valerie tapped the screen. 'The one with the white scarf.'

The few letters were quite general, but each one was laced with fanatic passages. 'God help us.' Valerie turned from the screen. 'Fancy having that lot ruling the world. Get off home, Jane. See you tomorrow.' She pulled money from her wallet and handed Winston a hundred. 'Thanks, I think you got more out of her than I ever could.'

Winston helped Jane's coat over her shoulders. 'Where are you going to look?' he asked.

'Food markets were the only lead Charlie could give me.'

'Well, if you need some help...' he looked at the twenties in his hand, 'just ask.' Valerie flexed her fingers before pushing them through her hair.

'Okay, Winston. Tomorrow. Come in with Jane; we'll start doing the rounds.'

# FOUR

Winston had replaced his suit with cream slacks, a blue Tommy Hilfiger Polo shirt, and tan leather jacket. 'As we are going around markets and such like, I thought I'd better dress down.'

'Yeah… right,' said Valerie, as Jane brushed non-existent creases from his jacket. 'Really slumming it.' She pushed an arm down a sleeve of her flying coat and threw the key across. 'Here, Winston, you probably know your way around the markets better than me.'

'Biggest first?'

'Let's go.'

Fifteen minutes later, Winston swung the Clio into Smithfield's underground car park. 'You know your way around here?' asked Valerie.

'Been here a few times.' Winston led the way to the stairwell. 'I suggest we start from this end.'

Valerie quickly followed Winston's long steps. 'Do you want another look at his photo?'

Winston shook his head as they emerged into the butchers' hall. 'I think the changing rooms and cafés are a good place to begin, any place the guys take a break. We'll leave it till later to start flashing the photo.'

Between stands piled high with cuts of beef, lamb and pork, wide walkways stretched the length of each hall. Down side alleys, turkeys hung high like grotesque decorations, lifeless heads at the end of broken necks. Some of the white-coated butchers behind the counters flashed boning knives on sword-like steels. Calls and whistles echoed around the arena as the stallholders vied for custom from the passing crowds.

Now and again, the two of them had to dodge recklessly navigated trolleys piled high with carcasses.

'Some place this,' said Valerie, skipping to one side. 'More meat on display than a bank holiday beach.'

Winston cut down a passageway towards a flexible plastic doorway. He held up a hand. 'Better wait here; it's one of the guys' changing rooms.'

Two cafés and a restroom later, Valerie said, 'I think we'd better get the photo out.'

The only response they got was from one of the poultry stallholders, who said he thought he had worked in the market at one time.

'Onwards to the next one, Winston. But that was our best bet, so don't hold your breath.'

After three days, and one stallholder telling them that he did some work at Smithfield a few years ago, that was it. So, with a blanket parking permit in the windscreen, Valerie sat around the corner from the British Museum, looking at the back of the VW Polo.

She'd followed the man, known to her as Albert, just once, on foot to a nearby Co-op, then back to the Clio. The thirty-minute walk made her a little wiser. He liked salami, tomatoes, spaghetti and the most exclusive virgin olive oil in the store. After the welcome stretch of her legs, the mobile broke the monotony.

'Valerie, hope Winston got a good payday.' It was Charlie with a minor update. 'Heard from a mate about that Halal slaughterer you visited south of the river. Bentley had been working there, and someone told him about your visit, so he won't be turning in for another shift. Just did it for cash, so there are no records. But my contact thinks he's not far from the butchers. Maybe down a side road somewhere.'

'Charlie, you're a genius.'

'Tell me about it,' he said. 'By the way, you're racking up a hell of a bill.'

'No problem. It ain't coming out of my pocket.'

'Oh, another thing,' said Charlie. 'I was right. He now calls himself John Barclay.'

'No cigar, Charlie. You put your money on Brown.'

'What do you want? Blood?'

\*\*\*

Across from the slaughterhouse, Valerie sat tapping a fingernail on the steering wheel. It was reasonable to assume that although Bentley no longer worked there, he may still be around. Speculating that single workers from the same business would live together also seemed plausible. At least in the same building. Following one may lead to the one she wanted.

As the shop started to shut, she followed the first one to leave. He turned down a side road but joined the queue at a bus stop. The wait was just a few minutes before the next worker came out. The observation was shorter than before; he opened a van door, took out a box and returned to the shop. 'Blood and sand!' She took out a fresh stick of gum.

Two workers then left together and turned down the same road as the first. Deep in conversation, they walked past the bus stop and carried on a couple of hundred yards before splitting up. Mentally tossing a coin, she followed the younger. After about half a mile, two children and a Springer Spaniel jumped all over him as he opened a garden gate. 'Most unlikely,' she said, dodging into a bus shelter.

She thought better of knocking on the door and asking questions. Getting back to Bentley that someone was persisting in finding his whereabouts would only put everything back to square one.

The next evening, the two men again left work together. Following the

33

older led down a side alley and into a cul-de-sac. At the far end, facing back down the street, was a large house converted into flats. Valerie returned to the car, took a brown package from the passenger seat, and a hi-vis waistcoat from the boot.

Before entering the building, she slipped on the jacket and tucked the parcel under her arm. Two brown internal doors were the only break in the yellowed walls. A worn carpet led up the stairs from the linoleum floor. On a piece of white card, *A. Conway* had been neatly written in felt-tip. It was attached to the doorframe by its four corners.

'Looking for a Mister...' Valerie looked at the package as her knock was answered by a middle-aged woman in a flowered, wraparound apron. 'Er, Mr Barclay. I've been up and down this road for the last half hour. This place is about my last chance.'

'Top room.' The woman started to shut the door but was stopped by Valerie's foot.

'Wouldn't know if he's in, would you? I don't fancy going to the top if he's out.'

'Should be. In most of the time, ever since 'e packed 'is job in a few days ago.' Valerie's "thank you" was said to a quickly closing door.

There was only one door at the top. Not knowing what she might find, Valerie drew the automatic. 'Delivery for Mr Barclay.' She knocked on the door with the pistol's barrel. 'Needs signing for.' She had to hit it again before hearing what sounded like a hasty tidy-up.

'What is it?'

'No idea, sir. I'm just delivering. Got a package that needs a signature.'

'Leave it next to the window. I'll get it later.'

'I can't do that, sir.' Valerie leaned against the wall to the side of the door. 'I need a signature.'

Secured by a safety chain, the door opened a few inches. 'What's in the parcel?'

'I've no idea, sir. I'm just a courier.'

A hand came out. 'Give it here.'

'It's too large. Please, sir, I need to get on; I've loads more to deliver. I'll be lucky to get home by midnight.'

The chain rattled against the door as it was released. Valerie held the parcel at arm's length, the gun to one side.

'Mr Barclay?'

She dropped the package and savagely rammed at the door, then half-tripped into the dim room. The gun was pulled from her grip as a fist sent her sprawling across the floor. The man was powerful and had her on the bed, hands behind her back, in seconds. He pinned her, face down, into a pillow soiled with something she didn't want to think about. He went through her pockets. The gun, along with ID, landed in front of her face.

34

'I can't breathe, you bastard!' She struggled, but a strong hand held her with ease.

'You come in and wave a Glock under my nose, and I'm supposed to worry if you can breathe?' The accent was smooth, but not from the UK. She felt a cable tie go around her wrists and then ankles. He put a scarf around her eyes and tape across her lips. Sitting upright, she was secured to the bedhead. His movements were fast; proficient. 'Don't want you falling off the bed and hurting yourself, do we.'

She heard the door shut. For two hours, the only company she had was from passing trains and faint traffic noise. Trying to pull her hands to the front only ended in the binding cutting into her flesh.

Worrying about what would happen when he returned, was pushed to the back of her mind as a filling bladder took all her concentration. So, when he did return, there was relief rather than fear. The scarf was taken from her eyes, and the tape ripped from her mouth. She was looking straight into the eyes of the good-looking guy from the retirement home video.

'Get these bloody ties off.' She twisted from side to side. 'I need the toilet, you bastard.'

'Don't think you're in much of a position to make demands.'

Letting her shoulders slump, she stopped struggling. 'Please.'

He took a Swiss army knife and carefully cut the restraints. 'Toilet's on the floor below.'

'So, who the bloody hell are you?' she said, returning. 'Leave me trussed up like the bloody Christmas turkey.'

'Can we start with you?' He pushed the pistol and warrant card towards her. 'Police don't carry sidearms, so you're not with them, Special Branch or not. And Glocks are carried by the armed forces in the UK. So, what are you?'

'Well, I ain't Little Red Riding Hood, am I?' Valerie reached into an inside pocket. 'You missed that,' she said, throwing the security pass over. 'Now, I've shown you mine. Do I get to see yours?'

He handed her an Iranian diplomatic ID.

'You're no bloody diplomat.'

'No, I'm not, and you're no copper.' He got up and held the door open. 'Our friend's far away by now and not coming back. Let's go and have a talk.'

Rubbing her wrists, Valerie followed him down the stairs and out onto the street. 'How did you get here?'

He nodded to the Polo. 'And you?'

'I've got a car outside the slaughterhouse. You can drop me off, and I'll follow.'

'Like before?'

Valerie got into the small VW. 'You noticed?'

'Let's say I had a feeling, more than noticed.'

***

Valerie followed the Polo back into the city and parked along from the British Museum.

'So, who or what are you?' she said as he led the way through the building's main entrance.

'Let's get something to eat first.' Inside the lift, he pressed the illuminated third-floor button.

The functional but pleasant apartment smelt of polish and cinnamon. The furniture was sparse; pine chairs were seated with blue vinyl. The settee and two easy chairs were tartans. Short, hard, contract carpeting stretched up to the laminated kitchen area. Leading the way, the man pointed to a high stool at the breakfast bar.

'What do you fancy?' He swung open the door of an American-style fridge-freezer.

Valerie perched herself on a chrome stool. 'You choose,'.

'Okay.' He took out cream, salami and what looked like homemade pesto. 'Made some linguine, a couple of days ago. It will still be okay.'

He put the salami and some olive oil into a shallow pan and gently shook it as cherry tomatoes and small red peppers were added.

'The name's Mohamed,' he said, 'Major Mohamed. My mother was half French, so I ended up as Albert. Silent "t". Most confusing in Arabic, but as everyone I work with calls me sir, it doesn't matter.'

Valerie relaxed; her nod was accompanied by a smile.

He placed the pasta into a larger, separate pan, then added pesto and cream to the first. Shaking the mixture, he ground in sea salt and black pepper. After a bit of stirring, he poured it onto the pasta. Tossing them all together, he asked Valerie to pass a large bowl from the cupboard.

'I think I can trust you. Yes? You're not from any regular department. Don't have to follow the rules too closely.' He put the linguine into the bowl and spooned on lumps of cream cheese, then, tearing up some basil, scattered it over the pasta. 'Plates are behind you.' He slid a fork across the highly polished surface, then put a chunk of Reggiano, together with a small grater, between them. 'Help yourself; as much as you like.'

Valerie ran the hard cheese across the grater, then twirled up a few strands of pasta. 'Blimey, this is good.'

'Why do you want Bentley?' The major reached into the fridge for a bottle of Perrier. 'Glasses are behind you.' He dropped in two slices of lemon, followed by ice and the water.

Making the lemon fizz, Valerie swirled the glass around. 'No chance of

36

something a little stronger?' She flicked a finger at the rim.

'Sorry.' He shook his head, 'Not in this flat.'

'Why I want Bentley? I don't know. I didn't ask.'

'You didn't ask? You go chasing off after one of the nastier pieces of work on this planet, and you didn't ask?'

'I need the money, Major. Just leave it at that.'

He took a sip of water. 'You do this for money? You're crazy.' He shredded more cheese onto his pasta, knocking any clinging remains onto the top.

'Please, Major. It's complicated. I need the money.' She dropped her fork and leaned back. 'Now, tell me why *you* want him.'

'Not for the love of your country?' he pressed.

With Valerie's prodding of the lemon slice the only response, he returned to the subject of Bentley. 'As I said before, I can trust you. Yes?'

'Sure.' She swung a finger around the kitchen, 'It stays in here.'

'I'm a major in the Iranian Army. Also, I'm in the Security Service. But this is private. Why I'm after Bentley is personal. I had to come into the UK on the quiet. All I've got here is this.' He waved his diplomatic ID. 'If you went to your boss, I'd be on the first plane back to Tehran.' The major pushed his plate to the side. 'Bentley was in IS.' He stood and went into the lounge. 'My baby sister,' he said, returning with a photo. 'She was sixteen, working on a year out of school. Charity work. Before we knew what was happening, Islamic State swept through the village where she was working.' The major stopped and pushed a hand through his tightly cropped hair. 'She was captured.' His voice took on a tremor as he continued. 'Bentley seized her as....'

Valerie picked up his glass. Passing the water over, she spoke quietly, 'Here.' The major took a drink while staring out into the night.

'He took her as a sex slave. Got her pregnant. As far as I can find out, she died in childbirth. They threw her into a pit, along with the baby. When we entered the area, I pulled a few strings and got in with my men first. I was in charge of the team that dug her up, along with some other poor innocents. None of them ever did anything wrong. Just didn't line up with the IS warped interpretation of Islam. I was lucky; my men wouldn't let me look as they took the remains away. It took six of them to drag me away.' He gave a derisive snort.

'Definitely her?'

'Yes, DNA, a report came back a few weeks later.'

'I'm sorry, Major,' Valerie got to her feet, 'I need a drink.'

Ten minutes later, Valerie was back from the Co-op with a bottle of Southern Comfort. 'Is it okay to bring it in? There won't be a celestial strike through the window, will there? I promise I'll take it away when I go.' The major stood for a few moments, looking at the green tissue surrounding the bottle.

'Don't suppose I'll be cast into the fiery furnace for just one bottle.'

Valerie went into the kitchen and took a knife to an orange. Throwing three slices in a highball glass, she put it under the ice maker. Surrounded by the amber liquid, the ice cracked.

She usually liked to hold the aromatic bourbon in her mouth, but this time drank half the glass in one go before going into the lounge and dropping into one of the comfortable chairs.

'Sorry,' she said, 'I don't seem to be as tough as I thought.'

'No one is confronted with the kind of barbarism I witnessed.' The major brought his glass through and sat in the chair opposite. 'You'd better call me Albert.'

'I don't need to ask you what you're going to do with him,' said Valerie. 'I'm going to have to see my boss, see if I can find out why they are so interested in this particular piece of sh... sorry. This particular person.'

'Do you know where he's gone?'

Valerie reached for her mobile. 'There's only one person that might know.'

Albert looked up, 'Who's that?'

Valerie shook her head, 'He's a friend. I don't want him caught up in this any further than he is.' She dropped the mobile as Charlie's phone went through to answer mode. 'How did you know I wasn't with the police?'

'You carry a MOD sidearm. You work alone. And how old are you? Twenty-eight, twenty-nine?'

'Twenty-seven,' said Valerie. 'Why?'

'Your warrant card says Chief Inspector, you're far too young. It might fool the ignorant, but... And you've got a blue security card. You don't pick those up at the post office.'

'So where did you check me out, when you left me trussed up like the Christmas bloody turkey?' She moved her jaw from side to side while stroking her cheek. 'And with a friggin' sore face.'

'Sorry, but you came in like the Royal Marines assaulting Omaha beach.'

'Think you'll find that Omaha beach was one of the designated landings for the Americans,' she corrected him.

'Or whatever,' he said, dismissively waving a hand. 'The second world war isn't one of my strong subjects.'

'The Normandy beaches the British and Canadians landed on were code-named Gold, Juno and Sword. But don't ask me which the Marines were on.'

The major acknowledged the history lesson with a disinterested nod, then shrugged his shoulders. 'One of the secretaries at the embassy checked you out,' he said, returning to the subject. 'Your warrant card is genuine, so with a Chief Inspector having to be at least early thirties....'

'I was a phoney.'

The major shook his head, 'No, the card is genuine, so you have to be Secret Service. MI5, MI6 or something?'

'Yeah, that's me, "or something".'

'Someone's got you under control.' The major took the bottle of Southern Comfort and topped up Valerie's glass. 'Not very nice people you're working for.'

'No,' said Valerie. 'Not very nice people.'

She picked up her mobile as the repetitive chords of Tubular Bells rang out. 'Charlie, thanks for getting back. We've lost him. Think he got away with about forty-eight hours to spare. Any idea?' She listened attentively before switching the phone off. 'Birmingham, maybe Wolverhampton,' she told Albert. 'He'll get back with any addresses if he can.'

'Big place, isn't it? Birmingham?'

'Yeah, and Wolverhampton ain't no village.' Valerie got to her feet, finished the last few drops of Southern Comfort, and grabbed the bottle by the neck. 'Shouldn't think Charlie will call back until tomorrow. I'd better get a taxi.'

'No need,' said Albert, 'I have a spare room.' He went to a bedroom off to the side of the lounge and rummaged around in a drawer. 'Pyjamas.' He threw a red rugby shirt over.

'Welsh?' said Valerie, letting the red jersey unfurl.

'Sure. Mine's French.'

'You must have one crazy, mixed-up mind,' she said, disappearing into the guest room.

# FIVE

Attempting to focus on the bottle across the room, Valerie rubbed at the pain between her eyes. One-third of the bourbon was gone. 'Jesus.'

She got out of bed and stared at the fury tongue cast back from the mirror. 'And Jesus again.' Turning her back, she looked at the red rugby shirt in the mirror. 'Couldn't pronounce it... even the right way around,' she said, looking at *Cymru* reflected back to front.

'Valerie, are you presentable?' The enquiry was accompanied by a polite knock.

'Not sure. Western world presentable, yes, but....'

The door opened. 'It's okay.' Albert came in with a toothbrush and tube of Colgate. 'Don't forget, I'm a quarter French.' Valerie held out a shaking hand.

'Knew there must be at least one plus in being a Muslim.' She shook the toothpaste at Albert, 'Don't have any of this for the brain, do you?'

'Shower's free, next door. There's soap and a fresh towel.'

In time with her words, Valerie rhythmically pointed with the toothbrush. 'You speak good English.'

'Yes, my mother was keen that I should speak French, which I do, but I concentrated on English. At one time, French was going to be the international language.'

'Well,' said Valerie, 'there was no way the Americans were going to put up with that. They can hardly speak English, so getting them onto anything else was a nonstarter.'

Albert laughed. 'Good job an international language isn't being decided now. Probably be Chinese.'

Valerie went into the bathroom and, pulling the door to leave a couple of inches, carried on with the conversation. 'Can't see the Americans getting their heads around that when Donald Trump doesn't know what a bloody thesaurus is.'

'Breakfast?' Albert called through from the kitchen.

'Orange juice, and lots of it. Please.'

With her hair wrapped in a fluffy towel, Valerie took the large glass of orange. 'Fresh, lovely. Slice of toast? Do you know what one of the avowed aims of Islamic State is?' Without waiting for an answer, she carried on, 'To have their black flag flying above Number Ten.' Albert put a rack of toast on the table, along with a tub of Bertolli, but only received a quizzical look. 'Butter?'

'Not the healthiest of people, are you?' said Albert.

'I'll take that as a no.'

'Flying the flag in Downing Street,' he said, getting back to Valerie's observation. 'They'd be more successful getting a date with The Duchess of York.'

'How's that?' said Valerie, nibbling a corner of toast, 'Fight them every inch of the way, the old Dunkirk spirit?'

'No.' Albert poured a little cream into his coffee. 'You British are just too bloody-minded. You'd almost certainly take no notice.'

'You're probably right.' Valerie dropped the toast and rubbed at her hair. 'They'd be ranting about how we should live, and the only Mecca we'd be interested in would be the bingo hall.'

Valerie's phone rang with news from Charlie. The conversation was short.

'Handsworth,' said Valerie. 'That's all he knows. Do we go?'

'We?' said Albert. 'Are we working together?'

'Looks like.'

'Okay, Valerie. But together means together, no secrets.'

'As much as I can. But all I've been told is to find this Bentley. And I doubt I'll ever find out why. My lot are very good at keeping secrets.'

'So, what have we got in Handsworth?'

'It's not the most salubrious place. But the best Balti restaurants are in Handsworth... they're next door to each other in some streets.'

'Balti?'

'Curry. Some argue it was a Pakistani invention, some an Indian, back in the seventies. Whoever it was, it's a work of genius. If you find the train times, I'll go and get a bag packed. Back in an hour. Oh, by the way, bring my pyjamas; I'm afraid you've lost that rugby shirt.'

***

A little after midday, the train pulled into New Street Station just as Valerie's phone rang.

'Where are you?'

'Birmingham, Colonel. Why?' Trying to cut out the background noise, Valerie put a hand to her other ear.

'Are you making any progress?'

'Maybe. What's the problem?'

'No problem, but we may have someone else looking for Bentley. Have you noticed any faces cropping up on your travels?'

Valerie looked across at Albert as he took down their bags. 'No, don't think so.'

'Okay, but look out for a man, Arabian looks, maybe a scar on one cheek.'

'Okay, I'll let you know.'

'By the way,' said the colonel, 'there's been a bit of a development.'

'Oh yes?' Valerie pressed the phone harder against her ear as an announcement echoed over the Tannoy.

'It's Simon.'

'What?! What's the matter, has there been a change? Is he worse?'

'No, no. There is no need to worry.' The colonel's voice was soothing. 'I've had him moved. A friend of mine is in charge of this military hospital in the country. When I found out about your situation, I asked him to let me know if a permanent bed became available.'

'What?! I'm coming back to London. Where is he?'

'No need for that, Valerie. He's quite safe. Getting the best of attention.'

'Why have you done this? Isn't holding the Inland Revenue and Customs over my head enough?'

'Valerie, Valerie, calm down. This is in your, or should I say Simon's, best interest. He'll be getting more than he ever got in a regular hospital. They don't have the facilities this place does. Everyday muscle stimulus and massage. The most advanced brain monitoring. Believe me, he's in a better place. You're helping us; I've done this to help you.'

'Help yourself, you bastard. I do as you say, or you switch him off.'

'No, not at all. Nothing can be done without your say-so. It's still the same; you're the next of kin. Nothing can change that.'

'Why am I after this Bentley?' she said, calming down.

'He's a terrorist and wanted for murder.'

'What else?'

The phone went dead.

'That all seemed a bit fraught,' said Albert as they left the train.

'Yes, I need a drink of water.'

Valerie unscrewed the top from a cold bottle of Evian and leaned against the kiosk counter. 'Sorry, I haven't any money, only a card, can you?'

'Sure.' Albert dropped some coins onto the counter and waved away the change. 'I booked us into the AC Hotel; it's on the old canal front.'

\*\*\*

After checking in and dropping their bags off, Valerie and Albert met up in the bar.

'Where to?' Albert took a drink of his mineral water and pushed a diet Pepsi towards Valerie.

'Same as I, and presumably you, did before. Go around the meat and food markets. But I ain't going to hold my breath.'

'Largest first?' said Albert.

'That's at Witton.' Valerie scrolled through her mobile. 'I'll get us a visitor's pass; pretend we're prospective tenants.'

Sipping at his drink, Albert looked around the modern bar as Valerie called the office. 'You seem to know a lot about the market,' he said as she hung up.

'It's the biggest wholesale food market in Europe, and I come from just down the road. Well, thirty miles down the road. So, it's a taxi at three o'clock.'

Albert looked at his watch, 'Just time for lunch.'

'Sorry, that's three in the morning. The market opens at three-thirty.'

Albert said something she didn't understand. She presumed it some kind of Arabic profanity.

'Doesn't matter.' Valerie swilled down the last of her Pepsi. 'This evening, I'll introduce you to the best Indian you'll ever eat. Right now, I'm off for a shower.'

\*\*\*

Three o'clock the following day, Valerie's knock was answered by Albert, still brushing his teeth. 'Come in; I'll be two minutes.'

The room was near identical to the one she occupied. He'd hardly disturbed the crisp bed linen. The French rugby shirt had been thrown on the pillow, together with a pair of shorts. Clean, modern furniture and polished wood flooring were the same. The only difference was that Valerie's room had been silent. Albert had Leonard Cohen playing from a memory stick pushed into the side of the television. To the side, a coffee machine spluttered its last drops into a small cup.

'Wouldn't have thought you'd ever heard of him,' said Valerie.

'Leonard?' he said as if talking about an old friend, 'Some of the most beautiful poems and music ever written.' Valerie picked up the cup of coffee, took a sip and handed it to Albert.

'You'll get no argument from me.'

After gulping down the coffee that had scorched Valerie's throat, Albert led the way to the lift and out into a still-dark morning. A taxi waited under the glow of a flickering street light.

Wearing hi-vis waistcoats for the tour, they had managed to drop the attention of their guide after half an hour. By breakfast time, they had a total of two quizzical looks for the time spent. In the café, Valerie ordered two bacon sandwiches.

'Not for me,' said Albert. 'Egg.'

'Sorry, I thought...'

'The salami back in the flat?' Albert picked up the overcooked egg that had been thrown between two thick slices of white bread. 'It wasn't pork.' Sitting down, he took the mug of tea from the tray Valerie was balancing.

'Don't look,' he said, 'but in the doorway, by the servery, we're being watched.'

'Is it our man?'

Albert shook his head and got up. 'Just going to find the toilets.' As he left, he whispered, 'Round the back of the poultry stalls. Two minutes.'

When Valerie got to the corridor, Albert had the man in a firm grip. He ripped the red and white apron from his neck and pushed him towards the car park.

'Why were you watching us?' Albert kicked the man's shin. The man attempted to run as they went through the door, but Albert caught him within a few yards and pinned him to the wall.

'I think you'd better tell him.' Said Valerie. 'He's got a short fuse... I know, once had me tied to a bed.'

The man looked around thirty years of age but was thin and drawn. Unkempt, long hair hung over a dirty collar. Dark, dilated pupils flashed between Valerie and Albert. The unmistakable smell of cannabis filled her nostrils, and by his psychotic appearance, it was skunk.

'Tell you what?' The reply was as nervous as it was unconvincing. Valerie took Bentley's photo from her wallet and held it up.

'Where is he?'

Crushed up against a pillar, he could only attempt a shrug. 'Never seen him before.'

'Look,' hissed Albert as he grabbed the man's throat. He took the photograph from Valerie and pushed it under the guy's nose. 'Look.'

'Hey!' A call came from across the car park as two men in yellow coats ran towards them.

Albert let go of the man and then pushed Valerie behind a row of cars. 'Follow him.'

Holding up his hands, he walked towards the security men. 'It's okay, the toe-rag took my wallet.' He tapped his chest, 'But I've got it back.'

Following the man down a ramp, Valerie looked over her shoulder. Albert was treating the guards as old friends, engaging them in animated conversation. The man who had run off was careless. Being more intent on getting away than covering his tracks, he didn't look behind. Down along the canal, he stopped several times, coughing, spitting and leaning on anything convenient. Gripping his side, he limped up a steep embankment and crossed the road.

Valerie stood at the end of a cul-de-sac. She watched as, giving a cursory glance over his shoulder, the man hammered at the entrance of a rundown tenement before being let in.

The peeling door that had once been an unfashionable green resisted her push. She knocked. When opened, a hard shove sent a young woman, equally unkempt, stumbling into the hallway.

'Where is he?'

'Who the fuck are you? And where's who?'

'The guy you just let in. Where is he?' Valerie looked up as the bannister above creaked. A head and scrawny neck jerked back.

'Leave 'im alone.' Still on the floor, the woman clung to Valerie's leg as she tried to climb the stairs. Scraping a trainer down across the woman's hand, released the frantic grip.

Running up, she was in time to see the man's backside and feet disappear through a dilapidated window and onto a flat roof. He slammed the window shut, but before he could drop to the ground, Valerie got through. Grabbing at his collar, she threw him down.

'Where's Bentley? John Bentley?' She pushed a knee into his chest as he wriggled towards the edge. 'I'll help you over there if you don't stop squirming about.'

His heels scraped at the bitumen in his attempt to get away.

Pulling him to his feet, she propelled him towards the window and back onto the landing. 'Which is your room?'

Stumbling to his knees, he nodded along the landing. 'The end door.'

He took a key and, getting up and limping the few yards, pushed it into the worn lock. The overpowering stench of cannabis blended with a mixture of sweaty feet and stale alcohol.

'On the bed,' said Valerie as she chose the cleaner of two chairs. She pulled it away from a sink piled with dirty dishes and sat down. 'Now,' she took a fifty-pound note from her wallet, 'where is he?'

For the first time, a smile appeared as he held out a trembling hand. Valerie flicked the note back into her palm. 'Information first. And if it's good information, this,' she said, waving the money under his nose, 'has a friend.' He sniffled, then wiped the back of a grubby hand under his dripping nose.

'He was around the market yesterday, but not for a job. He was asking for Terry. Terry Franklyn. I think they used to be mates.' Wrapping shaking arms around hunched legs, a hopeless gaze tried to focus on Valerie.

'You're not just on weed, are you?'

He shook his head, 'But a joint will settle me a bit.' He reached into the bedside drawer and removed a small pouch, along with a pack of Rizla.

'Take your time.' She watched his shaking hand as the cannabis danced around the cigarette paper.

He made several attempts, spilling the valuable stash, before Valerie took it from him. 'Give it to me.' She opened a new paper, then using the remains of the filling, rolled a fresh joint. She took out her Zippo and lit the cigarette. Careful not to let it stick to her lips, she handed it across. 'Excuse the lipstick.'

45

He pulled the smoke deep into his lungs, then let it trickle out through his nose. An unsteady hand took a half bottle of Voda from the side with perhaps half an inch in the bottom. One swallow left it empty.

'Okay?' She was sympathetic, her voice soft. A while ago, she'd been on heavy-duty painkillers after an accident. Coming off them after two months had not been pleasant.

'A bit, yeah, better.' Mixed in with the forced smile, there was a tremor in his voice.

'I take it you've got no alliance to this John Bentley?' She went to pocket the lighter but threw it across, 'Present.'

'No.' Another stream of smoke escaped from his half-open mouth. 'Only person I'm responsible for is meself.' He chuckled. 'And I'm not very good at that.'

'So, where is he?'

'I don't know, honest.' He shook his head. 'I should think your best bet is Terry Franklyn.'

'What do you know about Bentley?'

'He worked around here for a few months, but as far as I know, he was mostly in London. Think he was on a long visit with someone when he was here, but don't ask me who. We're talking a few years ago. I consider meself lucky remembering yesterday.'

'Okay. What about this Terry? Where am I going to find him?' She felt a slight pang as the guy's joint burnt its way down. The yearning for a cigarette was coming and going in waves. She took out a piece of Wrigley's and threw the wrapper onto the table.

'Castle Street, next to one of them Balti houses, can't remember what it's called. Pink door, gold lettering on the window.'

'Okay. Anything else?'

'No, he's just a worker at the market—a bit of a fanatic. You know, white guy that's seen the light. Attends these outdoor Muslim meetings.' He gave Valerie a description.

'Okay, er... What's your name?'

'Billy.'

'Okay, Billy, thanks.' Valerie opened her wallet, put another fifty with the first and handed it over. 'And this,' she said, producing a twenty, 'if you promise to get a decent meal with it.'

Billy wrapped his fingers around the additional note. It was an extra hit. 'You're going to trust a junkie?'

\*\*\*

'It's open.'

Pushing at the door, Valerie found Albert lying on his bed, reading *Classic Rock*.

46

'You're not exactly my idea of an Iranian agent,' said Valerie.

Albert placed the periodical on his chest. 'I see. You think we're all under a fanatical cosh, do you?' He locked his fingers together, covering the sepia image of Led Zeppelin on the cover.

'Not sure what I think,' Valerie took the jacket from her shoulder and threw it onto the bed, 'but you keep coming up with surprises.'

'Okay.' Albert put the magazine on the bedside cabinet and swung his feet to the floor. 'So, what did you come up with?'

Valerie told Albert of what she had found out.

'I see; it looks like we're back to your favourite food.'

'Sure. They'll be open around six.'

***

With a freshly painted pink door, the restaurant was next to the only domestic dwelling in the row. The banner, held by a multi-coloured elephant just inside the entrance, claimed the restaurant as the originator of the Balti curry.

'Sounds good,' said Valerie, 'pass the time while we wait for our friend.'

'Two Indians in twenty-four hours.' Albert shuffled into the window seat and picked up a red folder. 'Hope this Franklyn won't be too long; I've got a feeling that waiter over there will be expecting me to eat curry all night.'

'And a tip,' murmured Valerie, her head buried deep in a menu.

Rather than go in and confront him, they had agreed to follow Terry Franklyn if he, hopefully, went out. But the time dragged by, and they had to drop a couple of bribes to the manager to let them stay at the table.

More ten-pound notes were being offered when Franklyn appeared. Quickly folding the money, Albert shoved it back into his top pocket. 'Thanks, a lovely evening.' He pushed the table to one side and made for the door.

Valerie swapped to the far side of the street as Albert followed Franklyn towards the city. After a quarter of a mile, Valerie took over as Albert dropped behind. Passing a green neon sign, Franklyn trotted down a flight of steps and into a nightclub.

A suited, well-built doorman stopped his quiet whistling and held up a hand.

'Members only.'

'Sorry,' said Valerie, 'my membership card.' She pushed a twenty-pound note into the man's top pocket and smiled.

'Beg pardon, Miss. Didn't recognise you for a moment.' He waved them both through then, putting his hands behind his back, resumed his subdued tune.

Sitting in a secluded corner, Franklyn was in earnest conversation with a girl.

Valerie ordered a Southern Comfort and a Perrier. Moving into the next booth, she pushed the mineral water towards Albert before taking a small sip of the bourbon. 'Well, at least the beard makes him look the part.'

'Stop shaving and, hey presto, you're a Muslim.' Albert risked a glance around the corner before returning to Valerie. 'What is it about you westerners? You think you have some divine right to put your nose into any damn place you please.'

For the first time, Valerie studied Albert's mesmerising eyes. 'This country has been at it since Elizabethan times. Even today, politicians think everyone should do as they say. We've no muscle to back it up anymore, but the idiots still keep shouting.'

Albert idly drummed his fingers on the table. 'Okay, what now?'

'We're not in a hurry, are we? Let's just see what happens. In the meantime, try and blend in.'

'Blend in? How?'

'Pretend to be in love with me... instead of someone trying not to look like the bloody fuzz.'

Albert took her hand, led her onto the small dance floor and, pulling her into his arms, they drifted around in tune to the small combo.

'Like this?' he said, dropping a hand to her bottom.

'Very good,' said Valerie, draping her arms around his neck. 'Now try moving your hand up a few inches.' Albert's hand shifted to her waist.

'Thought you wanted it to look convincing.'

For ten minutes they swayed around, now and again looking at Franklyn. Then Albert put a gentle hand behind Valerie's head and kissed her.

'Sorry,' he said, 'but our friend was looking at us.'

Valerie drew back just far enough to focus on his face. 'That's all right.' Her reply was soft and made without any connection to the reason they were there.

Back at the table, they could only watch as the talk in the corner was in whispers. Valerie shrugged her shoulders. 'I think keeping an eye on him is all we can do at the moment.'

Looking out of place, a slim woman, around fifty, came across the room and slid in beside Franklyn and the girl. The two women shared high cheeks and the slight bump of a Roman nose. With their similar poise, Valerie guessed them, mother and daughter.

'And where do they fit in? said Albert. 'If anywhere.'

Valerie pursed her lips. 'Just hope no one else turns up. We can't follow more than two.'

Valerie pushed Albert as, half an hour later, the two women got up. 'You take the older one.'

'Oh?' said Albert.

'Okay, *I'll* take the older one.'

Two streets later, the older woman entered another tenement.

Giving it a minute Valerie crossed over.

Ringing the bell brought a scruffy man to the door. His unkempt, greasy hair hung over a grubby collar. Only when he had finished stuffing shirttails into shapeless trousers did he look up. 'Yeah?' A cigarette stub clung to a pouty bottom lip.

'Rooms?' said Valerie. 'Someone told me you might have a room to rent.'

'Oh, yeah?' He pulled green braces from around his waist, snapping them over his shoulders. 'And who might that someone be?'

'Terry. Don't know his other name. Got a beard, met him down the market.'

Ogling Valerie's breasts, the man scratched at his grey stubble. 'You'd better come in. You don't seem the type that wants a fleapit to live in.'

'It's what you make it,' said Valerie, looking up the stairwell. 'As long as the money's right.'

Shuffling along in his down-at-heel slippers, the man took a small plastic tub from a side table.

'Got one on the second floor. Room six.' Pressing the container against his chest, he prised the top away and pushed a stubby finger around the contents. 'You can find your own way.' He handed over a Yale-type key.

'The lady that just came in, Mrs... er, I've forgotten her first name.'

'Sally, room four, same floor.'

'That's it, Sally. Thanks.'

Valerie opened room six before knocking on four. 'Sally?' she said as the woman she recognised from the club peered around the door. 'Wonder if you can help?' With a look of slight aggravation, the woman said nothing. 'What's it like here? I've just been looking at number six.'

'It's a doss house. What do you think it's like?'

'I know, I know,' said Valerie. 'But I work long hours and need somewhere quiet when I'm off.'

'On the game, are you?' The woman stopped leaning on the door and came onto the landing. 'Can't say you look the type.'

Valerie kept quiet, but mostly from being unsure where to go next with the conversation. There was no point scaring away any help, no matter how tenuous.

'But you're not, are you?' Staring at Valerie, the woman spoke slowly. 'There's no way you'd be shoved up against some backstreet wall having the skin scraped from your arse... and certainly not for a couple of

49

tenners.'

'I need to find someone.'

'That's better. But you've not just put a pin in a map of the Midlands and landed on this shit-heap.'

'Not just floated up the Worcester Canal on a tea tray, have you?' said Valerie, craving a cigarette for the second time that day.

'So how about being honest?'

'It is Sally, yes?'

The woman nodded.

Valerie shut the door to room six and followed Sally into her place. The small bed-sit was immaculate. The furniture was worn, as was the kitchen equipment, but everywhere was spotless.

'Well?' said Sally, pointing to a chair.

'I'm looking for a guy called Bentley, but he's probably changed that to Barclay. John Barclay.'

'Like the bank,' said Sally, pouring boiling water into a couple of mugs. 'Sugar?'

Valerie shook her head, 'Just milk, please.'

'And why do you want this Bentley or Barclay?'

'I'd rather not say at the moment, Sally.' Valerie took the mug and blew gently across the top.

'You the police?' Once again, Sally scrutinised Valerie. 'No,' she said slowly, 'you're not the bogies.' Valerie accepted a coaster and put her mug down.

'He's a nasty piece of work.'

Only looking up now and again, Sally sat quietly, sipping at her coffee.

'What I'm doing is above board,' said Valerie. 'You'd not be getting into any trouble. As a matter of fact—'

'Above board, is it? That's a very genteel way of talking. Are you sure you're not into something over your head?'

'You could very well be right,' said Valerie, thinking it was rapidly looking like she *was* out of her depth for a second time. 'So, do you know him?'

'Just like that. You walk in, and I'm supposed to… I'm supposed to what? I don't even know your name.'

'Valerie Stone. You know him, don't you?'

'Maybe. But why should I tell you anything?'

'He's responsible for the death of a young girl.'

Sally went over to the kitchenette and ran a cloth around the sink. 'My daughter used to know him a few years ago. He was a bit of a lad, spreading it about, but there was no telling her. She was in love.' Sally tutted before carrying on. 'She'd be waiting outside the flicks, and he'd be in bed with some tart. Tried to put her straight, but she'd always believe his stories…

50

working late, looking after his mother.'

'His mother is around here?'

'Was she hell as like. Lived in London. But my daughter wouldn't have it. He was only in Brum a few months. When he went back down south, she would visit him any time she could. Now he's been in contact again. She called me. I've just been to meet with her.'

'Along with Terry Franklyn,' said Valerie.

'Yes. How did you know?'

'I need to find him, Sally. He's going to hurt more people, and probably sooner rather than later.'

'Well, you're going to have to tell me who you are. I'm not going to go any further without a good reason. You reckon more people are going to get hurt. I don't want it starting with me and my daughter.'

Valerie took the security pass from her wallet and handed it across. 'Have you somewhere you can go? You and your daughter. Somewhere where he won't find you?'

Sally shook her head, 'Look around,' she said, handing the ID back, 'I ain't no high flyer.'

'Have you or... What's your daughter's name?'

'Jennifer, Jenny.'

'Have either of you got a job, somewhere you're expected?'

'No. Why?'

'You're going to disappear.' Valerie pulled out her phone and called the colonel.

'Where?' asked Sally when Valerie had finished.

'They'll let you know when you're on your way. Not before.' Valerie finished her coffee and handed the mug back. 'We need to speak to Jenny.'

'I don't know where she'll be at the moment, and she's out of credit on her phone... for a change.'

'I know where she is.' Valerie called Albert and then relayed the details of a twenty-four-hour McDonald's to Sally. 'You know where this place is?'

Sally nodded.

'Okay,' Valerie got to her feet, 'fill a bag and grab your coat. And shut everything off; you're not coming back. At least, not for a while.'

*\*\*\**

Valerie and Sally managed to avoid Jenny seeing them as they joined Albert at a corner table. 'Strawberry shake?' said Valerie, noting the drink between Albert's hands. 'We'll have you westernised yet.'

Albert rose from the chair and offered his hand as Valerie introduced him to Sally. 'She's been here for the past hour, just came straight from the club.'

Sally took in Albert's rugged looks. 'I take it you two are from the same place?'

'Yes,' interrupted Valerie before Albert could say anything. 'We've been ordered to take Bentley into custody, then our job's done. We let the authorities sort it out. Better get something to eat; we'll stick out a bit with just the one drink between the three of us.'

Valerie punched an order into the auto menu and went to the counter. The restaurant was all but deserted, the staff outnumbering customers two-to-one. The service was quick. She was soon on her way back with the burgers and Coke when the side door opened. Expecting that it would be Franklyn if anyone, she was taken by surprise.

'Albert!' she screamed, throwing the tray to one side as she ran towards Jenny's table, 'It's Bentley!'

Albert jumped to his feet. 'Stay here.' He propelled Sally back into the seat as she tried to follow.

Yanking Jenny by her wrist, Bentley pulled a table into Valerie's path as they dashed towards the side door. Outside, he thrust a bin between the door and a safety post. Albert gave the jammed door a shove with his shoulder. It yielded only inches. Valerie turned and made for the front entrance, only to see them running away from the city centre.

Dodging the late-night traffic, she sprinted across the road. Pulling and swearing at Jenny, Bentley led the way down a dimly lit alley. Valerie kept them in sight as she avoided refuse sacks and the odd bicycle. She instinctively ducked as a gunshot rang out. The bullet broke open several black bin liners, spilling rubbish onto the cobbles.

Her Glock was left in its holster; with Jenny by Bentley's side, and the danger of a bystander being hit, drawing it was too much of a risk. Valerie caught up just as Jenny tripped and held onto Bentley's leg. Holding his arm and gun skywards, he kicked out as Valerie grabbed his wrist.

Struggling with the two women who wanted different things, Bentley thumped Valerie across the neck and kicked again at the anchor around his leg. Losing his footing he fell against the wall. 'Get off, you stupid cow!'

Valerie kicked him in the groin, then landed, knee first, on his chest as he fell to the ground. She ripped the automatic from his clenched fist and threw it along the alley.

Jenny grabbed Valerie around the neck and pulled her away. 'Get off him!'

'I'm trying to save you, you stupid bitch!'

Bentley hit out again, making Valerie gasp for breath as he caught her beneath the breasts. Getting to his feet, he took a final kick at Jenny and rushed out of the alley just as Albert caught up.

'Round to the right,' Valerie shouted, then laid back against the wall, taking large gulps of air. 'You're a right idiot,' she said, turning to Jenny.

'He's the biggest piece of scum *you're* ever likely to come across.'

They were still arguing when Albert came back. 'Lost him.' Hands on knees he bent over. 'God, he can run. I thought I was fit.'

'Yeah, well,' said Valerie, accepting his hand to get up, 'he's got an incentive to run, hasn't he.'

'So have I.'

Still regaining his breath, Albert led the way back to the McDonald's. Valerie put in a second order and told Albert to take Jenny into a quiet corner and educate her on Bentley's history.

'What's that all about?' asked Sally as Valerie placed fresh fast-food on the table.

I'll tell you about it later. For now, leave Jenny with him. If *he* can't persuade her, no one can.'

\*\*\*

'It's not true,' said Jenny, returning next to her mother.

Before eating a couple of thin fries, Valerie prodded them towards Jenny. 'If you think Albert here has come all this way just because your boyfriend nicked a couple of Rial....'

'What?'

'Miss Stone is having a little joke,' said Albert. 'The Rial is Iran's currency, and there's somewhere around fifty thousand to the pound. But she's right; I wouldn't come all this way for nothing.' He shuffled through the burgers and picked up the spiciest. 'So, you have to decide. Are you going to believe me or—?'

'Or,' butted in Sally, 'take the word of someone who makes a date for the cinema, then stays in bed with some bloody scrubber?'

'I know it hurts,' Valerie pushed more fries into the barbeque dip, 'but this guy is bloody dangerous. We need to get him into the right hands.'

Albert got to his feet. He took Valerie's hand. 'Have a word with your mother while us two go for a walk around the block.' Valerie grabbed a Coke and straw as she was gently guided to the door.

'What's that all about?' she asked when they were outside.

'If,' said Albert, looking through a Tommy Hilfiger window, 'she takes little or no notice of what I say... she may, just may, listen to her mother.'

'Psychological approach, is it?'

'Maybe. Her mother will tell her about the times he let her down and the rumours from friends. Things of which we know nothing. Anyway, ten minutes won't hurt, then we'll find out if it's worked or not.' He took Valerie's hand and escorted her across the road.

If Valerie had been asked, she could not have given any reason other than it felt warm and protective. But she did not release his hand until they returned to the restaurant.

'Okay, it may be reluctantly,' said Sally, 'but she'll answer anything you want to know.'

***

Along with Albert, Valerie ushered the two women into her hotel room.

'So where will he be now?' Valerie handed coffees around and then sat on the bed end.

'He won't be in Birmingham anymore.' Sally nudged her daughter, urging her to carry on. 'He'll be on his way back south, and I don't think it'll be anywhere but London. He's got no friends anywhere else.'

Albert leant forward and took Jenny's hand. 'Any ideas where Jenny?'

'I can give you a couple of addresses, but....' She shrugged her shoulders.

'I know,' he said, getting up, 'no guarantees. Give Valerie the details; I'm going out for a while.'

Knowing where he was off to, Valerie only raised her eyebrows in resignation. Two of them would be pointless, and besides, Albert looked a lot more frightening.

When she'd been given the little information available, Valerie told them to stay. 'I don't think it's necessary anymore, but there'll be a car along soon. Get whatever Jenny needs and just go with the two men. You'll be quite safe.'

# SIX

Valerie focused bleary eyes on her watch as Albert gave her a shake.

'Tea?' He put a cup on the side table and switched on the radio.

'Are you just back?' She pushed herself up.

He shook his head, 'No, earlier, but guessed you'd be whacked, so I let you sleep on for a while.'

'Crikey, Albert, we need to get going.' He gently placed a hand on her shoulder, preventing her from rising.

'No need. I think I now know where he's headed.' He nodded towards the rugby shirt she was wearing, 'You like it, then?'

'Albert, for goodness' sake, where is he? And what about Franklyn? He'll warn him.'

'All under control. I've ordered a late breakfast. Get showered, and I'll see you downstairs. Tell you about it then.'

***

The last few customers were finishing breakfast as Valerie weaved between polished tables illuminated by low-slung lighting. A single waitress dusted and rearranged black leather chairs.

Albert had not changed his preference for corner tables; he was beneath a cluster of pictures that left little of the magnolia wall visible. Sliding in next to him, Valerie pushed a hand through still-damp hair.

'I suppose, as you're not in a blind panic, then neither should I be.' She picked up a slice of toast and peeled the top from a marmalade portion. 'Well?'

'I managed to see his friend, Franklyn.' Albert speared the remains of a tomato with his fork. 'By the way, they were closing the kitchen, so I guessed that you're a scrambled egg and bacon person.'

'Smoked bacon?'

'Of course.' He waved for the waitress's attention.

'And coffee,' added Valerie before turning to Albert. 'Sorry, but I only drink tea in an emergency.'

'First of all,' said Albert, 'Franklyn is being entertained by friends of mine at the embassy.' He shook his head as Valerie frowned, 'It's okay, just got him somewhere safe until this is all over. Nobody will hurt him; just keep him on ice.'

'Thank the chef,' said Valerie as the waitress arrived.

'Madam?' Butter oozed from the pale-yellow mixture as she pushed it with a fork.

'Yes, he didn't make it twenty minutes ago and leave it under the heater.

It's fresh, and the bacon, too.' She cut a small slice. 'Tell him thanks.'

Wrinkling her nose, the waitress left the table.

'I think the idea that she'd bring you something heated up was a bit of an insult,' said Albert.

'Come on, give.' Valerie scooped up a small mound of egg and balanced it on the back of her fork. 'Where is he?'

'You try to hide it,' said Albert, looking at the fork, 'but you're quite an elegant lady.'

'What?'

'You try to be cold, pretend you're hard, but you're not.' He pushed his empty plate to one side. 'I only see the real you when your brain's not buzzing.'

'I do believe you're making a pass at me.'

'You think so?' Albert smiled. 'Well, maybe I am.'

Valerie stopped thinking about Bentley and began to study the man sitting next to her. The thin scar on his cheek must have been made recently; it had not mellowed. Unusual for someone from where he came, his eyes were not brown but grey, a cold grey, evidently from being quarter European. His black hair was not coarse; again, from not being one-hundred per cent Iranian, she thought. The moustache was de rigour; he would be incomplete without it. When he leaned forward, his shirt sometimes opened between buttons, revealing thick, curly hair. She was being drawn in.

'What are you thinking?' he asked.

She was abruptly pulled back. 'Bentley. Are you going to tell me where he is, or is it a guessing game?'

'He's leaving or left Birmingham. Making for London.'

'We're back to searching the metropolis,' said Valerie. 'Did you get an idea, from Franklyn, where?'

Albert shook his head, 'We might as well chase smoke.'

'So?'

'We wait until he gets to where he's going. Then we have a better chance.'

'Albert, you're infuriating.' She playfully struck his arm. 'Where?'

'Marseille.'

'Marseille?' Valerie put a cup that was halfway to her lips, back on the saucer. 'Why in God's name Marseille?'

'Because he's clever. He's breaking up his journey, shaking off anyone that might be after him.'

'To?'

'Italy, then North Africa, Libya and down into central Africa.'

'Joining up with insurgents.'

'Yes.' Stifling a yawn, Albert got up and stretched his back. 'I guess we've got about a week in London to sort ourselves out, then the south of France.'

'Why a week?' said Valerie, following him out.

'Because he's no passport. He'll have to get something to travel on.'

'That's not going to be easy. I mean a passport.'

Albert slowly stretched out her name, 'Valerie. Come on.'

'What, it's easy?'

'No. As I said, we've about a week.'

*** 

For the second time that day, Albert woke Valerie. This time with a gentle tap on the head with a copy of *Private Eye*.

'We'll be pulling into Euston; fifteen minutes.'

'Sorry, all I seem to do is sleep... nothing personal.'

'I've just had a call from the embassy. Someone important is flying in tomorrow, and they've put him in the flat. I need to find somewhere. Any ideas?'

Valerie yawned and took a Tic Tac from the box in her pocket. 'As long as you don't cut your toenails in the kitchen, you can stay with me.' Albert shoved the magazine into his grip and drooped a scarf around his shoulders.

'Are you sure?'

'You want me to change my mind?'

'They need the Polo back as well.'

'Oh dear,' Valerie ran the back of her hand down his cheek, 'you poor, abandoned secret agent. When we get in, I'll have to go to the office.' She took a couple of keys and gave one to Albert, then folding back a page of his magazine, wrote down her address. 'It's the first houseboat in a row of four. Make yourself at home. Your room is the first in the passageway to the stern.'

'The first?'

'Yes,' said Valerie firmly. 'The first.'

*** 

The colonel was busy when Valerie arrived.

'He shouldn't be more than ten minutes.' Trying to ignore her, Dennis carried on making notes between tapping the keyboard on his desk. 'Take a seat.'

'Oh God, Dennis, this is stupid. I'm sorry. Okay?'

Dennis dropped the pencil. 'Tell me,' he said. 'Back on the river bank. Would you have pulled the trigger, blown my brains out, if Simonds hadn't

58

come along?'

'Of course not. I was just so riled up. I wanted to get to the truth. There was no way I would have killed you, not in cold blood. I couldn't do that.'

He wasn't going to get an honest answer, mostly because she didn't know herself.

'Not what I heard. The one out on the fort, you blew him to bits.'

'Christ, Dennis, that was different. He was just about to rape me. Hardly what you'd call killing in cold blood.'

Dennis's intake of breath was stopped by the intercom. Valerie got up and held the door to one side as a woman backed out, carrying a pile of box files.

'Valerie,' the familiar voice rolled out. 'Well, what have you come to tell me? Is Bentley behind bars?'

Although some pictures had been changed, the colonel's office still looked like a gentleman's club. She sank into the brown leather chair opposite the man twiddling his cigar.

'You know he's not,' she said, secreting a piece of Nicorette in a tissue.

'So, what's to report, if anything?'

'He scurried off to Birmingham, then scurried back.'

'And that's it?'

'I had him by the arm.'

'What, and let him get away?'

'I had a feeling that wouldn't count,' she said, relating the chase down the alleyway.

'You had his gun?' A look of exasperation crossed the colonel's face.

'You're the one that wants him alive.'

To one side, a drinks cabinet stood under a rather nice Chagall. 'Wouldn't say no to some of your perks.' She poured mineral water into a heavy bottom glass and took a sip. 'I could have shot him, I suppose, but in the middle of the mayhem, working out what you wanted in two seconds....' Sitting back down, she left the rest unsaid.

'So, where is he now?'

'Here somewhere, but we'll not find him; he's on his way to southern France.'

The colonel picked up one of the two phones on his desk and gestured towards the door, 'Give me a few minutes, will you, Valerie.'

'What's all that about?' she said, trying to put some normality back into her relationship with Dennis, 'Wanting me out while he makes a call?'

'He'll be consulting with others on what to do next. He doesn't want you in on it while they're making decisions.' Dennis put his work to one side. 'I'm afraid you're going to be in this for quite a while.'

'What, this case? The guy's off out of the country. That's where my job ends.'

'I wouldn't be so sure of that. The colonel wants Bentley, and you're the one who seems to have the magic touch. He won't let you go. And as for getting out after, I'm not sure that is going to happen either. He may not show it but, after the last job and running this guy down so fast this time, you're his golden girl.'

A few minutes later, the colonel called her back in.

'Before you say anything, I want to know where Simon is.'

'Absolutely, no problem.' The colonel pulled a piece of headed notepaper from a tray and handed it over. 'He's in a wing at a military hospital.'

Valerie picked up the paper. 'We'll talk when I've seen him.'

***

The driveway was straight, maybe five hundred yards, and ran between a line of beech trees. Valerie slowed the E-Type pulled to one side halfway along and got out. Across a wheat field, a sizeable eighteenth-century building faced the afternoon sun. The ritual never varied. Before every visit, she stopped to gather her thoughts, each time hoping that this would be the day the courage could be found to tell the carers to cease the medication and let him die.

Ten minutes passed, this time without nicotine. She slid back into the seat and pressed the starter. The tarmac gave way to a gravel surround on which a dozen or so cars were parked. Leaning on the back of an ambulance a paramedic, enjoying a cigarette, watched as Valerie threaded her legs from the Jag.

Two columns stood to either side of an entrance that led to a pair of glass and mahogany doors. Inside, a small signpost stood on a black and white chequered floor. Valerie followed the relevant finger to inquiries. The man behind the desk had a thin, undernourished, almost sickly look. Like something out of a Dickensian novel, squinting eyes peered out below raised eyebrows.

As it was a military hospital, Valerie took out her security pass.

'I've come to visit Mr Stone.'

He was expecting her. 'Room three.' As if in short supply, he kept words to a minimum. 'Name's on the door.'

With loafers that felt like divers' boots, she climbed the broad stairway. At the top, the room number was to her left on the open landing. Again, as on the driveway, Valerie stopped. This time, instead of looking out across a field of yellow, she was staring at her husband's name. The decision to open the door or wait a minute was taken for her as a nurse came out.

'Mrs Stone, we received a call you were on your way.' She held the door. 'Please. Mr Stone's looking well.'

He had been in brain-damaged oblivion for four years and the puerile remark aggravated. But on seeing Simon, she was surprised. He was still in a coma, and the same medication was being intravenously provided. But he looked that, at any moment, he might open his eyes.

It had been in the last few months that she realised she was visiting no longer out of love but through a sense of duty. The stopping before each visit had been to pull herself up from the depths, a way of getting through. Now she had started being honest with herself because she no longer wished to be there. His personality was fading into the mist.

'He *does* look better,' said the nurse. 'Better than when he arrived.'

Valerie cleared her mind and looked up. The nurse wore an older style uniform, complete with a silver butterfly buckle on a tightly fitting belt. She had the look of someone from a bygone age. Blond hair pulled back in a short ponytail. Bright lipstick surrounded perfect teeth. And, as if supplied with the job, sparkling blue eyes.

'Yes, he is,' she said softly. Her brain suddenly snapped back to the present. 'Sorry, I just remembered I have an appointment. I'll call back in a few days.'

Valerie left the room with undue haste, trotting down the stairs. Holding the back of a fist to her lips, she ran into the car park. Standing still and closing her eyes, she breathed deeply.

In the hour it took to get back to the houseboat, her mind tumbled around. Something had changed. She was a step further away from the man she had loved.

\*\*\*

'What's that I can smell?' Valerie pulled the key from the houseboat lock that was reluctant to let go. She threw her jacket onto a hook and went into the galley.

Albert smacked at her fingers as she pinched a dried apricot. 'Lamb tagine over there.' He pointed a knife at the stovetop. 'Couscous in the steamer.'

'Steamer? Hope you chipped the rust off first?'

'Yes, I did observe that only the most basic utensils have had an outing. Anything slightly on the technical side is still in boxes.'

'Albert.' Valerie thoughtfully stretched out his name then sat on a stool, sucking at the plundered fruit. 'Have you ever been in love? I don't mean sex, having a good time and liking someone a lot,' she added quickly, 'but the real thing? Crawl over broken glass, lay down your life love?'

'That's a big question to come straight off the street with. What's brought that on?'

'Have you?'

Albert looked out from the small porthole and started chopping a pile of mint leaves.

'Careful,' said Valerie, 'you'll have your fingers off.'

'Don't worry, my fingers will stay where they're supposed to be. Taught by mother. Remember I told you she was half French.' He stopped and looked straight into her eyes, 'Have *you*? I mean, the real thing?'

'I asked first,' Valerie retorted.

'The real "crawl over broken glass for someone" love? Oh yes. Just once.' Albert upturned the couscous into a vivid red and yellow bowl, then poured the tagine over the top. He gently heated some pine seeds in a shallow pan and sprinkled them with the mint leaves over the dish. 'I've laid the table and put one of your bottles of wine in the fridge.'

'No, it's okay,' said Valerie, 'I'll have water with you.'

After complimenting him on the food, they ate in silence until Albert spoke.

'And you?'

Although knowing what he meant, Valerie grabbed a short respite by feigning ignorance. 'What?'

Albert shuffled a little tagine onto his fork and gave her a look devoid of expression. 'Love.'

'Yes, I have.' It was said quietly, reluctantly. Now regretting she had asked in the first place, Valerie tried to bounce the conversation back. 'Was she, or is she, pretty?'

'Not showy pretty, no. But she had an aura. Wherever she went, whatever she did, she carried this indefinable beauty, a beauty that comes from within. She radiated goodness and compassion.'

'I'm sorry,' said Valerie, 'I've upset you.'

'It's okay,' he said. 'I carry them here,' he put an open palm to his heart. 'And here.' He moved his hand to his head.

'Them?'

'She died in childbirth. I lost them both.'

'Oh Christ, I'm sorry, Albert. Big mouth, just trying to… don't know what I was trying to do.'

'And you?'

'I'm sorry, Albert. You've told me, but I'm not ready to talk about what has happened to me. Guess I'm a coward. My family know, of course, and I once told Jane when I was off my head with Southern Comfort,' Valerie explained. 'But that's about it... apart from someone I'd rather didn't know,' she added quietly.

'Jane?'

'My secretary. I have my own business as well as being entangled with the pros.'

Valerie was sure Albert would not press her but was still glad when the phone rang. She listened attentively until, just before finishing, she said, 'I'll need a passport, and you'd better get it filled with visas for all the countries you think I might need.' She threw the phone on the settee. 'How are we travelling?'

'You're coming?'

In the last twenty-four hours, she'd changed her mind about not chasing him to the end. 'Of course, unless you had other ideas?'

'No, no. Suppose we're a team now. Like Holmes and Watson.'

'Oh, good grief,' said Valerie, 'sure it's not Laurel and Hardy? So how do we travel, and what about a passport for you?'

'Not sure, probably fly down, and I'll get the embassy to sort a passport.'

***

The colonel handed Valerie some papers, amongst them a passport. 'That'll open most doors.'

'I'm going to take the Glock,' said Valerie. 'Any ideas about getting it abroad?'

'I'll get you a car; we'll fix somewhere to put it. They'll have to take it down to its last nut and bolt to find something as small as a pistol.'

'British plates, French?'

'French, I think. Don't worry, we'll have it over here by tomorrow; it'll check out. Any preference?'

'Golf R, with an auto box.'

'Don't want much, do you? I'll bet you even have a colour preference.'

Valerie opened the passport, 'Lapiz blue.'

'Passport okay?'

'Yes, sure. Diplomat attached to our Paris embassy. Nice touch.'

'Well, didn't think "Paid Assassin" would have got you very far.'

'Thought you wanted him breathing?'

'Yes, Valerie, we do.' The colonel started fiddling with a cigar tube. 'Definitely.'

'Am I allowed to know why this is so important?'

'We need to make an example of this one. You run Bentley down, give us a call, and then you can get yourself off to the nearest cocktail bar. By the way, have you noticed anyone else taking an interest?'

'No. You asked me that before. Why?'

'Just watch your back. Okay?'

Giving herself time to think, Valerie walked most of the way back to the houseboat. She was sure she could not get anywhere without Albert, and as to him wanting Bentley dead and she alive, that would have to be worked out when the time came.

Being expendable, she had no qualms about keeping the department in the dark. Lying face down in a cul-de-sac, Valerie would soon be forgotten after the colonel had sent the compulsory bunch of carnations, whatever Dennis's opinion. What she couldn't get out of her head was why the colonel wanted Bentley alive. Making an example of him was a load of guff.

There was also something nagging at her about Albert. If he were here on a personal mission, why was the Iranian embassy so helpful? She was beginning to feel like a very meagre piece of cheddar between two slices of Hovis.

\*\*\*

'This could get habit-forming.' Valerie poured mineral water into two glasses and pushed one across to Albert. The pieces of lemon fizzed as they floated to the top.   'You're beginning to be a bad influence on me.'

Valerie had driven them down a winding lane to a small pub on the edge of a hamlet. It had been through a lean time after the introduction of the drink-driving law of the sixties. Periods of being shut down had been interspersed by several would-be owners going broke. Then, fresh from a top restaurant in London, a twenty-three-year-old chef had hocked everything he owned and opened it back up. A few years later and it was one of the top dining places in the south.

Expensive cars, jostling side-by-side on the freshly tarmacked car park, were in stark contrast to the inside. The new owner had not touched the interior. The ceiling was stained yellow from years of nicotine. Electric cables hadn't been chased below the plaster but ran down wall surfaces to every socket and switch. Cracked and discoloured pictures hung around in clusters. There were no beer pumps on the bar; a row of barrels lined the back wall, all of them sporting shining brass taps. In contrast, the freshly scrubbed yew tables were topped with highly polished silver and crisp linen napkins.

Sipping his drink, Albert gave the room a quizzical look. 'I don't think I've been anywhere remotely like this.'

'Lovely, isn't it?'

Albert pushed his lips together and frowned before answering. 'I'll reserve judgment if that's okay.' He pointed through the window towards the E-Type. 'It doesn't look out of place. What's its history? It's considerably older than you.' Valerie shrugged her shoulders, then unconsciously wrapped her hand around the ring finger of her left hand.

Albert noticed the involuntary action. 'Sorry, it's to do with broken glass.'

Valerie nodded as their lunch arrived. As before, the feelings were no longer intense. The past could be brushed away; almost. Letting go was possible, but it would bring new problems and new decisions.

'Well? How's your lunch?'

'Brilliant food in a Victorian slum. You Brits are…' He shook his head and carried on with his vegetable curry.

'Now,' said Valerie, 'we don't want to go together, France, I mean.'

'You drive and pick me up from the airport.'

'What, Charles de Gaulle? Absolutely no way. I get in a tangle going to Gatwick. If you think I'm going to repeat that trick with a French accent, you can think again.'

'Okay, you can pick me up at Beauvais.'

'Easy to find?'

'Off the ferry and straight down the A16. Okay?'

'You seem to know the country well.'

'Spent a lot of time in France, so don't worry, we won't get lost.' He pushed his plate away, patting his lips with the serviette. 'How do you feel about keeping your people in the dark?'

'I do the job and get paid,' she said flatly. 'How I do it is my business.'

'You talk like a mercenary; don't you feel an allegiance?'

Valerie tried to change the topic, 'When do you think Bentley will leave the country?'

'You just do it for the money?' Albert's question had an intimate edge as he lowered his voice in the crowded room.

'The money's good, far more than I could earn doing anything else. But I do like to think they receive value.' Then, glancing at her plate, she added under her breath, '*At least, they did last time.*'

'Do you want a dessert?' Albert had been leaning over the table but now, picking up the menu, straightened his back.

'Yes, I'm a sucker for chocolate ice cream, especially when the chef makes it.'

Wearing a long white apron, the waiter came to the table, took out an electronic pad, and sent the order through to the kitchen.

'Are you close to no one?' said Albert, trying to draw out more.

'Yes, of course. I'm not some lone weirdo. Love my parents and brother like crazy. Couldn't get by without seeing them now and again. And there's Jane. I always liked her, but she was injured a little while ago, and it made me realise she means more to me than I'd thought. More like a younger sister.'

'Boyfriends?'

'Sometimes. Don't sit in the houseboat watching game shows and the teleshopping channel, if that's what you're getting at.' Albert pushed his fork into a slice of French apple tart. 'Good as mum's?'

He topped the golden apples with a bit of crème fresh. 'I wouldn't like to tell her, but yes, it's good, excellent.'

'Where are they?'

'Sorry?' said Albert.

'Parents?'

'Tehran.'

***

Down the end of a short mews, Sergeant Peterson was bending over a Golf's engine bay.

With only the one option Valerie addressed his backside. 'Hello Sergeant, nice to see you again.'

'Hello, Miss Stone.' Straining on a spanner, he kept his head under the bonnet. 'How have you been?'

'Fine.'

'You can put the Glock in here.' He pulled his head clear and shone a torch to the side of the engine bay. 'Not much room, I'm afraid, but no one will find it. And in the boot, we've made a little compartment under the spare. Again, it looks like part of the body. Enough room for ammunition and the holster.' He removed his latex gloves and dropped them into a bag. 'I understand you've driven one of these before?'

Valerie took the two keys, 'Yes, I know where everything is.' She thought it better not to say she'd left the side of the last one in a wall.

'Steering wheel on the wrong side, of course, but you don't want it standing out. And an R looks like an ordinary Golf at a casual glance. Nicely understated.'

At first, Valerie thought she'd been mistaken, but as the sergeant bent over the car again, she saw that she'd been correct. 'Johnny?'

Leaning on the car wing with his elbows, he looked back over his shoulder. 'Yes.'

'You have a blue sock on one foot, and a green one on the other.'

'I'm off to see my ex-wife later.'

'Connection?'

'We've been talking more and more... you know, when I go around to pick up the kids for a day out. Started with five minutes of polite chat, now it's not far short of half an hour.'

'All right,' said Valerie slowly.

'So, I finally got up the courage to ask her out to dinner, and she said yes. I think the spark has returned, or at least, it has for me.'

'Socks?'

'Going to make sure she sees them sometime during dinner.'

'No,' said Valerie.

'What do you mean, no?'

66

'I know what you're doing, and it's no. Your wife is not stupid, and I'm sure she's not looking for another child to mother, if she's thinking about getting back together. She wants a man. You go home, get a shower, shave and manicure. Put on a pale shirt with a nice tie, not gaudy. And not regimental. Suits?'

'Er, a grey one and a dark blue one with a subtle check.'

'Dark blue,' said Valerie. 'Black shoes polished until they'd blind a platoon of soldiers. Cufflinks, not buttons on the shirt sleeves, tiepin to match. If they were a gift from her, all the better. What are you taking as a present?'

'Er.'

'No, Johnny, you're not taking her an "er". Nice bunch of flowers. They don't have to be roses, just a nice bunch. Come to think of it, not roses, too slushy; you're a man. Give them to her at the house, so they can be left behind. She doesn't want to look like Eliza Doolittle in the restaurant. Aftershave?'

'Polo or Joop!'

'Very nice, both of them. Is one unopened?'

'Yes, the Joop!'

'That's the one then, fresh. Just don't chuck it on.'

Valerie got in the car and ran the window down.

'Thanks, Johnny, and,' she said, driving off, 'black socks. Two of them.'

# SEVEN

Luck and primary schoolgirl French got Valerie from the ferry and onto the A16 heading to Beauvais. Too soon, the rain started bouncing from the Golf's bonnet.

*'Hell's teeth and buckets of blood thought this kind of weather was reserved for the UK. It's bad enough driving on the wrong side without turning it into an Olympic sport. Thank Christ Johnny changed the car's language to English.'*

Blinding reflections from the lights of on-coming traffic became worse when she came up behind a van with its rear fog lights on. The flooded road became a dazzling light display. Using the voice command, she called Albert.

'Hello, Valerie.' He sounded relaxed. 'How are you? In France yet?'

'Albert, at the moment, I'm swimming down the A16 and in danger of drowning. Where are you?'

'I'm sitting in the lounge of the hotel, having a coffee.'

'Beauvais?'

'Yes, of course. I arrived yesterday. Just waiting for Watson.'

'Well, lucky bloody you.'

'Where exactly are you?'

'On the by-pass around Amiens... I think.'

'Have you gone over the Somme?'

'What?'

'The River Somme.'

'I think so. Series of lakes and then over a river.'

'That's it, less than an hour in good weather.'

Valerie looked at her watch; it was one-thirty. 'At this rate, expect me to surf in around six.' She slowed as a lorry thundered past, sending dirty spray over the windscreen. 'If I survive.'

Six o'clock had been a joke. But Valerie was still shattered as she turned into the hotel car park around three-thirty. The rain had eased when Albert came across to greet her.

'Bags in the back?'

'Just the one.' Sheltering under her jacket she pulled at the boot release with her free hand.

'You need a shower,' said Albert, shaking the water from his coat in the hotel doorway. He put the bag by the reception and gave out instructions to a girl.

Unsure of what was being said, Valerie went through to the lounge and ordered a coffee.

'Shower in a minute; I've been looking forward to this for the past hour.' She moved over, letting him onto the large sofa. The waiter put an apple Danish next to the coffee. 'Oh yes.' She took a large bite. Flaky bits of pastry dropped onto her lap. 'Now that's good.'

'Dinner at eight,' said Albert. 'I'll see you in reception around seven-thirty if that's okay?'

'Sure, are we eating here?'

'No, and we're not going to a dilapidated pub, either.'

***

Except for a pair of high heels, a simple black dress and short coat, Valerie was travelling light. After using the hotel iron, she made sure the tiny roses running up the back of each stocking were straight; slipped on the shoes and dress, then reached over her shoulder, pulled up the zip and put the jacket around her shoulders.

Whether through politeness or genuine surprise, Albert stood transfixed for a moment as Valerie descended the stairs.

'Well, you certainly don't look like a police officer. Not that I'm sure you ever did.'

'Will I do?'

'Fishing for compliments?'

Inclining her head, Valerie smiled. 'Maybe.'

'The restaurant's not far, do you want to walk, or...?'

'I take it it's stopped raining?'

'Yes, turned into a rather nice evening.'

She took hold of his arm.

***

One of the double glass doors slid open as Albert leaned against the round oak handle. As the Valet took Valerie's coat, she noted a Michelin Star to the side of a flight of three steps dropping into the restaurant.

The ceiling was low, individual booths were to three sides; tables in the middle had partitions and curtains. The central display, of water falling down a glass panel, glistened with pale green lighting. A waiter stood patiently as Valerie slid into the high-back bench. After being handed a menu, Valerie only caught one word in four as Albert talked with the young man. She turned to the menu, where she was on safer ground. A French menu is a French menu; it doesn't matter if it's in Beauvais or Brighton.

'Surprise me,' said Valerie when Albert had finished speaking with the waiter. She folded the menu and put it to the side. 'And I'll join you in a bottle of Perrier.'

69

'Sure? You can have wine if you prefer.'

Valerie shook her head, 'Told you, you're becoming a bad influence.'

When it arrived, the meal was not a complete surprise; she had recognised the order of sweet parsnip soup, with lamb loin and caramelised onion to follow.

'What, no *Pommes Frites*?' Feigning ignorance, Valerie giggled behind a cupped palm.

'No, you barbarian, and no salt and vinegar either.'

Towards the end of the meal, when Valerie was enjoying spoonfuls of chocolate ice cream, which she had to admit was better than the pub's, she ceased the frivolous small talk and asked about Bentley's whereabouts.

After patting his lips, Albert put the folded napkin to one side. 'Put his thumb out on the A6 or got his own transport. I'm not sure he would risk flying; the UK will have that covered. By the way,' he pulled out his wallet and showed her a photo, 'I've had that made up. Computer image of what he will look like without a beard.'

'You think he'll have shaved it off?'

'Wouldn't you?'

Valerie vigorously rubbed her chin and smiled, 'I suppose.'

'Well?' asked Albert as they walked back to the hotel.

'Yes, good. It was perfect.'

They stopped by the village square where a group of older men were playing boules. 'That's what I'm going to do when I'm old and grey,' said Albert, nodding in their direction. 'Minus the wine,' he added, noticing bottles of St Julien scattered around the tables. 'But I might smoke a pipe.'

Still holding onto his arm, Valerie pulled back, frowning, 'Um, maybe.'

Back in the hotel foyer, she took hold of his hand and kissed his cheek. 'Thank you, an oasis of calm in the middle of… Well, we'll have to see what it's in the middle of.'

'My pleasure, Valerie. I can't remember a better night.' Taking her head between his hands, he let a soft kiss linger on her lips.

Walking up the stairs, she could not remember being kissed by a man with a moustache before. In twenty-seven years, it had not happened once. She couldn't decide whether it was better or not, but she knew she had been kissed by a man who had put thought and gentleness into it.

\*\*\*

The next morning, after putting the bags in the boot, Valerie threw the key across.

'I might only have been on the road a few hours yesterday, but it was long enough to know I don't like driving on the wrong side.'

'On the way back,' said Albert as they skirted around Paris, 'we can stop off... Eiffel Tower, dinner at Maxim's.'

She did not protest at his self-assurance but found herself nodding in agreement. She'd known him a little under two weeks, but already, as with the kiss, he seemed to be taking control of the relationship.

'Any ideas as to where he'll be?'

'Bentley? The immigrant district is in the north. We'll start there.'

'Blimey, it's a big place. I hope we've got a little more to go on than hanging around street corners, looking for a guy with barber's rash.'

'Well, you were sitting on his chest down that alley. I was hoping you would be able to recognise him, beard or not.'

'Oh yes,' she said, remembering his fist striking her neck, 'I'll remember him.'

A couple of hours later, south of Lyon, Valerie unscrewed the top from a bottle of water and passed it across. 'The road's a bit quieter.'

'We're on an N road. The A roads are toll, but these are generally quieter. Pretty, too.'

'Pull in, will you,' said Valerie as a car park and toilet sign came up, 'I need to wash my hands.'

'You're very quaint, Valerie.' The car left the smooth tarmac and bumped over the uneven parking area. 'But then again, I find all you Brits that way.'

She took some tissues and a bottle of water from the door bin. 'Okay,' she said, getting out and stretching, 'I want to use the toilet... Or, if you want to be upper-class,' she put her head back through the open window, 'the lavatory.'

Entering, she felt like using the tissue for the handle but thought better of it. Inside the stall, the facilities looked like the last time it had been cleaned was by one of the builders. She ran a couple of tissues around the seat before using the toilet. Looking at the sink reminded her of the old joke: "After using these facilities, please wash your hands." She drenched her hands with the water from the bottle and used the last of the tissues. A rusty hand-dryer hung from the wall by a couple of bare wires.

'Less like a toilet and more like the Twilight Zone,' she said, putting her foot on the flush peddle.

'Okay?' asked Albert as she returned.

'Oh, yeah, just keep an eye out for symptoms of typhoid.'

'Think I'll go.'

She took another bottle of water and threw it across as he got out of the car. 'You're lucky; you don't have to sit.'

'Pity the pretty scenery doesn't run to the rest facilities,' he said on returning.

'Now who's being quaint?' she said. 'The last thing I'd want to do in there is rest.'

As the water cascaded around, Valerie reached for more shower gel. Unable to shake off the thoughts of the roadway toilet, she scrubbed the back of her thighs and continually rinsed her hands. As she shut off the control, there was a knock on the bedroom door.

'Valerie, can I come in?'

She wrapped herself in a large fluffy towel, let Albert in, and then sat on the king-size bed, rubbing her hair. 'Any news?'

'Maybe.' He put two coffees on the bedside table. 'We know where to start if nothing else.'

Only being in Marseille for a short time, Valerie once again wondered how Albert got the information so quickly. 'Where would that be?'

'The docks.' He reached over and took one of the cups. 'Dear Allah.' He lightly tapped a forefinger at the scar on her shoulder.

'Oh, just an accident.' She held her head to one side, giving her hair an extra rub.

He gently took her arm and, pulling her forward, examined her back. 'Accident?' His voice had a mild touch of sarcasm.' That's an entry and exit wound, small calibre, a handgun. Nine millimetre? Or are you Brits still working in fractions of an inch?'

'Clever, aren't we?'

'Clever enough. This isn't the first time you've been at the sharp end.'

Ignoring his comment, Valerie stood up. 'We could go down to the waterside cafés and bars this evening. See if we can spot anything. I'll meet you downstairs.' She glanced at her watch, 'Fifteen minutes?'

\*\*\*

With the main road and docks running along the seafront in Marseille, most of the cafés and bars are set back. Albert seemed to have an intimate knowledge of the piazzas that run from one to the other. Down an incline a narrow road opened onto a larger plaza. Tables and chairs stood outside various businesses, each distinguished from its neighbour by different coloured umbrellas. The largest and most impressive restaurant was to one end. Purple and gold furniture outside a large smoked glass front dominated that part of the square.

Albert shook his head as Valerie began to make her way towards the far side. 'The side streets first. And as your French is a bit, er….'

'Rubbish?'

'Limited, I'll ask and show the photos. Anyone that sneaks out, that's your department.'

'Why bars and cafés?'

'Because he'll stay out of anywhere obvious, and anybody can work in the wash-up. Yes?'

Valerie thought it all a bit thin but stayed to one side as Albert showed the photos at one café after another. She was also wondering why they were concentrating on one tight area when a crash, followed by shouting, came from the back of a small bar. Valerie ran after a girl escaping between crowded tables, pinning her against the opposite wall. A mixture of garlic and olive oil engulfed her as she held a wrist against the girl's throat. Telling her to keep still was returned by a French torrent, which she presumed was far from complimentary.

'Keep still, you stupid little cow.'

More abuse followed; this time accompanied by a face full of saliva.

'Bitch!' Valerie drew the back of a free hand across her cheek.

Albert came out and grabbed the girl by her wrists. 'Okay, let her go.'

Valerie jumped back as a swinging foot caught her knee. 'You sure?'

Albert held up a card to one side of the encircling crowd, 'Surete.' Still holding the id, he swung around and repeated himself. The girl was pushed through a small gap by the flat of Albert's hand as he ground out the words, 'Down to the waterfront.'

Confirming she must know something, the girl's face drained of colour. She had to break into a trot to keep up as, pulling her by the wrist, Albert led them across the main road. Finding a quiet bench, he forced her to sit.

Again, wondering how he produced the right card at the right moment, Valerie furrowed her brow. 'Surete?'

He said nothing.

Leaving the questioning to Albert, Valerie leaned on a lamppost as he squared up to the girl. Several minutes of French that Valerie was unable to follow continued between the two. She recognised a few food words, so presumed the girl was protesting about being kept away from work. The only other word she picked out was "running", and terrorist sounded the same in both languages.

Albert let the girl get to her feet, then helped her on her way with a kick up the backside.

Valerie took the freshly vacated space. 'Seeing a whole new side to you.' He was about to say something when Valerie stopped him. 'Can I see the card you flashed back there?'

Albert put a hand inside his jacket and pulled out a wallet. 'Here.' He momentarily held it between two fingers, then passed it over. Albert's photo was surrounded by French text, and an official-looking logo to the side.

'What's going on, Albert? Someone on a one-man mission does not carry one of these.' She passed the card back. 'And how did you know where to come? Never mind Marseille, you went straight to the right café… almost.'

'I have a friend in the embassy; I thought you knew that. Nothing mysterious.'

'In the UK, yes. But in France as well? There's well connected, and there's well connected. But you're pulling enough rabbits out of hats to start a bloody farm.'

'I have a good friend in the UK. He got in touch with someone at the Paris consulate and called in a favour.'

She thought it stretched the believable to breaking point but said nothing. If she was ever going to catch up with Bentley, there was no way she would do it without Albert. She decided to pursue the French warrant card no further.

'Was that girl of any use?'

He got up and pulled Valerie to her feet. 'He's here, or at least for the moment. The girl knows him from before but says she doesn't know where he is now.' He put a hand around Valerie's waist and guided her across the road. Only when back in the piazza did he remove his arm. 'Coffee?'

They sat at a table in one of the smaller cafés. 'Make mine a Southern Comfort, two slices of orange and a lot of ice.'

Albert raised a hand to a waiter. 'I've not completely reformed you, then?'

Valerie pushed the Cinzano ashtray to one side and lightly drummed her fingers on the table. 'So, what was it the girl said, something about running? I presume she'd heard about our friend scarpering again.'

Albert took his coffee as the waiter put a coaster, followed by a thick highball glass full of ice surrounded by the amber bourbon in front of Valerie. He kept quiet until the young man had left. 'From what the girl said, it wasn't "running away". She was talking about immigrants. Running people.'

'She seems to know an awful lot about someone she hasn't seen in ages.'

'I know, she probably has, but I didn't want to push it. I've got no authority here; it's all bluff.'

'This Bentley doesn't stay very faithful to anything or anyone.' Valerie took a sip of her drink and held it in her mouth for a moment.

'Himself,' said Albert. 'And that's about it.'

'And I presume *terroriste* translates into terrorist.'

Gazing at nothing in particular, Albert nodded. Around the square, a light breeze set the umbrellas fluttering.

'We seem to have gone through a succession of places I could happily live in. Beauvais, the valley south of Lyon… here.'

'What? Just disappear and hang your hat in one of these flats?' He waved a hand towards the open windows above the cafés.

'I'd need a bit more money than I have now, or I'd be washing up like that girl.'

Albert managed to combine a querying look with a smile.

Valerie stroked a finger in small circles around her forehead as if trying to start up her brain. 'Joining people smugglers, then. But they're not just going to let some guy come in and share the rewards.'

'No, he'll know a whole lot of undesirables. He'll be well known, and he's just the kind of scum they would welcome. Hard, well trained and ruthless.' Finishing his coffee, he threw some euros onto the table, 'Come on.'

'Where?'

'She gave me an address.'

'Hell, Albert, we should have gone straight off. That girl will warn him.'

He shook his head, 'I told her if she did, I'd come back and make sure she was deported.'

'Deported?'

'Yes, she's from Syria.'

'More bluff?'

'Of course. There's only one way I could do that... make her swim.'

'I need to get something from the car before we go.'

'Are you sure? If you get caught with that Glock....' Albert left the rest unsaid.

'I'd rather wind up surrounded by gendarmes than stare down the barrel of anything Bentley pointed at me. Especially with no more than crossed fingers for protection.'

***

Valerie shut the car bonnet and tucked the Glock into the small of her back.

Before realising it, Albert was catching the car key once again. 'I don't want to T-bone some Merc before we get to the end of the road.'

Neat, tree-lined roads gave way to a district dominated by poorly maintained tower blocks. A lonely, barricaded all-night store was more or less identical to the one in Birmingham. 'Just like home,' she said, craning her neck.

'About the same ratio of immigrants, I should think.' Albert stopped and shut the engine off; then pointed to a small building to the side of the parking area. 'There. You go to the front and knock. I'll go around the back and do the chasing this time.'

Valerie gave him a couple of minutes, then, drawing the Glock, knocked on the bright red door. 'Jesus,' she whispered, hearing someone inside calling out in English.

'What is it?' The door opened, and a clean-shaven Bentley looked down the barrel of Valerie's pistol. 'Bastard!' He pulled her arm into the gap and repeatedly slammed the door until the gun dropped to the floor. Holding onto her arm, she fell backwards as a clenched fist in the face sent her to her knees.

A booted foot connecting with her neck brought down a black curtain.

***

'Valerie?'

An involuntary flinch coincided with a spasm through her neck and shoulder. Trying to get to her feet, unsure legs crumbled as she stared through a misty veil.

'Christ, I can't see.' Supporting herself by leaning on the wall, she managed to rub a knuckle into each eye. 'Is that you, Albert?'

'Yes. Bentley...' He stopped. 'Are you all right?'

Valerie touched his face with an outstretched hand. 'Albert, I can't see.'

She felt herself being scooped up, before drifting back behind a grey fog.

A few seconds of consciousness came and went as the Golf screamed through the gears, along with braking that even the anti-lock brakes had a problem keeping pace with. All this was accompanied by continuous use of the horn and Albert swearing, she presumed, in Arabic.

Again, the curtain wrapped her away until she was jolted back by Albert running up the hospital steps. This time he was shouting orders in French. Blurred lights and the ceiling, she assumed, rushed by until she was laid onto something cold.

'Albert?' The squeeze on her hand was felt with numb fingers. 'Albert? I can't feel your hand properly.' A combination of shock and fear started her shaking. 'Albert?!'

'I'm here. Don't worry, you're in hospital.'

'Albert?'

'It's all right.'

'Don't leave me, Albert; I'm frightened. Please.'

The mist gathered again as his words echoed, 'I'm going nowhere.'

Only interrupted by Albert's face, fluffy clouds swirled through her mind. Bentley's footsteps bounced down a dark alley, and pain jabbed at her neck and arm. Falling into the fog, she began to feel warm and comfortable, then her mind gave up. The blackness returned.

***

76

A few days later, Valerie was awake. She could hear the bustle around her, but could see nothing.

'Albert!' A female voice answered her frantic scream, but in French. 'I don't understand; I'm English. Where's Albert?'

Although in a thick, southern French accent, the English reply was fluent. 'The gentleman has gone for something to eat. He's not left your side since you were brought in.'

'I can't see.' The panic in Valerie's voice was soothed by a pat on the hand.

'Your eyes are covered.'

Valerie relaxed slightly. She could feel the gentle strokes; the numbness in her hand had gone but had been replaced by tightness on the top of her head.

'Back with the living?' Valerie heard Albert as he approached the bed. 'You had me rather worried.'

'Do you know when I can get this off?' She ran a finger across the dressing.

'Right now, the doctor's on his way.'

Valerie felt the cold scissors across her cheek, then heard blades sever the bandages. A cloudy light replaced the blackness as the outer layer was removed. She could see light before, but it had been blurred. She kept her eyes closed as the final pads were removed.

'I can't, Albert.'

He ran a finger down her cheek, 'Of course, you can.'

Sight still blurred, she squinted around. Blinking brought an improvement. She blinked again, then, closing her eyes for a few seconds, tried once more. Albert was sitting on the side of the bed. Every hair of his moustache was crisply defined. Grapes and a vase of flowers were sharply focused in a shaft of sunlight. Saying nothing, she leant forward and pulled him towards her. The kiss was more than one of relief; the memory of their previous encounter flooded back as she held him close.

'No need to ask if you can see,' he said, making a joke of fighting for breath.

She fell back against the pillows. 'So, *you* let Bentley get away as well.'

'I heard you screaming and came through from the back.' Albert ran a finger around the bunch of grapes, then selected one from the centre. 'It was either run after Bentley or scoop up the pieces.'

Valerie pushed herself up. 'Can I get out of here?'

He dodged to one side as a nurse pulled curtains around the bed. 'No reason why not. I suppose they may want you back next week.'

Valerie swung her legs from the bed. 'Can you ask about my clothes?'

Albert stuck his head on the other side of the curtains and pulled a bag through. 'I went out. Thought you'd want clean things; I guessed your size. I didn't want to rummage through your stuff at the hotel.'

'I can understand an estimate for the top and jeans,' said Valerie, following Albert down the hospital steps. 'But how did you guess my bra size?'

'Guess?' said Albert, looking over his shoulder.

She felt the stitches above her hairline and asked what the doctors had done.

'There was a build-up of pressure that had to be reduced, a small piece of skull was removed and-'

'Yuk, stop for Christ's sake!' Swivelling it back to front, she pulled a baseball cap over the scar visible through the still-short hair.

***

'Bentley's place?' Valerie followed Albert to the red door.

'As he left in a hurry, I thought we'd have a look around.'

The front door led straight into a lounge area, with two doors separated by a wooden table on the back wall. No pictures broke up the light blue paintwork, and no carpet gave relief to the tiled floor.

Valerie pulled the single drawer from the table and emptied its contents onto the top. 'How do you know he's not been and cleared the place out?'

'Had someone watch it. I didn't want to leave you.'

Valerie picked up a biro and flicked through the desk litter. 'There's receipts and flyers, dated from before Bentley got here. What are we supposed to be looking for?'

'Not sure; I was hoping his passport might be here. Then we'd know he would have to hang around for a while until he got another.'

Valerie went into the bedroom and dragged out more drawers from bedside cabinets and a dressing table, then went into the small, adjoining shower room.

'Nothing,' she shouted, pulling out a tube of toothpaste and a couple of toilet rolls. The cistern was only full of water. Going back into the bedroom, she upturned the sheets and mattress. A British passport dropped to the floor.

She went into the kitchenette and waved the passport under Albert's nose.

'He's not far away then, is he?' said Albert as he opened it.

'Why not?' On a shelf by the sink, Valerie moved a few tins of ragout to one side. 'What if he has more than one?'

'Yes, I suppose. He seems to be a well-organised individual.'

'Except for nearly getting himself caught. And more than once.'

'Overconfident.' Albert threw a packet of basmati back into a cupboard. 'Come on, let's get back to the hotel.'

***

'My room,' said Albert as they got into the lift, 'somewhere we can talk. But don't worry, I'm sure there'll be something in the drinks cabinet that will take your fancy.'

Valerie shook her head, 'Not at the moment.'

Albert's room was slightly larger than the one she had. The king-size bed was on a raised plinth. The unremarkable prints scattered around the walls had been given a lift with heavy mahogany frames. An oversized television would have looked more at home in a theatre.

Valerie sank into one of the deep chairs and took the offered glass of water. 'Okay, let's hear it.'

'I think you could be right. It's the most probable conclusion... he's got more than one.' He tapped Bentley's passport on his fingertips before dropping it on the coffee table. 'So, he's off across the Mediterranean. But how? Fly?'

Valerie shook her head, 'Quietly, on a boat, or drive around to Italy, then Sicily? Malta? And across. But if you think I'm chasing that bastard around the Libyan dunes, you can think again.'

'Don't worry, I've got friends there. Anyway, he's headed further south. Probably.'

'Into bandit territory? Hell's teeth, Albert, have you got a death wish? And what do you mean, friends? I've no intention of joining a bunch of terrorists.'

'They are strictly on the side of the angels.'

'I've heard that one before. I didn't believe it then, and I don't believe it now. There's no such thing as angels.'

'What *do* you believe in, Valerie?'

She left her chair and sat at Albert's feet. 'I don't think I believe in anything anymore; there's nothing left.'

Avoiding the scar, Albert stroked her hair for a few minutes. Then she got onto his lap and brushed a finger across his moustache.

'What's caused all this pain?' He kissed her forehead and cupped a breast through her thin T-shirt. The intimate contact sent a message tumbling towards the top of her thighs.

'Why are you chasing Bentley?'

'I told you.'

'Yes, I know, but that's only part of it. I want the truth.'

'And why do you want the truth? You'll be paid for what you do. What's so important about why I want him, besides what you already

79

know?'

'I'm not sleeping with a man who tells lies.'

'How did you know?' Albert did not remove his hand but now began gentle stroking.

'Are you expecting me to purr?' Valerie removed his hand, kissed it, and put it back. 'And how did I know what?'

'The way I feel about you.'

'Oh, that's an easy one. I feel the same.' She took a handful of his hair and pulled his lips towards hers.

Albert got up and lay Valerie on the bed. 'Bentley is, or rather was, we're not quite sure, a British agent.' He took a sip of water and sat next to her.

'It's okay,' said Valerie, 'I'm way ahead of you. No wonder the colonel wanted him alive. He's got information about… About what?'

'He joined IS with your country's blessing, just to feedback as much information as he could. But he came across some sensitive stuff, and we're not sure where his allegiance is anymore... with the UK, IS or just himself.'

'And the sensitive material is about Tehran?' Albert nodded and was about to say something else when Valerie stopped him. 'No need for anymore; I don't want to know about Iran's security. None of my damn business. And in any case, I might be able to multi-task, but wanting you and talking about Bentley don't mix.'

'Business later, then.' Albert sat next to her and started stroking her breast again.

'That's the same one,' said Valerie, 'have you something against the other?' She momentarily sat up and removed her T-shirt.

'It is a good fit,' said Albert, moving his attention to her other breast.

'A good guess, or...?'

'Bra size?'

Valerie nodded.

'They just had to be. The perfect size, eighty c.'

'Eighty c?' Valerie sat up and looked at her chest. 'I presume we're talking European sizes?' Albert stopped her as she moved her hands towards the clasp. 'No?'

'No,' said Albert. 'A surprise present does not unwrap itself.'

'Surprise? You mean to tell me you don't know what's underneath?'

'Oh, I wouldn't say that. I think I have an idea.' He sat behind her and, removing her bra, cupped both breasts. 'Just had to be,' he said. Twisting around, Valerie offered her open mouth.

'Had to be what?' she said, breaking away.

'Perfect breasts tipped with exquisite pink nipples.'

Valerie stood up and let Albert remove the rest of her clothes.

'My turn,' she said, unbuttoning his shirt.

Finishing when they were both naked, her hand moved down, caressing him gently. Albert let go and stood back, just looking for a few minutes.

'I'm not made of china,' said Valerie, smoothing both hands down her hips. 'I'll not break.'

'Yes, I know.' He still did not move; only his eyes travelled over her body.

'Well?'

'With women, it's the touch, caressing, exploring.'

'And making love,' said Valerie. 'Don't forget that.'

'No, I'm not forgetting. But with men, it's the sight of a naked woman. Looking is so important. I feel sorry for the men who have a woman who will only make love in the dark. Why do you think the vast majority of people that watch pornography are men? It's looking. I can feel a tightening of my throat, and a tremble in my fingertips. I cannot take my eyes away.'

Valerie lay back on the bed. 'It's okay, I understand. Someone else told me the same thing, a long time ago.' Propping herself up on the pillow, she raised a knee, leaving a little less to his imagination.

Albert moved closer and stroked her cheek. 'There is one other part of you that demands attention.'

'Oh, yes?' She took his hand and bit gently at his fingers. 'What would that be?'

'Those, oh so mesmerising, emerald eyes.' He took a breast between his hands and ran an inquisitive tongue around a hardening nipple.

She pulled at his hair. 'And now it starts.'

'Yes,' he said. 'Now, it starts.' He sat beside her, with his back to the bedhead. 'Come here. Sit between my legs with your back to me.' Valerie squirmed around and lay back against his chest.

'Now what?' His hands took a breast each and stroked, then pulled, at her perfect nipples. 'I see,' she said, moving her legs apart. 'I'm at the mercy of a devious move.' Albert took a hand from under her breast and moved to her thigh.

'I hear no screams. See no one running from the room.'

'The screams come later.' She took his hand, kissed it, and guided it even higher. A few seconds later, he touched nerves that arched her back. Grabbing the back of his neck, she whispered sweet obscenities before gripping his exploring hand between the top of her shapely limbs.

Nibbling at her ear, Albert said nothing, tender, exploring fingers bringing the only words from Valerie. Only when Albert knew she was ready did he release her and turn her onto her back.

'Traditionalist.'

With an open mouth, she explored his mouth with her tongue.

Albert still said nothing as he brought them together. Valerie withdrew from being equal and whimpered as he began to tease with the slowness of his movement. Three times he took her to the edge of the cliff; three times, cries and sobs were dropping from her lips. Turning her over, he took her from behind, then finally let her fall from volcanic peaks into the raging seas beneath.

Laying back on the bed, the warm Mediterranean breeze blew through cotton curtains onto bodies that were drenched with sweat. For several minutes neither spoke until Valerie rolled over, kissed him, and went to the shower. Letting the cooling waterfall around, she looked at her watch. It had been fifty-five minutes since he had removed her clothes. It felt like fifty-five seconds.

With his eyes closed, Albert was still on the bed when Valerie threw a towel over. Sitting by his side, she rubbed at her hair. 'Would you like to dry me off?'

Reluctantly, he propped himself on an elbow and stared at her shoulders. 'What's this?' he said, kneeling behind her. 'Small scars here?' He gently touched the small of her back.

She left the bed, pulled the towel around her breasts and tucked the end in.

'Someone else liked to hear me scream.'

Albert jumped from the bed and went off to the shower. 'Ever thought of a different occupation?'

# EIGHT

Twenty-four hours later, each with a backpack of essentials, they landed at Malta International.

'I slipped, fell over.' She explained the stitches to the immigration officer when she removed her cap. 'Hair will cover it soon. Be able to throw this thing away.' She waved the baseball cap around.

Along with putting the car in storage, Albert had told Valerie to leave the Glock in the hidden compartment.

'You don't want to get caught carrying that through Customs. Maltese prisons are not the most pleasant,' he'd said. 'Especially the women's slammer.'

'Where in God's name did you pick up such slang, Albert? Slammer?'

'Back in the good old days, we used to confiscate American TV cop DVDs, along with Region One players, of course.'

\*\*\*

'Okay,' said Valerie as they went over to the taxi rank, 'how do we unofficially get off this island?'

'A couple of my men will pick us up from a quiet beach, and run us across.'

'There's such a thing as a quiet beach on Malta?'

'Well, nearly quiet. We want somewhere where there are pleasure boats around. They'll come in and take us out. No one will be any the wiser.'

'And if they are the wiser?'

'Who's going to chase a high-speed launch towards the Libyan coast?'

Valerie managed a smile, before adding quietly, 'Who the bloody hell wants to be on one?'

\*\*\*

'We've got a couple of days holiday.' Albert held the door to the first taxi on the rank. 'Are you going to check in with London?'

She sank back into her seat as Albert told the driver where to go. 'To tell them what? You're going to blow Bentley away before I can say, "You're under arrest"?'

'I'm sorry, Valerie, but….'

'Yeah, yeah, I know.'

Valerie could pin it down to that moment in the back of the taxi. There was more to this than Albert knew, and what he did know, he wasn't going to say. Adding to the confusion was the colonel wanting Bentley just to make an example of him; that was also looking pretty bloody thin.

'So, what are we going to do with our forty-eight-hour pass?'

Albert turned in the seat and smiled.

'Oh, of course. Silly me.'

\*\*\*

During the two days on Malta, Valerie used ten minutes to call the colonel.

'You can come back if you want, Valerie,' the colonel had said. 'As strange as it may seem to you, I don't want you dead.'

'Don't want me dead, or don't want me embarrassing the government by getting caught in the Middle East?'

'Valerie...'

'Yes, Colonel?'

'Get him in your sights and....'

'Okay, Colonel, but you'd better have a plan to pull me out and pull me out bloody quick.'

\*\*\*

In the late afternoon, when the two days were up, Valerie and Albert sat on their backpacks in a secluded cove. There was little wind, and the one or two sailing boats were stationary on the gentle swell. Speedboats ran back and forward from the neighbouring beach, the odd one towing skiers. The clear sea would have been inviting at any other time; now, it was just a highway they were sitting beside waiting for a lift.

'Are you not in touch with them?' she asked.

Albert shook his head, 'They'll be here.' He took her hand, squeezing it.

It was a bloody strange situation, going off with her lover to one of the most dangerous places on earth. She was about to ask if it wouldn't be a better idea for both of them to just "disappear" and live in the South of France when he stood up. He nodded to the end of the cove as a sizeable white launch came around the point.

'They've come around the coast from the west, less suspicious.'

With one man looking over the side, the helmsman manoeuvred the craft to the side of the rocks. Two minutes later, with Valerie and Albert on board, they were moving slowly away from the shore. Both men saluted as one started talking in what Valerie presumed was Persian.

'We speak English, Sergeant. The lady is Miss Stone.'

Again, both men saluted. The one Albert had addressed as sergeant bowed slightly. 'Sorry, ma'am.'

Valerie shook her head, 'It's not a problem, Sergeant.'

Both men were in their early twenties and looked as hard as Albert. She looked across to her new lover... maybe as hard.

The man at the helm opened the throttles halfway, and Valerie looked over the stern at the three Mercury four-hundreds churning up the sea.

'How long?'

'To the coast?' The sergeant counted the spare fuel. 'We'll get clear of the coast in about twenty minutes, then we can open it up. It's about three and a half hours at fifty knots.'

Valerie took the mobile phone from an inside pocket and dropped it over the side.

'Burning your bridges?'

'Don't want to get caught with it. Besides, I don't think dialling 999 in the middle of the desert would be of much use.'

'Pistol, Sergeant.' The young man unzipped a holdall and handed Valerie a Glock nineteen, complete with holster. 'Not as dainty as yours, but you shouldn't need it,' said Albert. 'I, or any of my men, will not be far away.'

Undoing her belt, she threaded on the holster, arranging it just above her backside. She pulled the clip from the gun, checked it, and banged it back in with the palm of her hand. Hoping she wouldn't need it, she pushed it into the holster.

The man at the helm checked the instrument panel and spoke in Persian again.

'You'd better ask the lady,' said Albert.

'Beg pardon, Miss, are you the major's lady?'

'Well, you get straight down to the nuts and bolts, er....'

'Lieutenant. I'm the major's lieutenant.'

'Yes,' said Valerie after a pause, 'I'm the major's lady.'

'That's good,' he said. 'That's very good.'

'You approve, do you?' She accepted a boiled sweet from the sergeant as he handed them around.

'Oh yes, ma'am. The major has been on his own for too long.' He turned to Albert, 'Begging your pardon, sir.'

Albert looked at his watch, 'Let's get going, Lieutenant.'

The boat surged forward as the helmsman pushed the throttles to the end of their respective gates. Albert was handed a pair of binoculars as Valerie pointed to a boat about a mile away.

'Coastguard. Let's go a little to port, Lieutenant.' He handed the glasses back, screwed up his face and spat the sweet overboard. 'Too much sugar.'

'Can we go any faster?' asked Valerie.

The helmsman smiled, 'There's nothing around here that can catch us, not at this speed.'

86

The lieutenant was right. Ten minutes later, they were back on course, the other boat lost to the horizon.

'Miss?' The helmsman consulted a satellite navigation screen. 'Can I ask something else?'

'Enough,' said Albert. 'Leave her with your questioning.'

'It's all right, I don't mind. What is it, Lieutenant?'

'Are you a good woman?'

'I can't say I've ever been asked that before.' Her slight snort was drowned in engine noise. 'I think you'd better ask the major.'

The young man remained silent as Albert explained, or tried to. 'Men from where we come from are a little more direct,' he said. 'And I'm afraid my men have become quite protective of me.'

'Then you must say, mustn't you, Major.' Emphasising the word major, Valerie gave him a smack across the thigh.

'We've known each other a short time, Lieutenant, and in a case like that, I would say I need more time. But with Miss Stone, I know. Yes, she is a good woman.'

Noticing there was no toilet aboard, Valerie shook her head at the offered water. She took one of the cushions and, putting it at Albert's feet, sat down and rested her head on his lap.

Although the boat thumped on the occasional wave, Valerie fell asleep. Albert took a jacket from one of the men and put it around her shoulders.

*** 

Aware of a gentle shake, Valerie rubbed her eyes. The night was clear. A near-full moon illuminated the shoreline.

'That's an oil installation,' Albert said, pointing at squat buildings and storage units. 'We're a little to the east of Zuwara. There's a wide beach further along, much easier to land.' He took up a small communications radio and started talking in Persian. A torrent of chatter returned. Albert let it continue for a few seconds before speaking again. 'Men are a little excited,' he explained to Valerie.

'Your major is much loved,' she said to the other two.

'Yes,' said the sergeant. 'We've been with him for a long time. We trust him with our lives.'

As they neared the beach, the lieutenant switched off the engines and raised the outboards clear of the surf. Men waded out and straightened the boat. A pair of solid arms gathered Valerie up and put her on dry land. She guessed there to be about a dozen men, removing the spare fuel tanks and steadying the boat as a trailer was backed down the gravel.

'Don't worry,' said Albert in response to Valerie's questioning look, 'we're well away from any habitation. No one will know there's been a

87

landing. The priority is to get the boat away. We have some secure storage a little inland.'

A saluting soldier passed Valerie her backpack.

Clapping his hands together, Albert encouraged urgency. 'English, please, gentlemen. I'm afraid Miss Stone does not speak our beautiful language.'

Men piled into the back. Valerie was squeezed between Albert and a driver on the lorry's front seat as it pulled the boat clear of the beach; above their heads, a thump on the cab roof signalled all were on board.

Either side of the road was scrub and desert, the occasional building in darkness.

Valerie looked at her watch. 'What time is it? I'm still on Malta.'

Albert let his head loll back on the seat. 'We're an hour on.' He stroked her thigh, 'We'll be there soon.'

***

Five hundred or so yards from the road, the lorry headlights lit what looked like a deserted industrial unit.

'Home, sweet home?' queried Valerie.

Albert swung from the cab and dropped to the ground. 'For a couple of days until we receive some information.' Banging his boots on the gravel, he held out his arms, helping her down. 'Grab your bag; I'll show you to our room.'

Like an aircraft hangar, the unit was vast. Metal beams ran from side to side, supporting a corrugated roof. Electric cables hung down, holding large circular reflectors, a large bulb in each. Several Humvees were backed up against an alloy wall that rattled with the breeze. The concrete floor was thick with sand that crunched underfoot. An open stairway led to a glass-panelled office area along the back wall, overlooking the eerie scene. Albert led Valerie under the structure and held a door to one side.

'Be it ever so humble,' said Valerie, surveying the two camp beds and table. 'Anyone?'

Albert nodded, 'Take your pick.' She dropped her bag next to the nearest bed.

'Any chance of a coffee?'

'Sure, I just need to get everyone together.'

A shrill whistle pierced the air as Albert climbed onto the bonnet of a Humvee. Men ran in and lined up. A series of sharp commands had them to attention in three ranks, then another had them at ease. Valerie stood quietly to the side.

Albert addressed them in Persian for a minute or two. Then, in English, he introduced Valerie. She counted the front row of men then multiplied by three: thirty-six men, plus the sergeant, lieutenant and Albert.

Jumping down, he explained that most of the men spoke English, only a few didn't. The approaching lieutenant asked to talk with Albert. They were in deep conversation when the sergeant came across.

'The major said you'd like a coffee.' He held out a hand, pointing across the parking area.

A connecting passageway led into a canteen. A few men that had gone in before were sitting around. As one, they jumped to their feet, standing to attention as Valerie walked in.

'Please, Sergeant, tell them to sit down.'

In an attempt to keep the wind out, panel screws and duct tape had been applied to gaps in the walls. An electric lead drooped from a hatch to a coffee machine on a trestle. The rising breeze wafted sand from the doorway as Valerie pushed a chocolate pod into the dispenser.

She sat for maybe ten minutes, exchanging pleasantries with the soldiers until Albert put his head around the door.

'Better go,' she said, getting to her feet, then followed the major from the room.

'Need to talk,' he said.

'Okay,' said Valerie when they were alone, 'you've got that "This is going to hurt" look on your face.'

'Not in that way, but it's going to stretch your loyalty to breaking point.'

'Go on then, Albert, or is it time to call you Major?'

'I've got new orders. They want Bentley alive.'

'Tehran?'

Albert nodded.

They were standing in a corner, next to a lorry. 'Bentley's carrying information that would be useful to us, I mean Iran.' Looking at his feet, he leaned on the vehicle's door.

'That would explain what I was told when we were on Malta. The UK want him dead, or at least if he can't be brought back to the UK.' Albert raised his eyebrows. 'It's no good giving me a confused look. I'm as much screwed up about this as you. And I'll tell you something else...' Thinking of killing an innocent in cold blood before, Valerie brought her fist crashing against the metal wall, 'I'm not murdering him. If he's blown away in a fight, that's different. But I'm not levelling a gun at a helpless victim.'

Albert took hold of her arm, preventing her from hitting the wall again. 'When this is all over, you make me a promise.'

'Okay.'

'You tell me about, you know... about before we met.'

Valerie grabbed his hair and pulled his lips to hers. 'Promise.' She pulled away slowly, savouring the moment, then looked him in the eyes. 'But where does that leave us? Tehran gets him, or London gets him, or we murder him. For Christ's sake, Albert, this isn't fair.' She threw her hands in the air. 'Listen to me, "fair". We're in the biggest immoral fuck up, and I'm talking about being fair.' She hit the wall again and screamed.

Letting the storm pass, Albert said nothing.

'Sorry,' she said, 'I'm acting like a child.'

'No, no. I don't want to give him to Tehran any more than take him back to London. And, the same as you, I'm no assassin.'

'So?'

'Let's catch him first.'

'Kick the can down the road. You're beginning to sound like a bloody politician.'

# NINE

A day later, Valerie was throwing her kit into a Humvee. 'Seems everything is happening in batches of forty-eight hours,' she said to Albert.

'Maybe.' He threw a small package across, 'Put that in your bag.'

'What is it?' she said, stuffing it into a side pocket.

'Hijab, you'll need it if we stop somewhere inhabited.' She grabbed the door top and pulled herself into the cab.

'Oh, sorry, wrong side. Automatically got into the left.'

'It's okay,' said Albert, getting into the passenger seat, 'you can drive; we'll not meet much out here.'

'Keys?' Valerie held out a hand.

'No keys,' said Albert. 'The switch to your left, put it to Run.'

'Nothing,' said Valerie.

'Wait.' The red light above the switch went out. 'Push it across again.'

'Crikey!' Valerie sat back. 'What a racket.'

'Six and a half litres… diesel,' he said above the roar.

'And doesn't it sound like it!' She blipped the accelerator, 'Gordon Bennett!'

'We'll wedge in the middle of the convoy. We're out third; the others will follow.' He slid down the seat and put his knee on the dash.

More men piled in the back as the large hangar doors were opened. Putting his hand out of the window, Albert banged on the roof and shouted for the convoy to start. The storage unit filled with fumes as the noisy engines echoed from the walls.

A couple of hundred yards along the road, the windows were closed.

'Thank goodness for that.' Valerie kept pace with the vehicle ahead, then looked at the one behind. 'Not too noisy with the glass where it belongs.'

A couple of hours passed before she asked where they were headed.

'Libyan-Sudan border.'

'And what's there?'

'Sand and rocks, but we have some friendly contacts, and….'

'Bentley?'

'Maybe… probably. It's a smuggling route, and we think he's gone into hiding with the gangs. Big money to be made. Bentley would be in demand... clever, ruthless, and above all, he knows people all the way back to the UK.'

'No guarantee,' said Valerie. 'What a business model. The refugees get caught, die; it doesn't matter. The money's in the bank.'

'Yes.' Albert took the top from a bottle of water and passed it across. 'Complaining just gets your head blown off. These people are frightening.'

'Psychopaths.'

'No.' A voice came from behind. 'These guys are ruthless, but they're not unhinged.' Valerie looked in the rear-view mirror. A young, clean-shaven man leaned forward. 'Don't make the mistake of thinking they're anything but intelligent. They won't let anyone get in their way. It's just that they're amoral.'

'That's Rachid. He had a bit of a scrap on the border last year.'

Rachid put his hand over Valerie's shoulder. 'Oh, not too bad,' he said with a vigorous handshake, 'just a little misunderstanding.'

'Ha,' said Albert. 'Same kind of misunderstanding that put those scars on your back, Valerie.'

'The master of the understatement are you, Rachid?' Valerie stood on the brakes as the Humvees in front stopped.

'He's not the only one in this cab,' said Albert under his breath as he got out. He shouted something across to the lead vehicle as he told Valerie to stay where she was. 'You stay with her,' he added to the men in the back.

'You have your pistol, ma'am?' Valerie nodded. 'Then get it out, and put on that hijab.' He passed her bag.

Tucking her hair beneath the black square, she put the gun by her side. 'Trouble?'

'No, no, it'll be okay.'

The men in the back laid AK-47s across their laps. Valerie lowered the window, but all she could hear was Arabic or Persian... or something. Albert's quiet monotone rumbled below other voices that became louder.

The first body to come by staggered before it fell. The second seemed to fly, then crunched into the dirt. The third man ran down the side of the Humvees with Albert in pursuit. The man tripped by Valerie's door. Pulling him to his feet, Albert kicked him on his way with what she presumed were some choice words.

Albert had only left the cab a few minutes before returning, brushing dust from his uniform. 'It's okay; we've been cleared through this checkpoint.'

Albert was deep into a map as they drove off; she turned to the men in the back for an explanation.

'Give the first checkpoint a stern talking to, and they will radio through to the others,' said Rachid. 'We'll find the barriers raised when we get to them.'

'And what if they decide they don't like being pushed around?'

'We're in uniform, and we're travelling in Humvees, so...' He shrugged his shoulders and relaxed back into the seat.

'Uniforms?' Valerie switched off the lights as the sun came up. 'What uniforms are you wearing?'

'Nothing in particular,' said Albert, folding the map. 'They're not Iranian if that's what you're thinking, but they look impressive. No one in these parts is going to confuse us with the Household Cavalry.'

Valerie's travelling companions were right. They passed three checkpoints during the day, all deserted, all with barriers raised. As the light faded, the vehicles in front slowed, then pulled off along a dirt track and parked up.

'Too many holes and rocks in the road to drive at night. We don't want to lose a vehicle.'

'Lose a Humvee? Are you kidding?'

Abert's words were only just audible. 'They're big holes.'

Sheltering from a rising breeze the Humvees were backed up to a dune. Each having a lean-to-tent strung from the roof. Soldiers went about refuelling and checking tyre pressures; others unpacked squat tables and what appeared to be collapsible stools. A fire was soon boiling water, and mugs of coffee were handed around. Valerie was the first to have a mess tin given to her, filled with what looked like a chicken stew.

'Boil in the bag, I'm afraid,' said Albert. 'We've not had a visit from Michelin... yet.'

Apart from the faint taste of plastic, the stew was quite palatable. Finishing their jobs, soldiers gradually gathered around the fire. The odd one ventured to engage Valerie in conversation, mostly about how she liked driving a Humvee.

Studying a laptop and a map, Albert was the last to join the group. Valerie rubbed the back of his neck as he closed his eyes and rocked his head from side to side.

'Can you spare some water for a quick wash?' she asked while watching a couple of soldiers practising what looked like taking a knife from an attacker.

Albert opened his eyes. 'I think we can spare a drop.'

Momentarily forgetting the wash, she wandered over to the soldiers. Albert looked on as one of the men handed her a piece of wood. The major said something in Persian that brought an immediate reply, accompanied by a salute from the would-be instructor.

Being beckoned on, Valerie attacked the soldier. A quick grab at her wrist, as he pulled her close, had the piece of wood falling into the sand.

'Again,' she said.

Once more, the imitation knife spun to the ground.

The soldier took the knife and, in slow motion, showed Valerie what was happening in the second that had seemed a blur. 'Never block,' he said. 'You have to use the opponent's thrust to your advantage. The attacker is off-balance when the knife is close; the advantage has crossed over to you.'

Twenty minutes later, Valerie was taking the knife in one slick move.

More unarmed combat followed until, after about an hour, Albert called a halt.

Shoulders dropped as soldiers, eager to show Valerie how to defend herself, drifted away.

***

Inside their lean-to-tent, Valerie rubbed at the top of her arms. 'It's getting cold.'

Albert said nothing as he picked up two sleeping bags and zipped them together. Taking her face in his hands, he kissed her parted mouth. She drew away and put her head on his shoulder. 'Let's go back to France. One of those little villages south of Lyon, find a cottage and never set foot from it in a month. We'll find some way of making a living. It doesn't have to be much. Just as long as you're next to me when I wake up.'

'And you think I don't want the same?' he said, undressing her.

'When did you know?'

'Same as you. It crept up from the first day.'

'How did you know it crept up?' she said, playfully hitting his shoulder.

'Because I am wise.' He gripped her naked bottom and squeezed.

'You might be wise, but I'm bloody freezing.'

She slid into the sleeping bag and watched him undress, then coyly pulled a finger across her bottom lip. 'I was just wondering.'

'Oh yes, what were you just wondering?' He knelt and kissed the back of her neck.

'Are all the men from Iran, you know?'

'What?' He got in beside her and pulled the zip up.

'So...' She began pulling at her lip again. 'You know?' He put his lips to hers, letting her tongue explore where it wanted.

'I'm afraid you're going to have to explain,' he said, flirtatiously putting her finger back against her lip.

Valerie now let a warm hand move down his chest and gently take hold.

'So big, er... I mean, large.'

'Too much?'

'No, it's not a complaint.' She put her hands further down, cupping what she sought with a thoughtful touch. 'Do you know,' she whispered, moving back to where she had first put her hand, 'couples that are close consider the man's penis as something that belongs to both of them?'

It was not a clinical description of what she held so lovingly. Falling from Valerie's lips, it was full of sensuality. She then took his hand, kissed it, and supervised its short journey. Subtle caressing took seconds to swell hardening nipples, followed by an electrifying jolt as she gripped his hands

95

between her thighs.

Albert kissed her cheek as she descended from that most delightful of places and relaxed.

'I can't see you,' he said quietly. Valerie pulled the zip away and stroked his forehead as he suckled at her breast. Then, rolling on top, she slipped down until they met. Albert ran his fingers along her back, 'More comfortable than that camp bed last night.'

'Shh.' Valerie closed her eyes while rolling her hips.

Albert brushed her pink-tipped breasts as she started to lead him to the mountain tops. She teased and pulled him higher, only to let him tumble back. Subtle tiptoeing had him cursing and begging. Never releasing him from her grasp but not letting him join her on the highest peaks.

When he had been tortured long enough, she took hold and propelled them both into the furnace.

She lay with her whole weight on him as the sweat from their bodies cooled.

He gripped her in his arms. 'Where in God's name did that come from?'

The pulsing deep inside diminished, but Valerie stayed where she was. She would not let him withdraw, keeping the precious visitor as long as she could.

'Valerie?'

'Shh.' She lay her face next to his.

Albert pulled the sleeping bag across her shoulders and said no more.

\*\*\*

When she woke, Albert was lying next to her, his eyes open.

'Been awake long?' she asked.

'Fifteen minutes or so. I just wanted to look. I have many images of you locked away, but this is the one I will never forget, the most treasured... you asleep, at peace.'

'I can smell coffee. And I suppose a shower is out of the question?'

'We're in the middle of the desert... coffee yes, shower no.'

'Have we enough water for a good wash?'

'Sweet Allah above... we've enough to brush your teeth, the rest we drink.'

Valerie pulled herself up from the sleeping bag, revealing pale breasts. She took Albert's hand, giving it a light kiss. 'You're travelling with a woman.'

'Yes, I can see that,' said Albert.

He pulled on khaki trousers. 'I'll see what I can do.' He let the back of a finger glide over a pert nipple before leaving the tent.

She was pulling a brush through her hair when he returned, carrying a bowl of hot water. 'Just the water, no soap, I'm afraid.'

'It's okay; I'll be out in ten minutes.' Valerie rolled over and pulled a bottle of Nivea from her pack. 'Don't drink all the coffee.'

After rinsing spare knickers through in left-over water, she dressed and joined the men having breakfast. The lipstick and lightly applied perfume were not lost on the men as she sat, cross-legged, by Albert's side. He raised his eyebrows but said nothing as he passed a mug of coffee across.

The sergeant clapped his hands and got to his feet, 'Ten minutes, then everything away. We need to be gone by half-past.' After a word from Albert, he looked at his watch. 'Make that twenty-five past.'

*\*\*\**

The dust and sand thrown up by the vehicles subsided as the column slowed.

'The border?' asked Valerie.

Albert nodded as he picked up his radio and said something in Persian. 'We'll see what's happening.' He dropped the communicator on the transmission tunnel as the Humvees pulled over to the side. 'Wait here.' He jumped from the cab.

Valerie searched her jacket for some gum. 'Anyone else?' She held the pack up between the seats. Two sticks were taken, followed by a murmur of thanks.

The two men in the back were more interested in the surrounding desert as the sun glowed red on the horizon. Valerie swivelled to one side and put a foot up next to the handbrake. Outside there was nothing to see except wind-scarred sand. No checkpoint, not even a fence. Libya melted into Sudan much as it had done for centuries. There was no sign anyone had been there in years.

'What about landmines?' she asked, squirming around to the two men. The two still concentrated on the desert, one of them only telling her quietly that it was most unlikely around here. There was so much desert; it was pointless.

Full of sand, the hinges protested as Albert pulled the door open and sat back inside.

He seemed as equally subdued as his men. 'We're sitting on the border now.'

'No one here to stamp our passports, then?' said Valerie.

'No,' said Albert, preoccupied with what surrounded them. 'We're going down to Al Fashir; there's a displacement camp to the north of it.'

'Okay,' said Valerie slowly. 'It's going to get a bit hairy, then?'

'No.' He signalled the men to top up the Humvees with diesel. 'The people in the camps have more to worry about than us. They've precious

97

little food and only get water for a couple of hours a day. And as for medicines, forget it.'

Feeling guilty about her flippant remarks, Valerie fell silent.

As the men piled back into the vehicles, the lieutenant gave the signal to start up before getting into the lead Humvee.

'Just keep following,' said Albert, 'we'll make camp when we're a few kilometres further into Sudan.'

As the sun finally disappeared, he looked at his watch in the glow of the instruments.

\*\*\*

With Valerie's offer of helping with the evening rations declined, she went off in search of Rachid for more instruction in unarmed combat. Albert sat on an upturned water container and watched as she improved her skills until they were called around the fire three-quarters of an hour later.

'I was thinking about when we go into the refugee camp tomorrow,' said Albert as Valerie sat at his side. 'Who to take in. It'll be best if only a few of us go.'

Valerie pushed the last few pieces of couscous to the side of her plate and stood up. 'No.'

'Before you get on your high horse, just sit down; I haven't finished.'

'You don't have to,' she said, 'I'm going in with you. Full stop. End of story.'

'Valerie, please,' Albert's voice was quiet, deliberate, 'sit down.' As she dropped back down, Albert continued. 'We'll be camping eighty or ninety kilometres away. I was going to suggest you stay with the others while I go ahead with one or two of the men.' He held his hand up, demanding Valerie keep quiet. 'But, I'm not sure that's a good idea. We have to look more like officials, even international workers, and we need you to come. Okay?'

'Oh, I thought...'

'It'll make it look more official if we have; what shall I say...?'

'A woman in tow?'

\*\*\*

Dust, sand and the occasional outcrop of rock sped past as they drove south towards the camp at Nifasha, near to Al Fashir. A short eastwardly detour took them to a particular, high escarpment.

Jagged rock climbed three or four hundred feet from the pale desert. The convoy made for a dark overhang to the side, protected from the sun.

When parked, men with shovels from the two lead trucks jumped out and started to dig in what looked like a small tunnel beneath the rock.

'Supplies,' said Albert. 'We need to top-up fuel and water. It was dropped off by a Mi 17 last night.'

'Mi 17?' queried Valerie.

'Russian built twin-rotor helicopter, like a Chinook.'

'I'm beginning to wonder who I'm working for.'

Swinging out of the cab, Albert's only answer was that he would drive from now on.

Jerrycans, some containing water but most marked *Diesel*, were put in the back of each vehicle, others strapped to the sides. As they got back in, Valerie asked about why they needed so much in the way of supplies.

Half closing her eyes as the Humvee rumbled along, Valerie began to reassess what was happening, what had changed. Albert had kept things from her from the start, that was certain, but now, in the last half-hour, he had distanced himself, or so it seemed.

But more to the point, was he still an ally? After being the "token woman" going into the camp, would she be dumped in the middle of a hostile country? The thought of being deserted by Albert added to the confusion.

\*\*\*

A gentle shake woke Valerie around one in the afternoon. Albert threw her a crisp, long-sleeved, olive-green shirt and hijab.

'Ten minutes, no lipstick, no perfume.'

She went behind one of the trucks, replaced her T-shirt, then slid the Glock into the slim holster, pushing it down the inside of her jeans.

One of the soldiers stripped the Humvee of anything that had a military look, even going to the trouble of hanging a pair of furry dice from the rear-view mirror. A blue pennant, not unlike the United Nations flag, drooped from the radio aerial.

Albert, the lieutenant and Rachid wore the same type of shirt. All four looked official, even down to some nondescript insignia sewn on the pockets.

Rachid leaned forward from one of the rear seats. 'Haven't got any of that gum left, have you, Miss? Got a parched throat for some reason.'

'Sure.' Valerie rummaged around in her jacket and passed a couple of pieces behind her.

'Better put that in the storage box,' said Albert, 'looks far too Western.' Valerie smiled. His voice had gone back to the one she had fallen for; firm but warm.

'How long before we get there?'

Albert looked at the sat-nav, 'We'll be there by two-thirty.'

Valerie switched the radio on but could only find an Arabian news channel. She was about to turn it off when Albert put his hand on hers.

'Leave it.' All three of the men sat in stern concentration as Albert eased off the accelerator. They trundled along at no more than thirty miles an hour until Albert reached across and switched the off radio. He pushed his foot back down.

'What was that all about?' Valerie looked at Albert before turning to the two behind her. 'Well?' she said. All she received in reply was silence.

'Rachid,' said Albert, 'would you care to enlighten Valerie?'

'Not really, sir.'

'Well, I think someone should say something,' said Valerie, 'if it's only get out and walk!'

The lieutenant leaned forward, resting his forearms on the back of the major's seat. 'I think someone had told you that Rachid,' he nodded across to the young man by his side, 'was caught up in a bit of trouble at one time.'

'Yes.'

'We had some Iranian nationals down on the Ethiopia-South Sudan border. They had been giving medical help. There were a lot of people going blind by using the water. River blindness, they call it.'

'Onchocerciasis,' said Rachid quietly. 'Caused by a parasite.'

The lieutenant cleared his throat. 'Yes, what Rachid said.'

'Educated man, our Rachid,' said Albert. 'Not sure what he's doing in the army with us illiterates.'

'Didn't hear about Iranians helping in Africa,' said Valerie in a slightly querying voice.

Trying to remove a lump of sand from the windscreen, Albert gave the wipers a sweep. 'We don't all shout it from the rooftops when we go out to help others, you know.'

'Not like the Yanks and us, you mean?'

'Well, the Yanks anyway,' said Albert.

As if trying to get consent to carry on, the lieutenant looked at them all in turn.

'Sorry,' said Valerie, 'go on.'

'Well, there was a bit of trouble, and the major took us down to bring them back home, at least until it all blew over.' The lieutenant relaxed back into the seat. 'We managed to get the medical team together, all except one. Rachid and one of the other guys went off along the river to the next village to find him. We thought it was all straightforward,' he stretched over and ruffled Rachid's hair, 'that's why we sent Junior here.'

'They found the medic they were looking for, but it was a trap. The bastards didn't fancy coming up against thirty guys from the Special

Forces, so they were happy luring just two. Putting themselves up against two is about all they can deal with.'

Valerie looked at Rachid, but he just stared at the desert, saying nothing.

'We managed to get the youngster back,' said Albert, flicking his head towards Rachid. 'The medic and the other soldier, we lost. Both had their heads hacked off.'

Valerie took it in for a moment before asking, 'And this is connected with the news on the radio?'

Albert forced a cynical smile, 'Yes, it is.'

She had to wait a few minutes before he carried on.

'A lot of these terrorist groups have given up on their original aims and gone into business on their own account. They're just as ruthless, maybe more so.'

Valerie raised her eyebrows, 'Freelance terrorists? Can't say I can imagine anything worse than an IS recruit.'

Albert appeared not to have heard. 'The ones we came across last time called themselves Allah's Children.'

'Very droll,' said Valerie. 'These gangsters do seem to be the masters of the soundbite.'

'Well, they're here. That is, on the Ethiopia-Somali border. Or,' he added quietly, 'what's left of the Ethiopia-Somali border.'

'That's what was mentioned in the news,' explained the lieutenant.

'Bandit country,' said Valerie.

'Yes,' said Rachid softly, 'bandit country.'

Valerie again turned around to the young soldier and asked him what had happened, but the only reply was a slight shake of the head.

'It's going to be a mud bath,' said Albert, 'look at the sand.'

Valerie frowned, unable to grasp what he was talking about.

'The sand,' he repeated, 'it's pitted. Been raining. The conditions in the camp will be appalling. They always seem to pitch these places where the smallest amount of rain brings filth and misery.'

\*\*\*

'I need something to carry,' said Valerie as the camp appeared on the horizon.

'What?' Albert furrowed his brow.

'I can't walk into this camp looking like an official if all I'm doing is examining my nail varnish.'

Rachid rose from the seat and turned on his knees towards the back of the truck. Rummaging, he passed a canvas bag over his shoulder. 'Knew there was one here somewhere.' He pulled out a clipboard, 'Can't get more official looking than that.'

He sat back down and handed the board to Valerie. 'You'll find some paper and a pencil in the storage unit under your seat.'

*** 

The camp was nothing like Valerie had imagined. They pulled up in a car park, of sorts. The village itself was marked off in grids. There were, more or less, permanent shacks and housing on each block. The walkways and roads were little more than swamps. Losing balance in the rubble, she gave up trying to walk to the side of the track. Gripping the clipboard, she followed through the sludge.

The children were the most robust, running around, hiding and shouting. The ones with shoes, usually the wrong size, were the exception. Most had mud squeezing between naked toes.

Adding to the surreal surroundings complete with advertising boards, they came across a supermarket.

'They're never going to get out of this,' she said, catching up with Albert. 'It's all too bloody permanent.'

'It's changed since we last came through. But there is a way out, and a lot will sacrifice everything to take it.'

'Bloody people traffickers,' said Valerie.

Albert nodded. 'Start jotting something on your clipboard. We're attracting attention.'

Taking the pencil from the clip, Valerie surprised herself by making relevant notes. 'Where're we going, Albert? We seem to be aimlessly wandering about.'

He said nothing. But indicating they had arrived at wherever he had in mind, held up a hand before disappearing into a building that looked a little more substantial than its neighbours.

Shrubs and an almond tree stood on a cultivated patch of maybe ten yards by four. Sprouting onions, and what Valerie thought was coriander, pushed for attention around large clumps of okra, cucumber and aubergine. Tomato vines were tied to a simple mud wall. Only the odd building in the area had the traditional thatch. The others, blue plastic sheeting; the lucky ones, rusty tin.

'Kind of a headman,' said the lieutenant as they waited outside. 'He helped us last time, told us where he thought the terrorists were.'

After fifteen minutes of staring at their feet and kicking imaginary pebbles, Albert returned. Tight-lipped, he led them away to the western side of the encampment.

'Nice coffee,' was the only reply Valerie received by way of information.

She took a bottle of water from her bag and took a sip. She kept quiet, deciding that asking anything about what they were doing or where they were going would be answered with the same generic explanation.

There was one comment from Albert. 'Put that away,' he said tersely. 'These people have to queue for hours to get water. The last thing they want is a bottle from a French spa waving under their noses.'

She could have pointed out that the bottle was a re-fill from the convoy's supply but didn't.

Along with Albert's short quips starting to rub her up the wrong way, she was conscious that the nearest friendly civilisation was a thousand miles away. If something had happened to make Albert now distrust her, she couldn't think what it might be, but it was becoming more and more likely that the colonel had once more hung her out to dry. She had been sent to run down Bentley and not told why. And it was apparent Albert knew more about why she was here than she did. The fact that he was fed information from multiple sources only made her more uncertain.

'Where are we going?' she asked, feeling less of an equal and more like a lackey.

Smiling, Albert became friendly again. He told her that Bentley had been through the camp, going south, but someone might help them. She thought, suspiciously, the friendliness was to keep her sweet, keep her in line.

The hut Albert led them to was more what Valerie had pictured when she was first told of the camp. Walls, barely able to hold themselves erect, had shredded Red Cross boxes pegged into the gaps and cracks. The roof of torn plastic sheeting was held in place by stones and rusty engine parts. The doorway, made of an old blanket, was held to one side by Rachid as Valerie followed Albert into the gloom.

Albert was well into questioning an old woman before Valerie's eyes became accustomed to the dark interior. They were in a single room. A plastic drum had been cut in half for washing. A single bed was up against the back wall. Tied together, cardboard boxes had been made into a makeshift wardrobe. Three legs and a stack of bricks held a table up, an upturned chair on top.

Turning around, Valerie found herself looking at piles of unopened Red Cross boxes, stencilled in several different languages. The prominent stamp was in English, "Medicinal Supplies". She raised an eyebrow towards the woman, who had been following her roving gaze. She said something to Albert that, Valerie presumed, was some sort of explanation about the boxes. Not knowing what was being said, Valerie went back into the small yard.

The sun, not far above the western buildings, threw long shadows across pale brown walls. Holding the clipboard to her chest, Valerie automatically put a barrier between herself and Albert as he appeared. She was going to ask why the small shack should have, perhaps, thousands of pounds worth of drugs and medicine stacked up against the wall but stuck with the original, single question.

'Any joy?'

'We missed him by just a few hours,' said Albert. 'My bet is he knows we've not given up and is travelling south as fast as he can. If he gets down onto the border, it'll get dangerous, he'll be among friends... his friends, that is.'

'Terrorists.'

Albert nodded. 'There's an international airport at Al Fashir; we can get you out of here by tomorrow. It may be safer. A woman captured further south will....' He let the words drift off as he led the way back to the Humvee.

'There's a United Nations presence here; it can't be as bad as all that,' said Valerie.

'They're in a tight community,' Albert replied, 'there's no way you're going to get the blue flag guarding us with what we have in mind. They are peacekeepers, emphasis on *peace*.'

'I'm not going back,' said Valerie. 'Besides, like the rest of you, I have no stamp on my passport.'

'That's not a problem,' said the lieutenant as Albert opened the truck door. 'We can get your passport brought up to date. We have ways. You can be back in London tomorrow night.'

Valerie put her clipboard under the passenger seat and slid in beside Albert.

'I'm not going back,' she said quietly.

*** 

'Why do you have an allegiance to the people that sent you here?' asked Albert when they were alone, back at the temporary camp. Keeping voices low, they were sitting against one of the Humvees.

'Why have you changed?' Valerie retorted. 'You're not the man I made love with last night.'

With his knees hunched up, Albert took a swig from his mug of coffee.

'Why are you chasing Bentley?'

'You know why,' she said. 'I told you all I know. But you've been given new information, given new instructions. You're no longer on a personal mission... not that you ever were, that's just a coincidence.'

Albert got up and fetched them both something to eat.

'You want a break?' said Valerie, taking the plate, 'Time to think about what you're going to tell me?' He scooped up a piece of chicken and shook

104

his head.

'Can't. Can you get in touch with your controller, and ask him what you're doing here?'

'I've worked for him before.' Valerie's answer was one of resignation. 'I didn't find out what it was about then. Had to work it out for myself. I doubt I'll know about it this time… at least, not until it's over.'

'By the sweet God above, how can you work for anyone on that basis?'

'Blackmail.' Valerie got up and scraped most of her meal into a black bin liner. 'That and a load of money,' she said, sitting back down.

'Money. Means a lot to you, does it?'

'Yes, it does, especially when you need it… and don't have any.'

With his head leaning against the truck, he turned towards her. 'Where does it go? On that car of yours?'

The suppressed laugh was sarcastic. 'Thought you knew me better than that.'

\*\*\*

Valerie woke with a start, then realised she was being shaken. She pulled her arm from the sleeping bag and blinked at the Rolex. 'Five past three! Something on fire?'

Albert pulled the zip down and took hold of her hand. 'Come on.'

'Gordon bloody Bennett, Albert. Where are we going?'

'Quiet,' he hissed, guiding them past a guard, then around a small outcrop of rock. 'You'll wake the others.'

The night was at its coldest as the moon threw finely defined shadows across the sand.

'Albert, for crying out loud, I'm not a ruddy soldier; I need my eight hours.'

'Sit,' he said, pushing her to the ground.

She rubbed at her eyes.

'Bentley,' he said, looking over to the vehicles. 'Dear Allah, I could be shot for this.'

'Then don't.'

'I love my country, but… Bentley, he's got something dangerous hidden away somewhere, maybe out here.'

'Okay,' said Valerie. 'What?'

Albert gritted his teeth. 'Biological weapon. Warhead, something.'

'Bloody hell.'

'There's worse.'

'There would be,' she said.

'Apparently, there is enough of the stuff to infect central Tehran, London, Paris, wherever.' He stopped for a moment. 'And…'

105

'And?' said Valerie, 'There's an and?'

'A delivery system.'

'Well, that's just dandy, isn't it? I take it that us and...' she nodded over the rock, 'the rest of the guys, are all that stands between the warheads and a couple of hundred thousand dead people? No good calling in the cavalry, I suppose?'

In the dim light, she could make out he was shaking his head. 'Flooding the place with a couple of regiments would be tantamount to pressing the trigger. Even if they couldn't hit one of their chosen targets, there are still plenty of big cities not too far away.'

'Yes,' Valerie gazed up at the stars, 'innocent people are innocent people, no matter where. Is that why you were acting-?'

'Yes,' he cut her short. 'I had the message come through earlier on. Didn't know what to think. Still don't.'

# TEN

'Are you sure you want to continue?' said Albert as they climbed into the Humvee. 'Al Fashir airport is not far. We skirt around it.'

Valerie said nothing. She checked the Glock, slid it into the holster inside her jeans, and asked for her hijab.

'That's some woman you've got there, Major,' Rachid said, handing over the square of black silk. 'If you don't mind me saying, sir.'

Keeping quiet, Albert held the young man's eye for a moment as he looked in the rear-view mirror.

Before picking up the main route south, the convoy had to put in a severe dogleg as it skirted the airport. They left the city's outskirts, following the road that varied little as it passed the occasional village. Now and again, Valerie looked at the compass that swung slightly west, then a little east as it unwaveringly pointed the way to the southern border. She must have looked at it for the umpteenth time before realising the instrument, fixed to the top of the dash with double-sided tape, had *Silva Sweden* written on the base. It was a tactical yacht compass. A device for racing, and having a good time in a safe world, was guiding her into danger.

The convoy stopped for a comfort break. Valerie and the men went in opposite directions around a roadside clump of vegetation and rocks.

'Drop of water?' said Valerie as she appeared again. One of the soldiers splashed a little water over her outstretched hands and handed her a small towel. She smiled and, after thanking him, apologised.

'That's all right, Miss. Have to make a few allowances for travelling with a lady.'

Knowing the men would not use the water for anything so frivolous, she took a sandwich from the offered tin before anyone could hand one across.

The stopping-off place had not been chosen at random: after about twenty minutes, two motorcyclists arrived. Dismounting, the riders quickly went into a huddle with Albert. While considering the earnest conversation, she chewed on the sandwich made with some kind of pita bread; laced with coriander and lemon, it bulged with goat's cheese.

Both riders wore short-sleeved shirts. One had jeans and the other leather trousers, making them look like they'd come straight from a nineteen-fifties motorbike gang. The one with the jeans had nothing on his head, his long hair reaching down to his beard. The other sported a squat helmet that resembled a battered pudding basin.

What had begun as understated gesturing became wild waving, mainly from the one with the long hair. Creating more flying dust and sand than necessary, the two cyclists returned to the road and turned north.

'Going in the opposite way to trouble, are they?' said Valerie as Albert gathered everyone around. 'Can't say I blame them.'

'I can still get one of the men to follow with you, and take you to the airport.'

Valerie approached Albert and punched him, a little more than playfully, in the arm. 'Any more of that, and I'll get someone to take *you* north.'

'Okay, we're in it together, then.'

Valerie looked around as the men either nodded, put their thumbs up, or just grinned.

'Okay. Rachid, before I fill everyone in on what we have to do, I want you to look after Valerie. Stick by her side, guard her with your life.'

With emphasised bravado, Rachid took his pistol and quickly pulled the slide back; then, letting go, pushed it back into its holster. Accompanied by catcalls, he stood at Valerie's side.

***

Sweeping down to South Sudan, then keeping to either one side of the border or the other, the convoy swapped between Kenya and Ethiopia on the way to Somalia. They picked up more fuel and water, plus a small package for Valerie. She had pulled Albert to one side when she found out more supplies were to be picked up.

'You know,' she said, pulling Albert to one side, 'time of the month just around the corner.'

The rest was uneventful. Rachid stuck to Valerie like a second skin. She did have to clear her throat to get a little privacy from time to time; apart from that, it could have been a safari holiday. With no indication they had crossed the border, the Humvees parked in the shelter of some Acacia.

'Welcome to Somalia,' said Albert, sliding from the driver's seat.

Casually, Valerie brushed the ever-present dust from her jeans and top. It was one of the most dangerous places on earth but felt no different from any other stops. A nearby herd of goats looked remarkably healthy, considering the scrub they were feeding on. Sitting on an outcrop of rock, a boy leaned on a crook several sizes too large for his stunted five feet. What was left of his T-shirt fluttered in the light evening breeze. He scrutinised his new neighbours for a minute, then, getting bored, turned back to his charges.

'There's a village over those dunes,' said Albert, pointing towards the setting sun. He gave a few orders before turning to Valerie and Rachid, telling them they should get going while there was still a little light.

There was another surprise in the village. Neat rows of small dwellings lined the main street where children were noisily chasing a half-inflated football. Village elders played backgammon in the shelter of a scrubby tree. Between neighbouring houses, brightly coloured clothes dried in the warm air.

'Are you sure we've come to the right place, Albert? It all looks so normal.'

'Yes, this is what it should be like,' he said. 'Trouble is, too many self-proclaimed saviours can't stay out. Giving everyone their version of a better life.'

He bent over one of the board games and had a few words with one of the players. A wrinkled forefinger pointed to a building across the street. Pulling at her hijab she followed the two men.

Inside, an old man rocked gently in an oversized oak chair. He exchanged a few words with Albert

'Last time we were here,' said Albert in answer to Valerie's querying gaze, 'I asked the village elder what he would like for the information. He asked for a large rocking chair.'

'Nothing like a nice rocking chair.' The old man surprised Valerie with his excellent English. He smiled at her furrowed brow. 'I used to work for the British embassy in Mogadishu, back in the day when Britain still had some influence.'

'Blimey,' said Valerie quietly, 'that must make you around a hundred and fifty.'

Laughing, he took a calabash pipe from the side table. 'I like your friend, Major. She's planted in reality.' Then added quietly, 'I'm getting short of tobacco.'

'There'll be as much as you can smoke in a lifetime if you can put us on the right track.'

There was a jar of homemade spills in the hearth. Albert selected one and put an end to the fire. 'Here,' he said, handing it over. The old man started producing smoke that smelt familiar.

'British,' he said, holding up a pouch, 'Saint Bruno.'

Albert took a photo from his top pocket and passed it over.

'Name's Bentley,' he said, 'may have changed it to Barclay.'

The old man inclined it towards the glowing oil lamp. 'Or something else entirely,' he murmured while scrutinising the picture for a moment. 'I'll want a bottle of scotch too,' he said, holding up his pipe.

'No problem,' said Albert. 'I'll throw in a brand-new Meerschaum.'

'You missed him, twenty-four hours. Heading south. He asked where the Badaadinta Badah were operating from.'

'The what?' said Valerie.

'Badaadinta Badah,' repeated Rachid, 'Saviours of the Sea.'

'Pirates,' explained Albert. 'With international navies, their activities have tailed off. But freelancers still crop up now and again.'

'Used to be considerable money in it a few years ago. But since international cooperation has more or less put a stop to it...' the old man shrugged his shoulders, then, with a stubby finger, pushed the loose ash into his pipe, 'those left have branched out into other activities. Got a lot more violent.'

'You mean they weren't before?'

The old man shook his head, 'Compared with what we put up with now, they'd have blended in with The Royal Yacht Squadron very nicely.'

Warming to the old man, she asked if he had any idea where they might be now.

'North of the capital, right up around The Horn. If they go out, it'll be into The Gulf of Aden. They can hide along the coast or even go over to Yemen.' He blew a huge cloud of smoke into the room. 'You've got to remember how these men think. They consider themselves legitimate, and like any big noise, they don't take kindly to others poking their noses in. They will do anything to keep their way of life intact.'

'And that includes rubbing us out,' said Valerie.

'Precisely.'

While talking, a woman, whom Valerie presumed the elder's wife, brought in a tray. Not having the old man's command of English, she gestured towards the beverages. Valerie took one of the offered cups. The sweet tea was balanced heavily with spices. She recognised cardamom, cinnamon, cumin and ginger as they danced around her taste buds.

'That's incredible,' she said. 'Your good lady must tell me how to make it.'

As the old man finished with his best guess as to where Bentley was, he jotted a few things on a piece of paper.

'Maybe condensed milk, if you haven't a goat,' he added, passing the recipe over.

'No,' said Valerie, wondering where she would keep one on the houseboat, 'no goat.'

She had never felt so detached from reality. For a moment wishing herself in the pouring winter rain outside some respondent's house, gathering evidence in a divorce case. Mind-numbingly dull seemed much the better option, not that alternatives were available. First thing tomorrow, they would be heading out with little more than fingers to cross.

'No goat,' she repeated, leaving the old man's house.

***

'That's appropriate,' said Valerie as the convoy departed for The Horn. She'd found a radio station from somewhere. Glenn Frey's *The Heat Is On* crackled from a single speaker.

'Decadence.' Albert pulled on the wheel as they rounded a deep rut.

'So speaks a Leonard Cohen fan.' She looked over her shoulder, 'Anything from the evil west you guys like? Music-wise, that is.'

The two in the back looked at Albert via the rear-view mirror.

He shook his head. 'It's okay, guys; everyone knows the genie's out of the bottle. Rachid over there is into The Who and Beyoncé.'

'Knew you'd be a Beyoncé fan,' said Valerie, 'but The Who?'

The convoy made good time as they kept up a steady banter on the various merits of British and American contemporary music. They were so relaxed, passing a bottle of water around, that the crack, when it came, took them all by surprise. Valerie received a shove from Albert, sending her into the footwell.

'Stay there!' he barked, bringing the Humvee to a halt. He grabbed an AK-47 passed from the back and jumped from the cab. Valerie squirmed around and, taking the Glock from her belt, pulled back the slide. She unfolded her legs that had been jammed under the dash and took a look over the door lip.

'Keep down.' Laying on his back, cradling a rifle, Rachid made the peculiarly polite request, 'Please. If you come to any harm, I'll be in it up to my neck.'

'Oh, perish the thought,' said Valerie, risking another look. 'For a moment, I believed you cared.'

He reached between the seats and pushed her head down. 'I do; just keep down.'

Valerie spat several obscenities as a bullet, entered by the door pillar, shattering the gear lever's top and leaving by the opposite door window. 'Come on, Rachid.' Valerie crawled over the transmission tunnel and opened the driver's door. 'Out. The last thing we want is a round bouncing about in here.'

Valerie made for the far side of some rocks, pulling the young man after her. With bullets kicking up the sand and ricocheting from the outcrop, they both sat with their backs hunched against the boulders.

'Lucky,' said Rachid.

'Lucky?' Valerie twisted around. 'Must remember to be this lucky again.'

Rachid checked his gun and took a look over the top, 'I mean this lump of rock being here,' he replied quietly.

Twenty yards away, amongst a ridge of sand, an explosion covered them in debris. 'That's bending the rules a bit,' said Valerie, 'bringing grenades to a gunfight.'

'No such things as rules out here.'

Valerie chanced a look across towards the Humvee. 'Who are they?'

'Could be any of half a dozen groups. They're after the vehicles. The bullet that hit us just now was probably a mistake, a stray. They fire a few rounds to stop the convoy, then pick us off. The lead truck must have come across an obstacle; otherwise, we'd be long gone.'

Valerie saw a man running towards them, recognised it was not one of the soldiers, and put him down with two quick shots.

'Couldn't have been one of us,' she countered to Rachid's frown, 'wild hair and beard.'

Whether it was because the ambushers thought Valerie and Rachid were a weak point or because they were nearer to the vehicles was of no consequence; several heavily armed men were attacking the position. Reasoning the insurgents would not use their weapons accurately while running, they both stood and fired together.

'Empty,' she said, getting back behind the rock. 'You got anything left?'

Rachid said something she did not understand, then hit the bottom of the magazine. 'Last clip.'

'Is this where I say save the last one for me?' Sitting down, she let her head fall back, gazing at the stars. 'How many of the bastards are there?' As if in answer, Rachid shot at two more, trying to outflank them.

Valerie let out a scream. 'Anyone about?'

A reply from the front of the convoy was inaudible.

'Ammunition!' Valerie's yell received no response. She looked back towards the vehicle. There were hundreds, perhaps thousands of rounds in the Humvee. 'Ammunition!' she screamed again.

Gunfire and the occasional explosion, echoing from the front of the convoy, were the only answer. There would be no help coming from that direction; they'd have to look after themselves.

There was little point in discussing what to do; or sitting behind the rock persuading Rachid what she had in mind was the best option. She told him to give what cover he could, then ran for the Humvee before he had time to argue. A shot whistled close, then sand kicked up around her ankles as she pulled open the door.

She threw the empty clip on the floor and grabbed a full one from the central storage unit. Pushing it into the handle, there was just time to turn and shoot one of the guerrillas in the chest as he appeared in the doorway. The dead body fell forward, knocking her back into the seat. Struggling, she pulled one leg from underneath the insurgent and planted it on his shoulder. A push released her other leg; she propelled the lifeless body out onto the sand.

Scrambling into the back seats, she rummaged around for ammunition. Among the rounds and clips was another Glock. Everything was bundled into a canvas bag before she ran back to Rachid.

'Here.' Taped to each other, she passed two clips across.

'For heaven's sake,' said Rachid, 'don't you ever tell the major what you did. I'd never see another sunrise.' He let an auto-burst go across the clearing.

Hunched up against the rock, Valerie let her head loll back. 'I wasn't going to let them wander over and casually put a bullet in my head. If they wanted me dead, then it was going to be in fucking flames.'

Being preoccupied with reassessing their position, they didn't at first realise the battle had finished. The whole action had taken little more than fifteen minutes.

'Got it,' said Valerie, searching through the bag. She took a bottle of Pepsi and unscrewed the top. 'Yuk! Warm.' She wiped the neck and handed it across.

'There wasn't any lemon, then?'

'Sorry… couldn't find the ice, either.'

Although quiet, Valerie and Rachid thought it prudent to sit and finish the Pepsi rather than risk revealing their whereabouts too soon and being mistaken for the insurgents.

After about five minutes, Albert looked over the top. 'Okay?'

'Just about,' said Valerie, getting to her feet. 'Do we know who they were?'

'It wasn't anything to do with Bentley if that's what you mean.'

'Have we lost anyone?'

Albert shook his head, 'One of our guys stopped one in the side, but he'll be all right. He's being patched up now. What happened to you?'

'Oh, we're okay, scared a couple away, but nothing too serious.'

Albert looked over the ground between the Humvee and where they had been hiding. 'Is that so,' he said, looking at the five bodies.

***

Valerie leaned on the Humvee door as the last of fifteen bodies were stacked under a rock ledge.

'We can't just leave them here,' she said to Albert. 'I know what they are, but we can't leave them.'

'We haven't the time to bury them, but the lieutenant is calling through now. There'll be a digger here before the vultures get to them.'

'Albert, no. You can't just dig a trench with a JCB and roll them in.'

Albert stared into her eyes, 'It's more than they'd do for you, believe me.'

'Albert.'

'Okay, okay.' He called over the back of the Humvee. 'Lieutenant, tell them to bring an Imam with them.'

Valerie pulled at Albert's arm and kissed his cheek. 'Thank you.'

'Thought you didn't believe?'

'I don't… but they did.'

***

'Best bet?' asked Valerie when they were on their way again. 'Bentley… from the information you got. Where is he?'

'There are a few places along the coast where these guys have central bases. Close to a village or even in it. He'll be in one of them.'

'And if not?'

'Don't even go there, Valerie. I'm trying to put that to the back of my mind. What I'm more concerned about now is how to persuade him to tell us where these weapons are.'

'And delivery systems,' she said quietly.

'They've got to be in the same place,' chipped in Rachid. 'Surely it makes little sense to keep them in separate places, or at least not too far from each other. But where?'

Albert slowed and followed the lead vehicles around a stretch of the missing road surface. 'Here, or across in Yemen… The UK.'

'Dear God.' Valerie's face whitened, 'The UK? Can't be.'

'Scary, isn't it.'

Albert re-joined the road and put his foot down as the Humvees in front drew away. 'Out here, in North Africa and across the Middle East, is far away. Out of mind. But if it's in the middle of London, it's different; you'll be going through what the countries north of Saudi and around here have had for the last thirty years.'

'Yeah. We and America have a lot to answer for. Throw troops into places where we have no right to be... then leave them to sort out the crap we've created.' Valerie gazed at the scrubland flashing past. 'How are you going to persuade him?'

'Bentley?'

She nodded.

'Don't ask.'

She sat for a while trying to square her moral conscience against, maybe, hundreds of thousands of lives.

'It all depends,' said Albert when Valerie didn't say anything.

'On?'

'A fanatic will say nothing, thinking he'll be on his way to paradise. But I'm not sure Bentley is a fanatic, not anymore.'

'So,' said Valerie, 'he's now in it for the money.'

'That's my opinion. He's changed sides before. It makes no difference to him as long as he comes out with a fatter bank balance.'

'And women.'

115

Between dunes, glimpses of sea sparkled on top of the rich blue. Some long sheds passed by the window. They skirted a small village and parked from sight by a thicket of thorns.

'You'll be okay to come this time.' Albert shook the dust from his shirt and trousers as he got out of the cab. 'We're only on the *edge* of the more dangerous part of the country.'

'How many times have you been around here?' said Valerie, flicking a towel across her back.

'Oh, once or twice.' He took a pair of binoculars and looked out to sea. 'Nothing. Not a single fishing boat.'

'You don't think he'll be here?'

'Not a chance,' said Albert, 'but we may learn something.'

A small car park next to a grocery shop had the usual smattering of Toyota pickups and twenty-year-old Mercs. Surrounded by protective traffic cones, a highly polished white Lexus SUV drew a whispered comment from Valerie.

'There's money around,' said Rachid. 'It's a right-hand drive. Probably stolen from Kensington High Street last week.'

'By the time some poor guy had looked out of his bedroom window and called the police, it was in a container and on its way to North Africa.'

In the shop, Albert dropped a ten-dollar note on the rickety counter and produced Bentley's photo.

'Not the Somali Shilling?' said Valerie.

'They'd rather have the Yankee dollar.'

A few words were exchanged before the shop assistant pointed along the street.

As before, 'Salaam' was the only recognised word as they entered a small garage. A driveshaft from its lofty perch on a car ramp drunkenly hung from an old Merc 200. The mechanic, pulling on a large spanner above his head, looked around at Albert's greeting. Valerie scrutinised her surroundings as, producing a hundred-dollar bill, Albert began a conversation in Persian.

The workshop was perhaps fifteen yards from front to back and eight or so across. A couple of vices and tools sat on an oily bench that ran along the back wall. On a table, fluttering in the breeze from the open door, American dollars were held down by a damaged piston head. Valerie caught Albert's attention and nodded towards the currency. Albert took another hundred-dollar bill from his pocket and pointed to the small table. Taking a cloth from his back pocket, the mechanic led Albert back into the sunlight. More discussion followed as, wiping his hands, he pointed back along the road.

Pushing the dollar bill into the man's top pocket Albert said something, and lightly touching his forehead, turned to Valerie. 'We've missed him again, but we're gaining. He part-exchanged that Mercedes up on the ramp and bought a four-by-four. Shogun.'

'Heading north?'

'Yes,' said Albert, 'heading north towards The Horn.'

\*\*\*

Two more ocean-side villages followed before Valerie turned to Albert. 'We must be breathing down his neck.'

She said nothing of the nagging thought that the situation was not what it seemed. Along with the soldiers checking kit, they were standing on a beach of finely ground shells. Two or three bright blue umbrellas underlined Valerie's feeling that it was all some kind of bizarre illusion.

'Not far behind,' was all he said.

The Shogun was a suitable vehicle, but there was no way it could outrun a Humvee on this type of terrain. And fuel? They were well supplied, but where was Bentley getting his? She was just about to tell him that she thought all they were doing was keeping pace when Rachid came across with a laptop, pointing to the next village on the Google map. Albert nodded while giving orders to make camp.

'Can I have a look?' said Rachid, sitting next to Valerie.

'What's that?'

'The Rolex.'

Valerie undid the buckle and handed it over. 'You like it, do you... the Submariner?'

'Yes.' He held it against his wrist. 'Looks good on a NATO strap. Why a man's, and why an old one?'

Valerie sidestepped the question. 'Expert, are you?'

'Not really. But on the dial, it has the depth in metres before the feet. That makes it around....' Rachid thought for a moment.

'Nineteen-sixties,' Valerie cut in. 'That one's sixty-seven. Rolex turned it around and put feet before metres in sixty-nine or seventy.'

'Yes, for the American market, hasn't changed since.'

'You seem to know a lot about them,' she said, slipping it back on.

'Going to get one. That's if I can ever get the money together.'

'You must pass through enough duty-free shops at airports: get one without having to pay a premium.'

Rachid shook his head, 'Don't want a modern one, want a *real* one,' he said. 'Nineteen-sixties, like yours.'

Rising above the sand and scattered bushes, the sun quickly warmed the morning air. Albert was no longer next to Valerie, and on questioning Rachid, she found that the major and sergeant had left early.

'Any idea why?' she asked.

Rachid shrugged his shoulders and passed her a small bowl containing a couple of eggs nestling in a spicy tomato sauce.

'I'll take you back home,' she said as he added a lump of goat's cheese, 'you'd go very well in my galley.'

She turned away as his gaze reminded her of another young man who had not survived an alliance with her.

They had to wait three hours until a brusque Albert returned, telling them to mount up. It was a further two hours before Valerie asked what was going on. Albert said nothing until the convoy stopped at the edge of a bluff. He left the cab with the lieutenant and told Rachid to stay and look after Valerie. The passionate kiss he gave her did little to reassure; neither did him saying that they would radio when it was safe for her and Rachid to catch them up.

What had happened, and more to the point, what was happening now could only be guessed. No longer sure of the situation, she said nothing, only giving a nod while squeezing Albert's hand.

Unable to watch him leave, she looked away as Rachid stared at the diminishing trail of dust the convoy left behind.

# ELEVEN

Valerie looked at her watch as the sun retreated behind the western horizon. 'How are we for fuel?'

'Plenty.' Rachid took a final mouthful of water and threw the empty bottle onto the back seat. 'Why?'

'We've been here long enough; I'm beginning to think we've been stood up.'

'We can't, Miss,' he said, anticipating her next move. 'You'll get me into trouble.'

'Trouble? We're on our own in the middle of the desert, if you haven't noticed.' Valerie slid into the driver's seat. 'So, it's wrestling me to the ground and tie me up, or....'

\*\*\*

The track levelled out at the bottom of the cliff as they progressed along the valley. Rachid leaned over the back and pulled an AK-47 onto his lap.

'Right, a quick lesson,' he said, switching on the interior light. 'Safety,' he pushed a small lever on the right, 'up off, down fire.' He then pressed a button behind the magazine, took it out, then slid the top lever back and forth. 'Make sure there isn't one in the chamber, just like a pistol.' He demonstrated the loading of the clip and replaced it.

'No wonder it's so popular.' She accelerated as Rachid shut the light off.

'Yes, about as simple as you can get. There's another in the back, but let's hope we don't have to use them.'

\*\*\*

A few hours later, Valerie stifled a yawn. 'We'll have to stop.' She squinted at the faint glow from her watch. It was just turned one. 'Six hours will be fine. We can be on our way by seven.'

'Miss?'

Valerie followed a short track to the side of the road and stopped by a stunted tree. 'Yes, what is it?'

'Any idea where they are or what they're doing?'

'No idea where they are, but it can't be far away. As to what they're doing....'

\*\*\*

Rachid drew her attention to it first. As Valerie poured fuel into the Humvee, he took hold of her wrist. 'Can you hear it?' She snapped the top back on the can and stood still. The surrounding desert was silent. Closing her eyes, she concentrated. Gunfire, from the north, was just about discernible.

'How far?'

'Not sure. It's far off, but just how far?' Pushing his lips together, he shook his head.

'It can carry a long way,' said Valerie. 'Gunfire, I mean.'

Rachid took a pair of binoculars and looked to the north. 'A very long way, especially in the still air like this.' He talked slowly, concentrating on the horizon. 'Nothing.'

She was utterly reliant on the young man. If anything happened and she was left on her own, her chances would not be good.

'How old are you, Rachid?'

He let the glasses drop to his waist, 'Twenty-three.'

'Why do you stay in the army? With your intelligence, it would have been easy to opt out and go to university.'

'Is that so?'

It was a while ago when she'd realised she was in the presence of someone with far more brainpower than she possessed.

'Hell, I could do with a cigarette.' He raised his eyebrows. 'Gave them up recently,' she explained. Indicating Rachid could drive for a while, she climbed into the passenger side.

Coming back onto the road, Rachid pointed a thumb over his shoulder. 'Better check our weapons.'

Besides the side arms and AK-47s, they both had what looked like enough ammunition to fight off the entire Islamic State.

'There are grenades in shoulder bags behind the back seats. Grab one if it looks like trouble.'

'Ha.' She spat the word out. 'Not sure I could handle one of those.'

'You'll soon get the hang of it if half a dozen insurgents come charging towards you. Just pull the pin out and throw... well, lob it, as you see in the movies. And get down,' he added thoughtfully, 'the blast goes a long way.'

'Yeah,' replied Valerie dryly, 'explaining you'd been hit by your own grenade could prove a trifle embarrassing.'

'You wouldn't be doing much explaining, I'm afraid.'

Once in a while over the next couple of hours, Rachid stopped the Humvee; focusing on the slightest sound, and each time, as they looked at each other, it was only with a shrug of shoulders. That is until Valerie spotted a few wisps of smoke behind some low hills.

'Northeast,' she said, looking at the compass.

Half an hour later, Rachid shook his head when Valerie asked why he'd headed off to an overhanging rock to park up. 'We'll hide the truck up to one side and....'

'Go in on tip-toe?'

She checked the Glock before shoving it back into its holster.

'Everything.' Rachid handed her one of the rifles and a bag of grenades. 'We might need everything.'

'Tooled up?' Trying to ease the situation, unaware that it would be the last time she would do so for a long time, Valerie smiled.

To the side of the dune, a crop of bushes surrounded rocks and a fallen tree. Emerging from cover, it became apparent from where the smoke had been coming: the remains of a Humvee was still smouldering. Several bodies lay about, some soldiers, mostly insurgents.

'Hell's teeth.' After crouching, Valerie stood up to see that she and Rachid were the only living things. 'We'd better check our guys first.' The tremor in her voice was accompanied by shaking hands. Putting the bag and rifle to one side, she went from one body to the next, removing tags from her Iranian comrades. 'Three of ours,' she shouted to Rachid, who was across the clearing. 'How many over there?'

Walking towards him, she was immediately halted. Rachid put himself in her way, holding her back.

She didn't have to be told. Gently pressing a hand to his chest, she went over to a body face down in a gully.

'Please,' she said quietly, 'help me roll him over.'

Stroking fingers across his face, Valerie closed Albert's eyes.

There was nothing on the still night air until Valerie's primitive scream split the desolate scene. Kneeling by her side, Rachid rocked back on his heels. He did nothing to stop the unworldly noise; it was repeated until exhausted, she fell back.

As if trying to bring him back to life, she grasped at ghostly images of her dead lover. Echoes of his laughter tortured a brain unable to accept the man's cold body, known for such a short time, in her arms.

Rachid said nothing. He didn't comfort her; lost in his misery, he didn't know how.

With an unrelenting grip, Valerie swore vengeance under her breath. Against whom, she did not know.

A minute or five or ten passed until she eventually relented and got to her feet. Shaking legs took her back to the Humvee's open door. She sat on the floor and let her head rest against the side of the seat. More time drifted by before she looked towards Rachid. He was kneeling by his major's side, recanting something; she didn't know what. The quiet words, no doubt in Persian, brought no comfort.

Feeling little more than emptiness, she went across and put her hand on his shoulder. There was something clasped in Albert's hand. She bent down and released his fingers; a small eternity ring fell into Valerie's palm. 'Belonged to his late wife, do you think?'

'I wouldn't know, Miss,' he whispered, 'but I wouldn't have thought so.'

Valerie felt physically numb. She looked around; nothing would register. Her mind blurred, defending her from reality. 'Can we get help?'

Rachid shook his head, 'We're too far from anywhere.'

'We can't leave them here.'

Rachid went to the Humvee and returned with a spade and pick.

'There's only us.' He dropped the spade on the ground and started kicking the dirt. 'It should be okay here.' He struck the ground several times with the pick before looking back at Valerie, 'As long as we don't get down to any bedrock.'

Valerie removed her jacket and began clearing loose stones. 'We can't dig separate graves,' she said as the sand and gravel piled up behind them.

Rachid did not break from the rhythmic swing.

Maybe thirty minutes passed before Valerie stopped him with an offer of water. With sweat dripping from his face, he drank close to a litre before handing it back. Valerie, who had been taking regular sips, finished what was left.

'We'll need rocks.' Rachid pointed around. 'There's no way we can go down two metres.' He removed his shirt and started shifting the loose dirt.

\*\*\*

With neither asking the other about a suitable depth, they kept going for two days.

'We'll have to put them in now.' Rachid sat on the edge of the pit. Over to the side, the bodies were covered by a green tarpaulin. 'Things are going to get very unpleasant if they're above ground another day.'

Valerie nodded her agreement. 'Doesn't seem right to put them in the same grave.'

Rachid jumped down and separated the pit with a rough line of stones. 'Okay?' He held out a hand, and Valerie pulled him out.

'Fine.' There was someone formulating decisions before speaking. Someone somewhere was pulling strings... but it wasn't her.

The two of them struggled for an hour to get the bodies into a reverent position until Valerie, eventually, pronounced herself satisfied. By the side of the grave, she lay on her stomach, folding each of their arms, lastly kissing her forefinger and pressing it to Albert's lips.

Filling in with sand and rocks, they finished off with stones that were more or less flat.

'Do you think he would mind if I kept the ring?' said Valerie, standing at Rachid's side.

'Probably why he had it in his hand.'

Rachid said a few words at the graveside that, once again, Valerie did not understand. 'Did you want to say something?'

Valerie shook her head, 'It would be hypocritical... I don't believe.'

With the hard toil over, Valerie's adrenalin dried up. Still, with a feeling of remoteness, tears did no more than glisten as Rachid started up the Humvee.

'Might be a good idea to try and contact the others,' she said after a while. The radio was fixed between them, above the transmission tunnel. Rachid picked up the microphone and, pressing the button to the side, said something in Persian. Releasing the switch, the only response was static. He tried again; the same crackling hiss came from the speaker.

'We're nearing the coast, but the road's running out. The Ogo Mountains run across our way.'

'Best bet?' asked Valerie.

'You guess,' he replied. 'Go to the east, but there's no road. North takes us around, but we can't go on forever.' He motioned over the back, 'Fuel.'

'I presume there are dollars in this vehicle somewhere?'

Rachid pointed to a storage unit behind them.

'Better get to the next village,' she said, pulling hundred-dollar bills from a leather pouch. 'You call it, east or north?'

Rachid flicked his fingers across the sat-nav screen. 'Nearest is north.'

He drove off steadily, partly saving fuel and partly dodging ruts in the road. After a while, Valerie passed him a bottle of water.

'How did you get into this?' he asked, taking a swig.

'Bloody good question. Don't suppose you'll believe devotion to duty?'

'No, Miss. I know next to nothing about you, but I know enough to dismiss that.'

'We could be heading into a load of trouble, couldn't we?' Only consulting the instruments, Rachid said nothing. 'Better call me Valerie, then.'

Bumping over the deteriorating track, she tried, unsuccessfully, to tune the radio to some music. Giving up, she let her head rest against the back of the seat and chose something more comfortable: assess her life. What was it about? And more importantly, where was it going?

She'd more or less begun to cut the ties with Simon, not because she loved him any less. He was becoming distant. And there was always the old cliché to fall back on: he wouldn't want her to carry on with nothing to live for. He would have wanted her to let go.

Albert had been known just a few weeks. And as to feeling guilty about not feeling guilty, she didn't even want to go there, except to find who was responsible for his death. But that could be out of her hands. The culprit may be lying by his side, under the rocks and sand.

She must have fallen asleep; Rachid was shaking her shoulder. 'Put your hijab on.' He drew up beside a faded Texaco pump and jumped out.

'Do you think it's the real thing?' she said, joining him by the pump. 'The diesel, I mean.'

'Could be anything.' A boy of no more than ten began filling the Humvee. 'If you get the cans out, we'll fill everything.'

'How far before we have to start worrying again?'

'We've long-range tanks, plenty spare in the back. But you can usually find diesel, even out here... hopefully.'

Back on the road, Rachid followed a narrow track to higher ground. 'See if we get anything out of the radio, a few hundred metres higher might help.'

Valerie stepped out of the cab and let Rachid try the radio once more. In contrast to the desert, the mountains they had passed through were lush, even at the lower altitude. Behind where they had parked, dark green foliage covered the rising ground that ended in a white cliff face. Two or three large birds, too far away to identify, wielded around on the warm currents above the rocky escarpment. There was no animal chatter, no sound, just Rachid receiving scrambled static in answer his calls. He shrugged an apology and put the microphone back in its cradle.

'Here,' he said, pointing at the satellite screen, 'there are a few fishing villages along the north coast... after that....'

'Can we fly out?'

'Sure, there's a holiday resort and an international airport, quite nice. But the nearer we get to it, the less likely we're going to find your friend.'

Valerie opened one of the rear doors and pulled out a small bag. 'Chewing gum?' She held out a couple of sticks. 'What will you do? When we get to civilisation, I mean. Fly back to Tehran?'

'Follow orders, same as always.' He screwed up the gum wrapper and dropped it into his pocket. 'And you?'

'Yeah, what about me?' She gazed out over the forest.

***

'Stop!' Valerie shrieked, pushing an arm across Rachid's chest. 'Over there.'

They were approaching the coastal resort. He pulled up and followed Valerie's gesturing finger.

'It's the airport,' he said calmly. 'I told you there was one here.'

He was about to start again when he saw what Valerie was getting so animated about. Along the eastern perimeter, the remains of a convoy were parked up. Rachid took the binoculars out.

'They're ours,' he said quietly. Anticipating her next thought, he added, 'They're not going anywhere; let's get cleaned up first.'

The hotel was three-stars and basic, but the two dusty travellers still drew querying looks as they approached the reception.

'Better give him a deposit,' said Valerie, seeing her reflection in the mirror behind the desk. 'They might think we'll run off without paying.'

The receptionist managed a half-smile as Rachid offered him some American currency. Valerie took one of the provided keys and, adjusting her hijab, followed her companion to a lift.

\*\*\*

Sipping a small coffee, Rachid was waiting at a foyer table when she came back down. Her voice was hushed and said from behind a raised hand. 'What now?'

'It's okay,' he emptied another spoonful of sugar into his cup, 'you're in a tourist resort; English is used around here.'

'Sorry, still getting used to comparative safety.'

\*\*\*

Along a chain-link fence, the Humvees were neatly parked. Apart from a bullet hole here and there, they were all tidy.

'I called ahead,' Rachid said as a man came towards them with a clipboard under his arm.

He looked Valerie up and down as he handed the board to Rachid.

'According to this,' Rachid flicked through the papers, 'they flew back yesterday evening. The Humvees will be picked up later, taken back to Libya.'

'And what about us? Just left in the desert? Bloody charming!'

'Not quite.' Rachid lightly scratched behind his ear. 'Someone was going to go and fetch us. I'm going to get into rather a lot of trouble. They will have expected to find us sitting around the campfire where we'd been left.'

'Singing *Ging Gang Goolie, Goolie*, no doubt,' said Valerie under her breath.

'What?'

She waved a dismissive hand, 'Don't worry, I'll tell them I pulled rank; you had no choice.'

'Well, that's the truth... more or less.' Rachid scribbled something at the foot of a page and handed the clipboard back. 'We've plenty of money left; I can get you on a flight to... well, wherever you want to go.'

'And you?'

Rachid raised a sardonic eyebrow, 'Back to the hotel, get in touch with….' The rest, he left unsaid.

Valerie was becoming aware that Rachid had more about him than a common soldier. 'I'll stay awhile. I can fly out when you do.'

While Rachid was busy with a borrowed laptop, Valerie took Bentley's photo and went along the beachfront cafés. Even though Rachid had told her English was used, she was still surprised when sign language wasn't needed. Towards the far end, fishing shacks replaced the tourist businesses. Most were secured with chunky padlocks, but outside a small, sun-bleached shed, an "Old-Man-of-the-Sea", his feet resting on a table, was leaning back in a dilapidated cane chair.

'Straight out of Hemingway,' she said quietly.

'You read Hemingway?' A local but educated voice came from behind the unkempt grey beard. He rocked the chair on its rear legs, patiently waiting for Valerie's reaction.

'The usual,' she said after a pause, 'For Whom the Bell Tolls, Farewell to Arms….'

He leaned forward, letting the chair fall onto all four feet. 'And, The Old Man and the Sea.'

Valerie smiled as he got to his feet, 'Yeah, bare necessities for school.'

'Oh, educated lady… been to school.'

'Yes, well, this educated lady could do with a little help. Trying to find a friend of mine.' She gave him the photo and gazed towards the horizon. A brilliant, clear sky let sunlight dance across breaking wavetops. 'Lovely view from your front door.'

'Friend? You sure keep strange company.'

Valerie turned, 'You know him?'

The man started making the same tea concoction she'd had before. 'Grind it fresh,' he said, ignoring Valerie's question, 'makes the difference.' He took a small kettle that had been simmering in the corner and poured it over the spices. 'Milk?'

'Please.' Not pushing for information, she settled into *his* pace. 'Goat's?'

'Of course.' He passed over a cup, splashing in a little milk.

After taking a drink himself, he pronounced it satisfactory. 'People like you don't usually drink it.'

'People like me?'

'Northern European.'

'It's worse than that; I'm one of the old colonialists.'

'I know,' he said slowly, 'when a third of the world was pink.' He handed the photo back. 'You look a little perplexed.'

'Yes, you're the second person I've met in this country that is a lot more….'

127

'Intelligent?'

Valerie shook her head, 'No, we've all got brains, just some of us don't know how to use them.' She held up her cup as he dropped a little honey into first her tea and then his own. With a prod from her finger, she encouraged the golden lump to dissolve. 'You know him, don't you?'

'Your friend?'

'Not a friend,' she said, chancing a different approach. 'I'm afraid he's a dangerous man.'

He took back the photo and pulled it closer to short-sighted eyes. 'What's he done?'

'IS.'

'So, your way of life is more righteous than his?'

Valerie tried the usual observations, 'What, beheading people that don't agree with your way of life? Telling those around you what to think, what to do?'

The man said nothing, leaving Valerie to answer her own criticism.

'Don't suppose it would help if I said I wasn't around when the British Empire was dishing it out? I wouldn't have been part of it.'

Handing the picture back, he kept sipping his tea.

'A lot more dead when we were in charge, is it? Don't you think apologising for something that happened way back is just a little… what… hypocritical? If he's not found, many people could wind up dead, and I mean a lot. Maybe Hiroshima all over again.' She put down the part-full cup of tea and stepped from the small veranda. 'You might be able to live with that, but don't expect me to join in with your skewed view of life.'

'Okay, okay,' he said calmly. 'He's gone. He was taken out in a small boat, but I don't think he'd got fishing in mind.'

'When?'

'Ooo, not long. Had some soldiers asking around yesterday, but he'd been gone the day before.'

'How do you know? When he went, I mean.'

'I pushed them off the beach.'

\*\*\*

Rachid tapped the computer screen as Valerie looked over his shoulder.

'Gone over to Aden,' he scrutinised the map, zooming in on the Yemeni port, 'must have… leaving this beach, there's nowhere else to go.' He asked Valerie to order them something to eat while he sent off some emails. 'Grab a table out on the terrace.'

'There's a flight out tomorrow,' said Rachid, joining her as the food arrived. 'You can be back at Heathrow early evening.'

'And where are you going?' She stabbed at a slice of beetroot and

128

smothered it in mayonnaise.

'Aden. I've got to try and keep up with Bentley... that is,' he added thoughtfully, 'I've been *ordered* to keep up with him.'

Saying nothing, Valerie took hold of the laptop and emailed the colonel. *Leaving Somalia. Going East. 24 hours behind. Valerie.*

\*\*\*

Rachid stood by Valerie's bedroom door as she thrust the few things she had into her grip. 'There's no need to come,' he said, 'you've done your bit.'

'Can we get our automatics past security?' She held up the Glock, 'I'd feel a lot better with this stuffed down my knickers.'

Rachid shook his head, 'No way, especially out here. We'll throw them into the sea. Don't worry, you'll have one stuffed down... er, wherever you want, thirty minutes after we land.'

Not for the first time, Valerie had teamed up with someone she knew little about.

\*\*\*

On touching down at Aden, the elderly Boeing 737 bumped a couple of times before making firm contact with the tarmac. Valerie gazed from the window as the engines went into reverse thrust.

'Couldn't we have found something a little more up-to-date?'

'It's all right.' Rachid received a withering look from the steward as he undid his seatbelt while the aircraft was still rolling. 'They're well screwed together.'

Littered with Middle East visas, immigration gave Valerie's passport more than a cursory glance.

'I'm with the British Embassy in Paris, helping with research for clothing companies. I'll be visiting quite a few countries.' The stamp came down, dismissing her from the desk.

'Pity you want an old one.' Valerie pointed to the Rolex duty-free shop as she slung the grip over her shoulder. She went over to the window and found herself looking at nearly every model they made. 'What a racket. Can't get them for love nor money at a normal outlet.'

'Come,' Rachid quickly led the way out, 'they do a rather individual cup of coffee in the old city.'

The coffee house was interesting, which was more than could be said for the unremarkable brew. Dark walnut panelling dulled the interior. With half the bulbs blown, a heavy chandelier struggled to bring light to the few tables. The man behind the counter was like most in the Middle East: while making their woman toe the line in clothing, they wore jeans and shirts bright with Western adverts.

Screwing up her face, she pushed the coffee away.

With a nod from Rachid, the man at the next table dropped an oilcloth shopping bag next to Valerie and walked out. Rachid drained his cup and stood up. 'Don't forget your shopping.'

Guessing what was in the bag, and hoping they wouldn't get stopped, Valerie followed Rachid. Ten minutes, maybe fifteen, of crossing roads and following alleys, he stopped down a side street next to a grey Landcruiser. He waved a hand across the door handle; the locks gave out a solid clunk.

'Magic?' said Valerie.

'No, keys in the bag. Throw it in the back; we'll get out of town first.'

Valerie leaned over to the back seat as Rachid pulled up overlooking the Gulf of Aden. 'Scenic route or a hunch?'

'Neither.' He pointed at the satellite navigation, 'Route's already programmed in.'

She passed over one of the Glocks and stuck the other into the glove compartment. There was a bulky envelope and keys. She also gave it to Rachid. Two hundred and fifty rounds of Winchester nine mil joined Valerie's pistol in the glove box.

'Now that's what I call forward-thinking.' She held up two bottles of Coke. 'Someone's on the ball.'

'Think you'll find more in the boot, along with the extra fuel and water.'

'Something to eat?'

'Yes, there'll be food.'

An hour down the road Valerie took a sip from the cola bottle and then handed it to Rachid. 'Think it's about time you came clean. You know all about *me*.'

'What do I know about you?' The young man who seemed to be maturing by the hour laughed, 'You work for the British government.'

'Not much else to say, is there? We both want Bentley. But you keep receiving information, which is more than I do. With what we've been through, don't you think I'm owed a little more? Take me into your confidence?'

After a few seconds of silence, he said, 'He's not far ahead. We're just keeping pace, as much as we can.' He took a mobile from his shirt pocket. 'Open it up, top right app.'

Valerie switched it on. A map filled the screen. In the centre, a blue circle. 'Us?'

Rachid nodded. 'The other,' he pointed to a yellow triangle near the top, 'that's Bentley, we managed to get a tracker into his vehicle.'

She propped the phone up in front of the gear lever.

'Why just us? Why has the cavalry stopped following?'

'Change of tactics, make him think he's got away. He'll hopefully lead us, that is, you and me, to where the weapons are.'

'So, your boss knows I'm with you?'

'That's right. Said I could take you along, although he wasn't quite as gracious as that.'

'I can imagine.'

'They said it was better to keep quiet; you'd probably kick up too much fuss.' Rachid laughed, 'I told them that was putting it mildly.'

'And when was this all going on?'

'Oh, the once or twice when I was on my own. I said I'd suggest getting you on the plane back to the UK but wouldn't recommend pushing it.' Rachid had been gripping the wheel and Coke bottle with one hand. 'Here,' he held the bottle in front of Valerie, 'you finish it.'

'We just follow him until... somewhere out here,' she waved her arm in a generally easterly direction, 'he leads us to this bomb?'

'I have a theory about where it is. But first, let's see if he's picked up anybody else along the way.'

Around ten in the evening, Valerie and Rachid were sitting in the Landcruiser, now and again glancing at the static image on the screen.

'Come on.' Valerie jumped from the cab.

The night air was cooling as they covered the quarter of a mile to Bentley's parked-up vehicle. From a slight rise in the ground, there was a clear view of a dwindling campfire where he was casually chatting with two others, their collars pulled up.

Valerie sat down; her back to a tree. 'How did you get a tracker into their car?'

'We had someone at each of the car hire outlets; there's not many in Aden. Just waited for him to come in.'

'And you think he's going... where?'

'Airport, then fly into Iran. He's just taking care... small boat, car, plane.'

'Not careful enough for you, is he?'

Rachid turned back towards the four-by-four. 'We'd better get some sleep.'

'Why Iran?'

The young man said nothing.

\*\*\*

The driving was shared over the next seven hundred miles. And as Rachid had predicted, they were now over the border in Oman, sitting in an airport car park.

'We'll have to leave the guns again.' Rachid took out his phone and sent off an email. 'Someone will pick the car up and dispose of the Glocks when we're gone.'

Adjusting her hijab, Valerie followed him towards buildings that looked more like large sheds.

'There's a flight out later today,' said Rachid, consulting his phone again. 'They must be on that one; there's no way they'd hang around longer than necessary.' He stopped by a jacaranda and carried on tapping the screen. 'We're on the same plane. You'll be pleased to know it's Iran Air, nice and modern.'

\*\*\*

Sitting next to the window overlooking the wing, Valerie took Rachid's word that Bentley and his companions were out of sight towards the back.

'What we're looking for is in Iran, then?' She stopped as a stewardess walked past, checking seatbelts. 'I presume immigration will wave them through.'

'Customs will open his case as soon as it comes off the plane, see if there are any clues.' Rachid shrugged, 'I doubt it, but you never know.'

'Okay, so where is the warhead?'

'Only my opinion,' Rachid opened the complimentary pack of almonds, 'one of our eastern borders.'

'Our borders?'

'Iran. I think he's going to hit Tehran.'

'Oh, Jesus, why? What is he, some kind of nut?'

The Airbus surged forward. Never liking air travel, Valerie gripped the seat arm as the plane made the usual tiny dips in the first few seconds of flight. Wondering how many tons of aeroplane could hang in the air, she looked out at the flaps moving back from the take-off position.

'Not like flying?' Rachid offered the small bag of nuts.

Valerie shook her head.

'Sorry, Iranian aircraft don't carry alcohol.'

'Pity, if there's one thing I could do with right now, it's a large Southern Comfort... How long?'

'Three hours.'

Valerie pulled down the window blind and shut her eyes.

\*\*\*

Rachid shook Valerie's arm, but she'd been awake every minute of the flight.

'Seat belt?' she asked.

'Yes, we'll be down in ten minutes.' Valerie disregarded the armrest and took hold of Rachid's hand. 'You don't like it, do you.' With his free hand, he patted Valerie's arm.

When taking off, it was the last few seconds approaching the ground that had her tense. As the pilot brought the aircraft in contact with the runway, the minor adjustments were just as uncomfortable.

'Didn't notice it on the first flight.'

'No,' said Valerie, 'I managed to lock it away. It's a second trip coming so soon after the first, I suppose. Couldn't keep the courage going for a second time.'

'Not sure it's courage you lack,' he said quietly.

Rachid held up an arm to an immigration officer standing to one side. 'Come on,' he said, picking up his bag, 'express check-through.'

Taking a passport stamp from his pocket, the official put an inky imprint on each document. Showing a badge to an inquisitive customs officer, he led them out onto the taxi rank. A few words passed between him and Rachid before the car door opened, and they headed for the city.

Valerie looked back through the rear window. 'Now that's what I call a customs clearance. What next?'

'We need to see someone.'

Valerie didn't ask who or where they were going but took an interest in the city around her. Buildings passed by, some the colour of calico, others faced in slate. The road was bustling with cars and cycles; the one or two buses painted red looked quite odd in the Middle East. Like anywhere else, pedestrians played chicken with the traffic. The taxi driver swerved at the occasional youngster and, she presumed, gave vent with a profanity.

Their destination, apart from being a modern building, was much like "The Art Department". A square, flanked by a museum, mosque and art gallery to three sides, was surrounded by slender cypress trees. A side street ran past a café and narrowed. The taxi stopped outside a dark glass frontage. An emblem, of four semi-circles divided by a central bar, was etched in gold onto the double doors.

Rachid returned a salute from a soldier in dress uniform as he showed his pass. He was joined by a young man in a western suit, his immaculate, jet-black hair short, his beard closely trimmed. Giving a short bow, he said something to Rachid.

They both followed as he led them up a broad curving stairway. The steps' centre was covered in a richly decorated blue carpet, each tread held in place by a gold rod; the sides were finely veined marble. The first landing was extensive, leading to half a dozen doors. Sumptuously varnished bannisters were of a dark, almost black wood. Rachid ushered Valerie into a side room, telling her there was coffee on the way and he'd be back shortly.

133

The room overlooked an enclosed quadrangle. Cypress trees, smaller than those in the street, surrounded seating that faced a fountain. In the room, oversized brown leather chairs flanked a coffee table of honey maple. On the wall, the eyes of two portraits followed her around. Valerie presumed them to be the supreme leader and president. She knew the name of neither.

Carrying a silver tray, the same young man that had greeted them came in. Valerie assumed his throat clearing was in preparation for the little English he had at his command.

'Coffee.' Matching the gleaming tray, he placed a large pot on the table; milk, sugar, honey and a fine bone china cup and saucer followed. A bow, similar to before, indicated his duty was complete. 'Madam.'

Wondering how much English he had at his fingertips, she poured out coffee that was definitely 'noir'. Bracing herself for the bitter liquid, she spooned in thick honey, then nibbled at a small macaroon that had been hiding beside the milk. It was excessively sweet; she took a sip of the coffee. Not for the first time since leaving Europe, she'd misjudged the taste, and to balance the honey added more coffee.

Thinking she was in for a long wait, she flicked through the few magazines on the table, selected one with more photos than the others, and settled into a serious critique. When deciding where to rank the fourth picture, Rachid put his head around the door.

'Okay?'

'Sure.' She threw the magazine on the table and got up. 'Where're we off to?'

'See the boss. Didn't know you could decipher Arabic?'

'Photos don't need translating.'

'No, I suppose not.'

After ascending another flight of stairs, Rachid held back a door, not unlike the colonel's. The man, who rose from his chair behind the desk, looked very much like her boss. The hair and moustache would have been indications as to his profession, except none was needed. He wore an olive-green shirt; a white belt with gold buckle was looped around perfectly pressed, black trousers. Campaign ribbons were stitched across the top of his left pocket. She was unsure of the insignia on his shoulders, but Rachid resolved the problem with an introduction. The crossed swords beneath ferns and the Iranian emblem clarified his rank of brigadier. His handshake was firm, his English clipped, but good.

'Miss Stone, I believe we owe you thanks in all this mess.'

In the colonel's office, smart remarks and the disregard for authority ran through her mind; but here, she kept them firmly under control.

'It goes both ways, Brigadier. I wouldn't be here if it wasn't for Rachid and the others.'

'Rachid?' She thought the colonel's approach somewhat cold, but this one didn't even know his operative's ruddy name.

'Yes, when we were ambushed. He's a courageous man.' The brigadier's gaze had her wondering if he'd seen a report or resigned it to the waste bin. She was going to give her version of events, but, holding a hand towards a chair, he opened a file.

'Rachid,' he stressed the name as if for Valerie's benefit, 'will follow this English....' A slight cough was the only apology for highlighting Bentley's origin. 'This man we're after. The best assessment of where he has the weapon is in Iran. And if that's so, Tehran is the target.'

'Why?' asked Valerie. 'For goodness' sake, what's the point?'

'We've had a demand.'

'What? Turn Iran into their version of an Islamic State, or we'll launch this weapon on your capital?'

'No.' The brigadier fiddled with a sheet of paper, 'Money. Ten million dollars in a Swiss account.'

'How come the bloody....' Swearing by a woman, no matter how mild, brought a frown to the brigadier's face. Choosing her words carefully, Valerie repeated her question, 'How come the world turns on the US dollar?'

'How come the world turns on everything American?' chipped in Rachid.

'You could keep quiet and pay. But of course,' she added, 'there's no way of guaranteeing you'll get your hands on the weapon. We've got to get Bentley, the warhead and delivery system all at once. If we miss the hardware...'

'We?' asked the brigadier. 'You can be on the next plane home, would you not wish that?'

'No, I'll see it through. Besides, we've become a bit of a team, haven't we, Rachid?'

Resignation was the best description of the response displayed by the young man.

'It's still just the two of you, then.' Rising to his feet, the brigadier flicked a switch on a small intercom and gave a few orders. 'Well, I'll not keep you any longer,' he released the control, 'I'm sure you want to get on.'

And with that, they were dismissed.

\*\*\*

Rachid led the way out and into an underground car park. It was not large, just one level. A small, white SUV of a make Valerie did not recognise was parked at the side of the stairway.

135

Rachid took out a set of keys, 'Just a twenty-minute journey.'

They were quickly out into the sunlight and on their way out of town. Valerie looked up at the building cranes scattered around many parts of the city centre. Ignoring the air-con that was keeping the cabin cool, she lowered the window. The sounds and smells could have been any city in any part of the world. Shouting, mixed in with honking horns and two-stroke engines, wafted around. Petrol fumes and fresh ground coffee added to the metropolitan atmosphere.

'Where to?'

'Get cleaned up and find out where Bentley is.' Rachid leaned forward as they approached a roundabout. A screech of brakes had him muttering to himself as a moped swerved in front. 'We have him under observation,' he said, recovering. 'Then it's up to you and me.'

'Dear God,' said Valerie, 'that's a hell of a responsibility heaped on us.'

'Asking for God's help?'

'Yeah, I know, it's a bloody cheek... asking for the help of the chief executive when I don't believe he or his organisation exist.'

'Can I ask you?' asked Rachid, 'Is it just bravado, or do you truly not believe?'

'Sorry, Rachid, I'm not trying to wind you up; I'm a fully paid-up atheist. When you're dead... you're dead!'

His response was quiet; measured. 'Then I'm truly sorry for you.'

She was about to continue telling him that anyone who thought there was paradise floating around in the clouds had lost their grip on reality when she saw the look on his face. She said nothing.

Following a valley, they drove out in a north-westerly direction.

About three miles past the last sign of habitation, Rachid drew up in front of a chain-link double gateway. He showed a pass to an armed guard, and after an exchange of words in which Valerie presumed her presence was being explained, they were waved through.

The only colour breaking up grey buildings was an occasional flag. Lines of dusty beige vehicles were to one side of a parade ground. As they drove past, a close inspection confirmed it was dusty beige camouflage, not dusty beige dirt. A column of desert-uniformed soldiers was being drilled; the crunch of boots broken only by sharp commands. It could have been anywhere, except that the sun cast short shadows, and shirts dripped wet beneath armpits and down straight backs.

'Would you like to get cleaned up first?' Rachid asked as they left the car.

Valerie took advantage of the offer and was under a steaming shower within ten minutes. Then, rinsing through her few clothes, she mused at the ridiculous situation of keeping clean while chasing down a terrorist.

Leaving her few things hanging from the window, she selected a mineral water from a small fridge. The room was bare; magnolia walls were only broken by the Iranian flag and a few photos of regimental platoons. She sat on the only piece of furniture; a basic settee draped in a gold cover.

A knock on the door came at the same time as Rachid called out her name.

'Just a moment.' He may have misheard, but it was too late. Naked but unfazed, Valerie reached for a towel as he walked in.

'I…'

'It's okay,' she smiled, 'I'm sure I'm not the first naked female you've seen.'

Rachid was back in uniform. Underlining his correct and polite manner, he didn't take his eyes from hers. Unless thought Valerie, he was… No, she studied the young man for a second; he was straight.

'We don't know when Bentley will be leaving the city, so we'd better get across to the armoury.'

*** 

Rachid held to one side, what looked like a blast door. Inside, a large hatchway cut the only space in a concrete wall. To see them, the sergeant behind the counter had to duck as they came in. A few exchanges between him and Rachid followed before two pistols and ammunition were pushed across.

'No Glocks, I'm afraid.' Valerie followed Rachid onto a firing range. He handed her a worn nine-mil Browning. 'It's okay,' he said in reply to her enquiring look, 'old but in perfect working order.'

There were no similar targets to the one she had used before, just something that looked like a small archery board.

'Don't worry,' Rachid handed her a full clip and a pair of ear defenders, 'I know you can shoot. Just want to make sure you're comfortable with this gun. Not that you've got a lot of choice.'

The Browning was larger and heavier than the Glock, but she still centred six rounds into a tight pattern. A soldier came from behind with another gun, heavier, larger, together with a chunky magazine. Rachid pushed the clip behind the trigger guard and handed it over.

'Have a go with that; it's an Uzi. Fully automatic.'

The gun was solid, giving the impression of a serious piece of kit. She pulled back the bolt and let fly at the coloured board. A dozen or so rounds later, the target was gone, leaving only the supporting post and confetti-like fragments floating gracefully to the floor.

'Hell's bloody teeth, you could cut down trees!'

'Drug dealers love them.'

Handing over a shoulder holster, Rachid told her that she could wear the Browning. 'Get used to it; the rest will be put in the back of the car.'

'Don't wish to be demeaning towards that SUV, but I'm not sure it's up to getting us to where we want to go.'

Leaving the gun range, Rachid told her it would be staying behind; they'd be using something a bit more 'up to the job'.

# TWELVE

'Up to the job?' Valerie said as they threw everything into the back of a long-wheelbase Defender.

Rachid checked the guns and ammunition. 'Thought you'd be a little more patriotic.'

'Spraying it in camouflage paint doesn't make it reliable.'

'They're tough vehicles. We have a few in service, got hold of them in a kind of round-about way.'

'Yeah, tough maybe,' she said, 'but it ain't of much use if you're under the ruddy thing with a set of spanners!' She looked about the square, 'Is there nothing else?'

'Tank?'

'I was thinking of something from Japan.'

'Sorry, no… I'll pack my Swiss army knife.'

'You know what they say in Australia?'

'Go on, what do they say in Australia?'

'You can go into the outback in a Land Rover or Landcruiser, but if you want to come back alive, take the Landcruiser. Good job I packed my nail file.'

\*\*\*

Valerie watched the tracker as they passed through the camp gates. 'He's not in much of a hurry, is he?'

'No, we're up against someone cold, confident and well-trained.'

'It's a pity we can't take some back-up. How quickly can your guys get to us when we shout for help?'

'An hour, less... it'll be fine. We just do a little tip-toeing, then call… when we're sure, of course.'

Rachid's calculations seemed to be correct as, after exiting the valley, they turned towards the border.

'Tell me,' said Valerie, feeling through her pockets, 'back in Tehran, your boss, or whoever didn't seem to know your name, or at least your given name?' Rachid said nothing as Valerie found what she was looking for. Some helpful person back at the barracks had fitted a shiny new stereo. She pushed a memory stick into its USB socket. 'Well?' she asked, skipping over Leonard Cohen and selecting Van Morrison.

'Code name.'

'Oh, good grief, please don't tell me it's a bloody number?'

Rachid laughed, 'No, I'm afraid not.'

'Well, go on. What is it?'

140

'Pipit.'

'What, the bird? Thought you'd have at least been some kind of ruddy great eagle, talons like swords. But anyhow, I now know you're not just a soldier.'

'What about you?' he said, changing the subject. 'My bet is Nemesis, or better still, Boadicea.'

'Agent Nemesis, now there's a thought. I'm sorry to disappoint you, but you already know my name.'

Rachid nodded slowly, 'I think I prefer Valerie.'

The compass on the satellite navigation swung rhythmically about its axis. Still, it always returned east, in the general direction of the rising sun. They followed the giant electricity pylons to the side of the road.

On the second day, as the road deteriorated, they started climbing. Gazing at the steady readings given by the instruments, Valerie screwed up her nose, 'Been praying to the great Land Rover god in the sky, have you?'

Rachid stood on the brakes. Just down in a shallow drop, the blip on the tracker was stationary.

Switching off the engine, he let the Land Rover roll back under a row of trees. Valerie pulled the Browning from her holster and followed Rachid along the track.

'You're getting a bit serious,' she said, noting the Uzi slung over his shoulder.

'If what we want is here....'

To the side of some bushes, the SUV was parked next to a flickering fire.

Lying on his front, Rachid passed a small pair of binoculars across. 'Just about the best small delivery system in the world,' he said, as two of the men loaded boxes and what even Valerie could see was a rocket.

'Just the one.' Valerie's voice was quiet.

'That's all they need. It's so compact, that's the problem.'

They watched for maybe ten minutes as the rest of the equipment was loaded.

'That's the warhead,' said Rachid as a container no more than two-foot square was pushed in last. The outer covering of alloy was protected on the edges and corners with stainless steel. 'As long as it's in there, it will remain stable... outside, and it will be deadly.'

The cold sweat on Valerie's neck was immediate. The familiar cocking of a pistol twisted at her abdomen.

'You seem to have a new companion, Miss Stone.' Rachid's half-twist was halted, 'Stay still, my friend. There's a forty-five pointed at the back of your head.' Rachid released the grip on the Uzi as a hand came from behind. 'And you, Valerie, I'll take that... Browning... Big gun for a little

141

girl.'

One at a time, they were ordered to stand, and then turn around.

'Bentley...' said Valerie, 'should have pulled the trigger when I had the chance.'

'Indeed, you should've.' He thrust the Browning into his belt, then gestured with the Uzi towards the other men.

Down at the campfire, Bentley pulled the bolt on the automatic and pushed the muzzle into Rachid's face.

'Where is it?'

'Where's what?' The strike from the gun butt was sudden and savage.

'Don't piss me about, arsehole! Where's the tracker?' Rachid spat blood and a chipped tooth from his mouth.

'I don't know, I didn't plant it. Could be anywhere.'

'Leave him alone, you bastard!' As in the past, the thought of putting herself in jeopardy was forgotten as Valerie's anger swept self-preservation aside. 'You piece of fucking shit!' Held back by one of the terrorists, wild kicking only ended in her falling, face down, to the ground.

'Got a little fireball here,' said the one that had been holding her as he dropped a knee into the small of her back. She gave out a choking screech as the air emptied from her lungs. 'I know a sure way to calm her down, same as any woman.'

Rachid pulled a sleeve across his bleeding mouth and lunged forward, pulling the terrorist away. 'Touch her, and you're dead! I swear to the Prophet, you're dead!'

'Enough!' Bentley let a round go into the air. 'We need to find this friggin' tracker. You!' he handed Valerie's Browning to the one on the ground, 'See if you can keep them quiet.' He turned to the other, 'Benny, get the lot out. We can't go anywhere until we find it.'

Everything removable from the truck was taken out and stacked up. For the next half hour, the two men went over the vehicle. After crawling underneath, Bentley got to his feet and stared into the engine bay.

'It could be fucking anywhere.' He brought a fist crashing onto the wheel arch. 'Here,' he tossed the keys across to the man who was guarding Valerie and Rachid, 'see if you can bring their transport around without any mishaps.'

'A bullet in the back of his head would relieve us both of a lot of bleedin' trouble,' said Benny as the other man disappeared over the crest.

'To say nothing of the extra money,' laughed Bentley.

'Honour among... honour among what?' said Valerie. 'Just what are you?'

'Entrepreneurs?' said Rachid.

'Keep your smart remarks to yourself, or I might decide one hostage is enough. And you ain't the good-looking one.'

'What is it?' said Valerie as she and Rachid were made to sit next to the alloy box. Neither Bentley nor Benny spoke.

'We think Sarin,' said Rachid, leaning back on some packing cases.

Not for the first time, Valerie dismissed her lack of faith, 'Dear God. You could kill thousands.' Bentley pushed himself from a rock where he had been resting as the Land Rover came over the slight rise.

'Oh, I don't think it'll come to that.'

'Which one of you is the chemist?' Rachid asked.

'He's driving your Land Rover.'

'Chemist?' Valerie turned to Rachid, 'Why do they need a chemist?'

'In the case,' said Rachid, 'it's not Sarin, as such. There'll be a compound and a precursor. Sarin has a short shelf life. You mix it just before deployment, and that's best done by an expert.'

'Oh, bloody marvellous, we've got a nutter for a safety officer.' Valerie scrambled to her feet. 'Look, Mr Bentley... or can I call you John?'

'You can call me whatever you bleedin' well like. What is it?'

'Surely we can come to some sensible agreement? You get the money; we get the box. No need to go any further. Then you can go off to South America or wherever else you had in mind, and the rest of us can go home.'

As the Land Rover drew up, Benny started loading the back.

'Very simplistic view of life you have.' He took the guns out, 'Haven't come to play footsy, have you?' He took the other Uzi and placed it next to the passenger seat. Again, Bentley shoved a gun into Rachid's face.

'No smart-arse answers. Is there a tracker in this piece of Solihull crap?'

'The Land Rover,' Valerie explained quietly, 'he wants to know if our vehicle is tracked.'

Rachid shook his head, 'No, no tracker.'

'If I see anything coming up in my rear-view mirror, you'll be the first to get one in the head. Got it?'

Bentley took one of the cans and loaded the last of the spare fuel into the Land Rover. 'Get a light into that,' he said when he'd emptied the diesel across the seats of the discarded SUV.

'Why?' Valerie still didn't know the name of the one who shrugged his shoulders as he spoke, 'What's the point?'

'Because, idiot, if it all goes up in smoke, then there's a good chance the tracker will go as well. How in God's name can you be a scientific genius and be so bloody thick when it comes to everything else?'

'Stop calling me thick!'

'Get in the back with these two; *I'll* fire the truck.' Bentley turned to Rachid as they climbed in, 'Child locks on these back doors?'

Saying nothing, Rachid was again hit across the face.

'Child locks,' said Valerie, 'must be those in the door ends.' She turned to Rachid, 'It's not worth getting beat up about.'

Locking them in, Bentley took a box of matches and, taking out half a dozen, pushed them into the end. He lit the protruding sticks and carefully placed the small incendiary on the cab floor, then swung into the driver's seat of the Defender as the flames took hold. With no backward glance, he drove off.

By the time they had left the scene, it was late in the day, leaving only three hours before they had parked up.

'Smithy.' Benny opened the rear door, giving out orders to Valerie and Rachid's guard. She now knew the third one's name, not that it made any difference. 'Get them to sit up against the Land Rover. We're going to have to take turns guarding them. Is there nothing to tie them up with?'

Bentley took a pack from the back and dumped it on the ground. 'There's a service station a hundred miles or so further along. They'll have something. But tonight…' he kicked the sole of Valerie's trainer, 'we watch and don't fall asleep. I'll take the first four hours.'

As his stint came to an end, he shook Smithy, 'Your four hours.' He took the automatic from his holster and handed it over. 'Bloody well, keep alert. I don't want to be woken up by you chasing them across the friggin' desert. Or,' he pulled a sheath knife from Smithy's boot and hooked it into his own belt, 'find you with a ventilated throat.'

Rachid was asleep when Valerie judged that Bentley had also dropped off. 'They're going to kill you, Smithy. When you're no longer of use, one of them is going to put a bullet in your brain.'

'They're my mates, they wouldn't….'

With his knees drawn up, he sat hunched, waving the gun in the general direction of Valerie. The elastic around the top of his underpants was visible where he'd tucked his shirt in. He was clean-shaven but looked like he only had to use a razor every other day. His hair, although short, was unkempt. Any money that had passed through his hands hadn't been spent in a dentist's chair: it looked like the celestial technician had hastily installed his teeth at the end of a busy day.

'How did you get mixed up with these two?' Valerie yawned, trying to keep things low-key. 'You're not like them.'

'Shut up, just shut up.' With only the lightest of probes, Smithy had got more than a little agitated. He wasn't thick, just immature and out of his depth. Valerie got up. 'Sit.' He levelled the gun, 'Sit back down.'

'No need to get upset.' She made her way over and sat a couple of feet away. 'I'm not going to do anything, just want to have a chat, that's all.' Smithy shifted his weight as he faced Valerie. 'There's enough in the back of that truck to kill thousands, maybe hundreds of thousands. Do you want to be part of that? Women, children… babies?'

'Keep your mouth shut.' He brought his face close, hissing stale breath. 'You don't know what's going on; just keep your friggin' opinions to yourself. You'll screw everything up.'

Valerie paused for a moment. Smithy was on a different wavelength.

'Do you know something they don't?' She nodded across the fire to the others. 'What's going on?'

'Stop it, just stop it.' He started waving the gun around, 'You'll fuck the whole thing up.'

'Okay.' Gesturing with the palms of her hands, Valerie got back to her feet. 'Okay... but do yourself a favour, think it over.'

Protecting herself from the ever-cooling night, Valerie pulled a blanket around her shoulders.

\*\*\*

'Up!' A sharp kick in the ribs had Valerie reaching for a gun that wasn't there.

'A cup of tea and gentle shake is the usual way of greeting someone in the morning.' She stumbled to her knees and looked around. Rachid was pouring coffee into a tin mug.

'Room service finished half an hour ago.' Bentley gave her another sharp kick, this time in the backside.

Rachid was on the point of saying something when Valerie gave her head a slight shake. 'Got one of those for me? My mouth's like a rugby player's you know what.'

He handed her the mug and poured another for himself. After taking a sip, she spat the coffee out. 'Never mind letting me lie in next time, just give me a shake. I can make better than that.' She went over to the Land Rover and took out a bottle of water.

Bentley drew his foot back and forth over the dying embers of the fire, then, kicking the ashes from his boot, ordered all of them back into the Land Rover.

From where Valerie sat in the rear, Benny's face was reflected in the oversized wing mirror. She hadn't taken all that much notice of him up until now. With little else to do, she scrutinised the sunburnt features. He was not overweight but had the small eyes usually associated with the obese. He was, she guessed, around thirty-five, but it was hard to tell. He tried to disguise prematurely thinning hair, but from whom, out here, was a mystery. She thought it unlikely he was trying to impress her. She engaged him in conversation with nothing else to do, thinking he would hardly turn and put a bullet into her.

'You shouldn't do that,' she said as he pushed his hair back into position. The move had been unconscious, automatic.

He half-turned. 'Shouldn't do what?'

'Men with thinning hair make a big mistake. Okay, at first you get upset

145

about it going, try to hide it. But the way to go is to cut it short. Say to hell with it, I'm a man and don't care.'

'So, what makes you such a bloody expert?'

'What, you serious? I'm a woman, in case you haven't noticed. Unless you're…?'

'No, I'm bleedin' not.'

'Okay, don't get worked up. Anyway, gays don't lose their hair. Well, not usually. Something to do with….'

'You looking for a fist in your mouth?'

'Steady.' Bentley butted in. 'And you,' he turned to Valerie, 'stop winding him up.'

Valerie persisted. 'How come you're in this with two such bloody oddballs?'

'Stop the fucking truck!' Benny reached for his gun, 'She's dead!'

'She's right, though.' Underlining his position in the trio, Bentley put his foot down. As they bounced over a large rut, he grabbed the gun and put it under the seat. 'Good question, Valerie. Smithy,' he nodded over his shoulder, 'that's easy… need him to put it together. I'm pretty sure I could do it myself, but I don't want any of the bleedin' stuff getting on me.' The laugh was cold, totally devoid of emotion. 'But this one, the one that wants to blow you away… I didn't find him at the job centre. Did I, Benny?' Benny said nothing, preferring to scowl out of the window. 'No, Benny, I found when working for queen and country before seeing the light. The light shining above obscene amounts of money that is. Didn't take long to lead him from the straight and narrow.' Again, the laugh was hollow. 'Used to believe, didn't you, son? A couple of months of no fags, and even less Scotch, had him listening to me.'

Valerie relaxed back into the seat. 'Where did you pick up….' She stopped for a few seconds, uncomfortable at letting the name of the chemical pass her lips. 'The weapon?'

'Oh, a bit of a mix-up there. Couldn't believe me luck. I had to go and pick up some gear… guns, ammo, bits and pieces. I was all on my own. It was in this warehouse. There in the corner was that little lot. I knew what the rocket was but at a bit of a loss about the rest. Anyway, the helpful buggers that had left it there also shoved a manual under the straps. "Dangerous" and "Top Secret" were stamped in red on the cover in half a dozen different languages. Well, that got my attention straight away. Talk about landing on your feet.'

The self-congratulations stopped after a while, and he pulled off the road behind a small mound. He kicked Rachid and Valerie out and turned to Smithy,

'Look after them. That service station is just along the road; we'll get the truck topped off.'

146

Twenty minutes later, he was back, waving a bunch of cable ties. 'Should be able to get a little sleep tonight.'

\*\*\*

For the next two days, the compass pointed north, now and again showing a little west. When trees and the occasional lake passed by, the destination became a little clearer.

'Very shrewd,' she said as they passed a hydroelectric dam. 'I take it we're not far from the Caspian Sea?'

The slight smile on Bentley's face was one of satisfaction.

'What are we, seventy, eighty miles from Tehran?'

'Sixty.' Bentley looked around, seemingly taking in the beautiful surroundings.

'Well within range, I presume. And who's going to look for an attack coming from a holiday resort.'

'Quite.' The smile broadened. 'We can now look forward to a large amount of spondulix landing in our account.' He could subdue the smile no longer, and a hysterical cackle erupted as he slapped Benny's shoulder, 'Come on, sunshine, time to admit your leader's a genius.' The laugh was ended by a coughing fit.

'Not one for that *all for one and one all for one* nonsense,' muttered Valerie.

'You have to have a leader, my dear Miss Stone. The brains and courage to see it through. Now, if only I could convert you. What do you say? How would you like to come and live with me in paradise?'

'All in all? All in all... I think I'd rather see you at the end of a rope. You still have capital punishment in Iran.' Although looking to Rachid, it was a statement rather than a question.

He nodded. 'In public, not very nice. And no drop,' he added quietly.

It was then that Smithy lost it. 'I've had enough! Let me out!' He thumped the door and then, leaning back, started kicking at the glass.

'For fuck's sake!' Bentley took advantage of a side track and drove into the woods. Opening the door, he pulled Smithy out and pushed a pistol into his face. 'You're not going to have to wait for no hangman, you friggin' turd. If you don't get a hold of yourself, this is going to be where you die.' Kicking Smithy's legs from beneath him, he booted him several times in the chest. 'And you...' although Valerie's hands were tied, he also pulled her out, 'keep it zipped up, or you're going to wind up in a hole. Get it?' A backhander sent her to the ground. Banging her head, she struggled with ties that cut into her wrists. 'Smithy!' Bentley viscously spat the words out, 'Give me a bloody fag, for Christ's sake!'

Rachid could only look on as Valerie struggled to her feet. She managed to twist her neck and wipe the blood from a broken lip on her collar.

Drawing deeply on his cigarette, Bentley cast a look at Valerie that demanded obedience.

'Okay,' she said, 'okay, I understand.' She slumped against the Land Rover as a small part of the vision in her right eye blurred. 'Oh Jesus, no, not again.' She shook her head. It got no better, but to her relief, no worse.

'What's the matter with you?' Bentley raised his hand again.

'Nothing, nothing.' Escaping his wrath, she slid back into the rear seat.

'Valerie,' Rachid moved across, out of her way, 'what's the matter? You okay?'

'Sure, sure.' She shook her head. Nothing altered.

The Land Rover swayed from side to side, inducing a fitful sleep. When she awoke Bentley was backing up against a bungalow in an enclosed yard.

'Nice and private,' said Bentley, ushering her and Rachid from the cab. 'We could sit in the kitchen and launch it from here; no one would know. Woosh, just like bonfire night.'

Anxious about her damaged sight, Valerie said nothing. She and Rachid had their hands released and were pushed into a side bedroom.

'You sure you're okay?' repeated Rachid as she lay on the bed.

'Just a little tired,' she replied before asking for a drink of water. With nothing to be done about the blurring, she kept it to herself.

'Should be okay to drink.' He went into the en-suite returning with a plastic cup.

Pushing herself upon the pillow, she took short sips. 'We've got to stop them. Smithy and Benny are easy; I think we could talk them out of it. But Bentley, he's round the bloody bend. I think the stupid bastard would go through with it.'

'Let's hope they pay up, then.' Rachid sat on the corner of the bed and finished the last few drops of water.

'Do you think they might not?'

'I don't know. What would the British government do?'

'That's a bloody good question. Ever wondered why terrorists go for French hostages and the like?' Rachid shook his head. 'Because they and others pay up. The Brits... never. They say it just leads to more hostage-taking. And they're right, of course. We hardly ever have anyone taken because they know they won't get paid. But with a quarter of a million lives at stake... no, they wouldn't refuse. At least, I don't think they would.'

'So, what do you suggest, jump Bentley and hope the other two will fall into line?'

'Doesn't sound all that good a plan when you say it out loud. The big question is, are you willing to put your life on the line for the sake of a city?'

'Yes, but it's my country, my fellow citizens. My mother and father are in Tehran. It's a no-brainer, as you Brits would say. But you, it's not your fight.'

'There's no such thing as frontiers when it comes down to this kind of shit. Don't worry, I'm in. I know you'd do the same if we were in the UK.'

Valerie's opinion of Bentley was strengthened when he opened the door and told them to come and get something to eat. 'Just wanted to show you something first.'

He waved them into the back like an enthusiastic kid. Painted in drab brown and olive was a launch platform. To the side, in a long box, the unarmed rocket lay in wood shavings. It was over two metres long but not as big as Valerie had imagined. She thought several sections would add up to… well; she didn't know what to, but certainly well over a couple of metres. Wires led from the platform into the kitchen area. A control panel, with various coloured switches and knobs, sat in front of two computer screens.

Momentarily forgetting the blurred edge of her eye, she asked him if he was serious about using it. 'Eat,' he said, pointing to the table.

They sat to the one side, opposite Benny and Smithy. Like a general attending a meeting with his men, Bentley smiled from the end chair. In the centre, a large bowl of spaghetti was covered in tomato and sausage, with sliced jalapeno scattered over the top. Grated cheese was to the side.

After finishing the meal, Valerie and Rachid were left to wash up, with Smithy standing guard. When the other two were out of earshot, she looked at their reluctant warden.

'Smithy,' she said quietly, 'you have to help us; this is utter madness. We know you're not like them. It's obvious you thought a few threats would get you money beyond your wildest dreams, but then Bentley comes up with this filthy, bloody weapon. I'll bet he told you he'd got it after you'd joined them, right? Then you found out he'd had it all along; that's why he chose you to join in with the riches. He didn't want *you*; he just wanted your know-how.'

He said nothing as she was cut short by Benny's return.

Both Valerie and Rachid dragged their feet with the washing as they looked for a way to appeal for help. Slowly drying a plate, Valerie weighed up the risk of a fist to the side of the head and worsening her sight. Easy enough when viewing the moral dilemma from the outside, but not so easy when it's you.

The chance of doing anything faded as they were bundled back into the bedroom. Valerie pushed at the en-suite door; a red towel hung from the corner of a rail that sloped to one side. Inside the shower cubical the hot and plentiful water splashed from Valerie's upturned face. With only a few sachets of shower gel on the cubical shelf, she thought the sparsely furnished bungalow was probably some sort of holiday home. Drying herself off, she wondered if there was an outside chance of cleaners arriving and raising the alarm. The idea was dismissed: if Bentley had got this far, he'd hardly have overlooked something so bloody basic. She towelled herself down and got dressed

An argument started in the kitchen; crashing and shouting sounded like it carried on into the yard. The rumpus escalated into swearing and breaking glass. Five or so minutes passed before it was all brought to a halt by a gunshot.

'Bentley... maybe?' Valerie raised her eyebrows, more in hope than anything else, as the door was opened. It wasn't who they had hoped. 'Or not,' she added.

It was Rachid that Bentley went for when he eventually came in.

'It was you that put him up to it, wasn't it?!' Grabbing his collar, he put a knife to Rachid's throat as Benny looked on. Behind them both, the last of the blood was seeping from the lifeless body. Smithy's body. 'I've half a mind to use this on you.' He pressed the point into Rachid's gulping Adam's apple.

'Leave him!' Valerie still kept to one side while trying to calm Bentley down. 'It wasn't either of us. When you left him alone with us, he started moaning about the rocket and said he didn't want to be part of it anymore. We said nothing, honestly. Isn't that right?' She looked appealingly towards Rachid. 'All we did was listen.'

Rachid nodded, 'That's right, we said nothing.'

Bentley eased his grip around Rachid's throat and, as if blaming Smithy, kicked his motionless head.

'Ease up, John.' Benny gave him a friendly tap on the shoulder, 'We don't need any more corpses on our hands.'

Bentley let go and sat on the only chair still on its feet. 'What a friggin' mess.'

Behind them, the control panel was smashed, and one of the screens was in pieces on the floor.

Valerie surveyed the useless guidance system, 'Bit of a mess.'

Not seeming to listen, Bentley took out a cigarette. 'Idiot. Bloody idiot.' He took another kick at Smithy's body, 'What the fuck did you think you were up to? Arsehole.'

'I don't get it,' said Valerie when she and Rachid were alone. 'There was something, I've got no idea what, but there was more to Smithy than just being a terrorist or gangster... or whatever.'

'Such as?' Rachid lay back against the bedhead, 'Seemed just as mad as the other two.'

'I wish I knew.'

***

Both bound hand and foot, Valerie and Rachid sat in the Land Rover while Benny and Bentley loaded up in the rear.

'Good job the pillock forgot about the detonation system when he set about the controls.' Benny's glib observation drew no remark.

Bentley braced his feet as he slid the alloy box in, along with a large briefcase. As if ridding himself of the troublesome Smithy, he banged his hands together and got into the cab.

'You just going to leave him there?' Out of his reach, Valerie risked a minor quip about the body still on the kitchen floor. 'And what about the rocket and controls?'

'Should be found in the next couple of days.' They drove out of the yard and turned towards Tehran. 'They'll know not to piss us about... we've still got the bits that count.'

In less than an hour, the Land Rover entered the outskirts of Tehran. Not for the first time during the journey, Valerie tried to ease the tie cutting into her wrists. But worse than the pain was the fear for her sight. She wasn't sure if it was just anxiety tormenting her, or was the blur to the side of her right eye spreading.

The truck swung through a line of traffic and dropped into an underground car park. Benny got out and, opening one of the back doors, pulled out a flick-knife.

'Feet out.' He cut through the cable tie around Rachid's ankles, followed by Valerie's. Using the knife, he directed them to a stairwell. At the rear of the Land Rover, Bentley pulled the alloy case to the edge and eased it onto a small trolley, along with the briefcase.

'You take that up by the lift, Benny; I'll escort these two up the stairs.' He pushed Valerie and Rachid ahead.

'It's a regular Cook's Tour with you, ain't it.' She shook her head, hoping for a change in the eye. It remained the same, but at least it wasn't worse. The sooner she got back to the UK, the better; see a specialist. 'What's next?' she asked as they stopped outside an apartment door.

With a key half into the lock, Bentley looked back over his shoulder. 'We wait, see if they come to their senses.'

'And if not?'

'Then they get this little lot,' he said as Benny came wheeling the trolley around the corner.

Like a wasp stuck in a saucer of treacle, Valerie felt helpless. Bentley pushed her and Rachid into a bedroom and replaced the wrist and ankle ties.

'We've got to get out of here, get some help.' Valerie rolled towards

151

the window and struggled to her feet. 'There's a way down. Drainpipes look okay.' A look of aggravation on Rachid's face intensified, but he said nothing. Valerie smiled, and with a bit of difficulty, brought her hands from behind her back and under her legs. 'Been trying to do that for the last few days, but they didn't leave enough slack.'

'I'm sure that's going to help a lot.' The scepticism in his voice was evident as Valerie held her hands in front.

With some difficulty, she undid one of her trainer laces and threaded it between the tie around her feet. Holding one end between her teeth, she took the other in her hands. Sawing back and forth, the binding broke.

'Here,' she said, passing one of the ends between Rachid's fingers, 'hold that... tight.' Once again, holding the other end in her teeth, she repeated the movement to release her hands.

'Merciful Allah, where did you learn that?' he said as he was also freed.

'Where all secret agents get information... YouTube.'

Rachid opened the window. 'Will you be all right getting down that?' He leant out and gave the drainpipe a firm shove.

'Don't worry about that, just give me a hand with this furniture... and bloody quietly!' she hissed.

They put the bed and bedside cabinets against the door.

'Well, come on, double-O Pipet. You go first; give me something soft to land on.'

Rachid put his hands behind his back and pushed himself onto the windowsill. Then swung his feet around.

Valerie caught a vase as it rolled towards the edge. 'Not very good at this covert work, are we.'

He squirmed around, feeling for the drainpipe with his feet. 'I'd hoped to get back behind a desk before this job came up,' he said, disappearing below the ledge. He flinched, shutting his eyes as something from above creaked. When nothing fell, he carried on, tentatively feeling each step on his way down. Towards the bottom, something metallic hit his hand, but the pipe still felt secure. When touching the ground, he tugged and banged the fixings before waving Valerie down. 'And be quick; something's loose up there.'

Valerie swung out, reassuring herself that she was lighter than Rachid, if only by a stone or so. She crouched as another piece of metal fell from above; a bolt landed silently in a small bay tree. A bracket followed, striking her on the shoulder before bouncing off and landing at Rachid's feet.

'Quickly!' Rachid called as loud as he dared, 'The top's coming away.'

A length of guttering started a stream of fittings and pipework to fall. Separate from the noise of disintegrating metal, shouts and crashing bed furniture came from the window. Half calculating, half hoping, Valerie let go.

As Bentley leant out of the window, Valerie missed Rachid's outstretched arms and crashed onto his chest. Grabbing her winded comrade, she pushed, pulled and dragged him through the barbed shrubbery and into the street.

'Over there!' She carried on leading, swearing and cajoling towards a café. Propelling him through the door, she pushed him up against the wall. 'Ask him for two coffees,' she said, looking for a secluded table.

Coughing and fighting for breath, Rachid managed to hold up two fingers before pointing to a table beside the bar.

She looked at the young man still struggling to get air into his lungs, 'This is the last place they'll think of.'

He nodded before managing a strangled, 'Suppose so.'

Concentrating on the calm, deliberate intake of breath, he wiped tears away with his sleeve as the coffees arrived. It was possible to see Bentley from their table as he took little time looking up and down the street.

Rachid's breathing returned to normal. 'Well, that was a good guess.' Pushing her lips together, Valerie raised an eyebrow. 'Okay... good judgment,' he said as Bentley ran back into the building.

# THIRTEEN

With little change remaining in his pocket, Rachid left the guard to pay for the taxi as they went up the steps and through the double glass doors.

'Think I'd better leave the explaining to you,' said Valerie, turning off on the first landing. 'If you could send in a coffee?'

'Déjà vu,' she said quietly, as the same young man came in with the same coffee service. She sat in the same chair and picked the same magazine that looked as though it hadn't moved from the last time.

There was now a slight pain in her eye. Very little, on a scale of one to ten, it only just crept up to one, but now she considered her job done, the sooner she was back in London to a specialist, the better.

It was a search through the city as far as Rachid and the Iranian security service were concerned, but where? The only place to rule out was the flat. There was the sound of a great deal of running up and down the stairs outside the room, off, no doubt, to where they *wouldn't* find Bentley, Benny, or the bomb. But they had to start somewhere.

Now on her own in the quiet building, she put herself in Bentley's place. '*Where would I go? What about the money? Just how hell-bent would I be on pulling the trigger?*'

She gave up trying to get into his brain as far as the money and monstrous weapon was concerned. Where would she leave it? She put her head out of the door. Beneath another portrait of the Supreme Leader, the young man was waiting patiently.

'Is it possible to use a laptop?' She gave him a reassuring smile. 'I'll have to get a flight back to the UK.' She wasn't sure if she'd be allowed to use a computer; peculiar reasons for a refusal ran through her mind. She smiled again, 'Please?'

He vanished through a nearby door, returning a few seconds later.

'Apple!' The absurdity of an American icon in this country that had more reasons than most to hate the USA struck as a little more than ironic. 'Thank you.'

She returned to the anti-room and typed in Sarin, although she had to do without Google. It kept coming up in Persian.

She put her head out of the door again. 'I'm going to need your help.'

The young man left his seat and entered the room. 'Please,' she said, patting the cushion to her side, 'I need to get something up in English.' On seeing the screen, he immediately pushed himself away, but she grabbed his wrist. 'Do you know what's going on?'

He shook his head.

'Thousands of lives are at stake. Lives of your countrymen. Men, women, children. For God's sake, find me some way of understanding this bloody thing.' She tapped the screen. 'Why do you think everyone is running around like the bloody Israelis are banging on the front door?'

He moved back towards her and took hold of the laptop. 'I'll get into trouble if anyone finds out that I went onto this site.'

'You'll be in even more bloody trouble if you don't. Starting with me!'

He handed it back, with a search engine she had never heard of on the screen, but at least it was in English. She tried again, S A R I N.

'Sarin?' The young man watched as Valerie searched for information.

'Yes, Sarin.'

'Is that why everybody's acting like the building's on fire?'

She nodded, half her mind on the search engine, the other half wondering about the sudden and excellent command of English.

He took the laptop and, in a few moments, had Google on the screen. He typed in Sarin, 'What do we want to know?'

'How to use it. That is, what's the best... excuse the expression, place to set it off? Kill most people?'

'Tehran?'

Valerie rubbed a couple of fingers across the top of her eye. 'Yes,' she said quietly, 'Tehran.'

His eyes scanned the screen as he clicked on several links. 'It's heavier than air,' he said after a few minutes, 'so, up a height.'

'Like the top of a tall building?'

'Yes.'

'Or crane... all this work going on around the city centre, hoist it up and....'

'These people, whoever they are, they want to get away? Not die in the attack?'

'Yeah, he's not a fanatic... at least, not in that "die for the cause" sense of the word. He'll want to get away. How far does he have to go... to be safe, I mean?'

'Well out of the city, several kilometres.'

'Crane's out then. It's a tall building... it's got to be out of sight.'

'No shortage of tall buildings in a large city.'

'We're left with evacuation.'

He shook his head, 'We'd never get them out in time. And anyway, what's... what's his name?'

'Bentley.'

'What's Bentley going to do when he sees everyone fleeing?'

'Yeah, he's not short of options. He can even postpone it and go into hiding.'

'And what about the money? Is he no longer wanting the money?'

'As far as I know,' Valerie put the laptop to one side, 'I can only presume the ultimate aim is money, but this guy isn't stable.'

The intake of breath was swift. 'Well, I would say that's an understatement, Miss.'

'Yeah, I know, who runs around with thousands of lives tucked under his arm? But there's more to it than that.'

'What about your flight home?' he asked after a pause.

'Yeah, I should go... trouble is, Bentley's a Brit and—'

Valerie was cut short by Rachid coming in to tell her what she'd already concluded. Bentley had gone, along with Benny and the Sarin.

Later in the day, Valerie attended a meeting. Rachid, the brigadier, a colonel and two clerics had left a chair for her at a highly polished table. The young man who had helped with the laptop sat to one side with a notepad. As they spoke Rachid kept up with a quick translation.

'The money's been paid?'

No one seemed to have mentioned anything being paid into a Swiss account. As the room fell silent, Rachid told her that it had, and they were waiting to hear back. 'About twenty-four hours ago,' he added, pre-empting another question.

'That's crazy; this guy wouldn't hang around that long. He'd want to be out of here.' The brigadier looked at each person around the table before settling on Valerie.

'You have something on your mind, Miss Stone.' It was a statement; he wasn't inviting random thoughts. Rachid quickly translated as the two clerics understood the tone, if not what the brigadier was saying. They kept quiet.

'He'd have replied within minutes of getting the confirmation.'

'All right, so where does that leave us?'

'Right...' She laid her hands on the table, her fingers moving slightly as she marshalled her thoughts. 'First, as I said, Bentley would have replied straight away... so he didn't get the email.'

'He must have; it hasn't bounced back. It was the address we'd been given,' Rachid butted in, but the brigadier held up a hand and shook his head.

'Okay, yes, you sent it, and no doubt to the address you'd got, but...' she looked around the table at each man in turn, 'what if this part of their operation was being handled by Smithy? Now he's dead; after their ultimatum was sent, there's no guarantee the other two would have access to his account. There was no need; they were all in it together. They're either trying to figure out another way to get in touch or as far as Bentley and Benny know, you've ignored them, called their bluff.'

The young man with the notepad echoed all their thoughts, 'How do we contact them?'

The brigadier's frown deepened, 'There's more, isn't there?'

Valerie nodded. 'Second, what if they didn't trust each other? They've

156

got your email but can't access the money because they each have a third of the account number; that way, no one person could grab the money and run; they all had to turn up. So now they're wondering what to do next. Don't want to get in touch because they don't want to show their hand. Want you to sweat instead of them.'

After Rachid's quick translation, one of the clerics spoke.

'The Ayatollah said he wasn't sure if he wanted to hear any more of your thoughts,' explained Rachid.

Giving the holy man a facial shrug, she carried on. 'The last is the worst, I'm afraid. They've got the money and don't give a damn, they'll explode the bomb, sell it on... abandon it.'

Again, the man with the notebook asked what they had all been thinking. 'Why on earth would they let it off if they've got the money?'

'Not sure about Benny, but Bentley is a vicious psychopath. I was talking with the major before he was killed... he told me a few things about what he'd done before.'

'Any suggestions?' The brigadier gazed around the table, having repeated the question in Persian. The young man raised his pencil.

'I think we need to get someone into all the high buildings.'

Rachid again began to translate as the brigadier raised his voice.

'I get it,' said Valerie before he could finish, 'he wants to know how you're going to get someone into all the suitable buildings.' Rachid nodded. 'It can be done.' Attempting to ignore the slight increase in pain behind her eye, Valerie got to her feet. 'Police, the military,' she smiled at the nearest holy man, 'clerics... Get a map, get the personnel contacted... and do it now, this minute.'

The brigadier said a few words to the colonel and pointed to the door. The senior officer was calm, slipping into the difficult situation. He said something else in a low monotone as the colonel left. Everyone else, including Valerie, recognised that the decisions were now going to come from the brigadier. All proposals must be put to him.

The cold reality had always been there. But now it had been sharpened, Valerie was not going to cut-and-run. She raised her hand. The only indication the brigadier gave was a slight nod of the head. 'It's being put into place? Getting someone out to the buildings most likely to be used?'

The total weight that was on his shoulders showed; the nod was small.

'I know it's an outside chance, but is there enough personnel to put someone on the building site gates, the ones with a crane?'

The brigadier pushed down a button on his desk console and lowered his head as he spoke. Rachid told Valerie that it was in hand.

The more senior-looking cleric said something, but Valerie missed the translation as she racked her brain, trying again to put herself in Bentley's place. 'It might help if I was a nutter myself.' The few words were all but inaudible and were ignored by the others. 'Is there anything else you need us for?' she asked.

'Us?' Everything said at the meeting seemed to irritate the brigadier.

'Rachid and myself. If you don't need us, we can go and put our heads together.' Raising a hand from the table, the brigadier flexed his fingers dismissing them.

'The clerics,' asked Valerie when they had left, 'how do they fit in? Should have thought it was down to the armed forces. Them and the police, of course.'

'The top two, the President and Ayatollah, don't attend. Like your Prime Minister and Queen, they leave it to others. The two you met are the next most important. They'll report back up the line.'

'If and when they get time,' she said quietly.

'Where are we going?' Rachid checked the mobile, 'And what are we going to do?'

'Where?' Valerie led the way through the doors, 'Somewhere, we can get a coffee and some sort of pastry heavy with sugar. And what are we going to do? Think!'

'Not sure we're going to have much time for that.'

\*\*\*

Valerie pulled her hijab closer as Rachid brought over a coffee, a folder under his arm.

'Lovely out here in the open,' he said. 'Hard to think what's hanging over us.'

Valerie stirred some honey into the coffee. 'Money was put into that account?'

'Yes... at least, that's what I've been told, and there's no point in lying, is there?'

'No, no.' Pieces of flaky pastry dropped to the plate as she took a chunk out of the sugary delicacy. 'Come on, Rachid, ideas. You've got a brain the same as me. What's the bastard doing?'

'One thing that's been bothering me... or rather, it's puzzling. Ten million, it's not a lot... well, not a lot given what they are threatening.'

'No, peanuts, in fact.' Valerie remained silent for a moment, but when no explanation was forthcoming, said, 'Is that it?'

Rachid shrugged his shoulders, 'Is there more to this than we can see at the moment?'

'Jesus, aren't we blind enough without throwing imponderables into the stew? What's in the envelope?'

'Oh, this.' Rachid upended the contents onto the table. 'Anyone that has been associated with Bentley over the last year or two. Don't know if it will help, but….'

Valerie took the first sheet from the pile. There was a police-type photo and a short history of a man of forty-three, born in Toulouse.

'A good few from France must be the revolutionary blood.' She put it to one side, picked up the following description and then discarded it when she noticed "deceased" stamped in the corner.

She carried on until Rachid spoke. 'You can disregard that one too; he's also dead. Don't know why it hasn't been brought up to date. He was killed in an explosion last year.' Rachid reached over, but Valerie pulled the sheet back.

'Killed?' She scrutinised the photo. The date beneath was two years ago, and there were no scars. The man's face had been well-defined when the nurse had frozen the monitor back in the residential home. The video had been interrupted just as he stopped moving. 'This one isn't.' She tapped the description with her forefinger. 'At least, he wasn't a couple of months ago.'

Rachid took the paper. 'No name, just a reference number.' He slumped back in the chair, reading through the short report. 'Are you sure, can't be mistaken?'

Valerie shook her head, 'He's alive, and I'll bet we're going to trip over him sooner or later.'

'I'd like to know what he's doing. Is he chasing Bentley or helping him?'

Valerie took the photo back. 'Well, one thing's for sure, he ain't on our side.'

Rachid's phone rang. Although she didn't know what he was saying, the few replies he made were despondent.

'We've people at all the likely places,' he said, dropping the call.

'Jesus, that was quick!'

'There are compensations to living under a... strict regime.' He slipped the mobile back into his pocket. 'Where else.'

'It's definitely heavier than air?'

'Yes, why?'

'Just thinking of where a rat would hide.' He did no more than give her an inquiring look. 'The sewers… Oh, dear God.'

'What?'

'Water, he's going to put it in the water.' She jumped to her feet, sending coffee and pastries across the slate floor. 'Get on the phone, tell them water treatment plants, water storage units, anything that supplies the city with water.'

'Calm down, for goodness' sake, we don't know that.'

'It's got to be; it's the easiest.'

Being persuaded, Rachid rang the brigadier, then more calls to find out where the water plants were.

'Lived here most of my life and never knew where they were,' he said, driving to the first one.

'Not sure that's such a good idea,' said Valerie as flashing lights and sirens became apparent. 'We don't want to scare him off; we need him caught, get the bomb, that's the most important thing.'

The car had hardly stopped when Rachid jumped out, giving orders. Lights ceased to reflect from the water as the place fell silent.

'Better get on to the others, Rachid, tell them stealth is what's required.'

She thought it too late, but maybe all the shouting had bought a little time. With a bit of luck, Bentley would think again, perhaps even for another forty-eight hours.

\*\*\*

When they got back, Valerie asked the brigadier if she and Rachid could carry on following up on their own thoughts.

'Yes, of course, it's all prevention and clearing the city... if we get permission. What thoughts?'

'We'll think of something. Won't we, Rachid?'

'We will?'

\*\*\*

'Let's see what we've got.' Valerie laid maps and road atlases on the coffee table.

From one of the easy chairs, Rachid leaned forward. 'What are we doing?'

'He's gone. Over the hills, but not so far away.'

'Guess?'

'Umm...' she opened one of the larger sheets and spread it out, 'let's try and make it more of a guesstimate.'

'There's a lot of lives at stake.' He pulled the ring from a Pepsi can and passed it over.

'That reservoir we passed on the way to the Caspian Sea, is it one of the main ones that supply the city?'

Rachid reached across and pulled the laptop towards him. 'It's one of a few.' He scrolled through a few entries, 'Largest... but it's a bit of a guess, isn't it?'

'Why is it?' She took a drink from the can. 'It's the easiest to get to, runs by the road, then reaches up to the foothills.'

She went back over the map, persuading him that it was the best option and that other supplies were all but inaccessible.

160

'I'll get on to the Brigadier.'

Valerie put her hand across his phone as he picked it up. 'There's nothing they can do that we can't. And I know it's Iran's crisis, and you have every right to handle it the way you think best, but we don't want hundreds of men descending around the lake.' She stopped and held his eyes to her own. 'It's not bravado, Rachid. I'm not playing heroes. From where I'm looking, this is the best way... as long as he's there, of course. If not...' She shrugged her shoulders.

Rachid sat back, drumming his fingers on the mobile, weighing up the lives of his countrymen. Pondering which way to jump and that, probably inevitably, whatever he chose, it would be wrong.

'One thing we can't do,' said Valerie, 'and that's nothing. The clock's running.'

He got to his feet and slipped the phone back into his pocket.

'Took the liberty of booking these out,' he said, taking a canvas bag from under the settee. Valerie shook her head at the offered Uzi and took the Browning automatic and shoulder holster. She pocketed several ammunition clips and checked the pistol was loaded.

'Any other goodies in there?' She took a six-inch sheath knife and threaded it onto her belt. 'No,' she said when Rachid held up a hand grenade, 'bloody things frighten me... I'll take that though.' She picked out a twenty-four-inch twelve-bore and cartridges.

\*\*\*

'We're still keeping the faith, are we?' She pointed towards the Land Rover.

'Don't think much about your country, do you?'

'It's not the country, Rachid. It's the idiots running it into the ground. They can't see that there is no foundation to what they are doing; everything is built on sand.'

They flung equipment into the back and checked the extra fuel.

The short run to the reservoir was uneventful, apart from the self-doubt Valerie felt. Like videos on a loop, visions of Iraqi villages after chemical attacks wouldn't fade. Babies, children, fathers and mothers, old men and old women, lying in the streets as if asleep.

'All very quiet,' she said as Rachid turned off onto a small area of sand.

'Yeah.' His nod was slight. 'No one around, the last thing we need is innocent people running about... presuming your reasoning is correct, of course.'

'Better idea?'

'No. Everything else is covered... at least everything else we can think of.'

161

He took the Uzi from the bag and pushed a pistol into his belt. Valerie pulled on her jacket, covering the Browning and holster.

The shotgun looked even shorter now as she checked the chambers. 'This been cut?'

'Yes, it's used when going into confined spaces.' He eased on a flak jacket and attached several grenades. 'You sure you don't want one or two?'

Valerie shook her head. 'Just make sure I'm not in the firing line when you pull the pin. I shouldn't want you explaining that one to my secretary.'

'You have a secretary?'

'Yeah. Just an ordinary private investigator before I got dragged into this lot.' Patting her pockets to check for ammunition, she slung the shotgun over her shoulder, then laughed.

'What's funny?'

'A friend of mine once said she thought I had a small perfume shop.' She looked at Rachid, then caught a glimpse of herself in the wing mirror, 'Jesus, we look like Bonnie and friggin' Clyde.'

'Or something out of The Godfather,' he replied quietly.

'You've seen The Godfather? You guys never fail to amaze me.'

'I could say the same thing.' Starting between the pines he ducked a low branch. 'Perfume shop!'

Along the eastern shore, the trees ran out. The track surface was hard, mostly stones, impossible to tell if anyone had been along recently. The inaccessible far side rose from the waterline in a sheer climb to the mountain peaks.

Rachid reckoned the length of the reservoir to be about five kilometres. At the head, a small delta stretched out its muddy fingers.

'Sorry,' said Rachid, 'but it looks like we've made the wrong decision.'

'It's okay,' Valerie sat on a rock to his side and took the offered water, 'I called it, it's my fault.'

He took no notice of the apology but pointed up the valley. 'What's up there?'

Valerie shook her head, 'No idea, the map runs out more-or-less where we're standing right now. Shall we take a look?'

'Might as well.'

Rachid got to his feet and took out a small pair of binoculars. 'There's some sort of structure up there... a couple of kilometres, maybe.'

'Okay.' The acceptance was reluctant. Valerie thought there was little point in going any farther.

It was when they were about halfway that Rachid laughed. 'Look, someone's not going to get very far without that.' He pointed to a boot that had fallen down the slope towards the river. Valerie hopped and slid the few yards to where it lay.

'It's not *any* boot.' She threw it up to the pathway. 'They're here.'

Rachid picked it up then held out a hand, helping her back onto the path. 'Could be anyone's,' he said, pulling her up.

She shook her head, and taking hold of the boot, turned it upside down. 'Ex-army… British army. Look, the arrow on the instep.'

'One of them can't be hopping around on one foot.'

'Probably got something else on. The boots may have been tied to a rucksack, and came undone.'

Examining the sole, Rachid stroked his chin. 'Yeah, suppose so.'

'You'll be lucky,' she said as he switched his mobile on. She put a loop in the bootlace and hooked it onto her belt.

Rachid glared at the lack of bars on the signal indicator before looking up at the high mountains. 'Now what?' He slipped it back in his pocket.

Around the next corner, Benny's body was propped up against a rock, his head hanging to one side. A trickle of blood glistened on a bruised lip.

'Christ!' Valerie took the hand of the lifeless body. 'No rigor mortis. He's still warm.'

With no obvious signs as to how he died, she pulled him forward. The shirt was drenched red, four deep knife wounds punctured his back.

'Argument?' Rachid's voice was devoid of emotion.

'Must have been.' She carefully let the body rest back against the stump. 'What do you think? Benny started to get a conscience. Come on.'

Struggling to keep upright on the sloping path, Valerie went on ahead. The rocky trail gave way to sand and shale. Leading towards the small building fresh footprints and slip marks appeared.

'Something to do with the reservoir,' said Rachid, 'water monitoring station or the like.'

'Quiet,' hissed Valerie. She crouched down, pulling Rachid with her.

Twenty yards beyond the small blockhouse, Bentley was sitting to one side of a struggling fire. More smoke than flames rose from splinters of damp twigs. Moving a billycan closer, the fumes drifted into his face.

'Bastard.' Coughing, he put the back of his hand to his mouth, waving the other at the grey fog. Valerie took the boot and threw it next to the fire.

'Having trouble, Cinderella?'

'What the fuck!' He got to his feet, only to be confronted by the barrels of the shotgun.

'Where is it?'

'Where's what?'

'I haven't come halfway around the world to get dumb answers, arsehole.' Valerie levelled the gun at Bentley's face, 'Where is it?' she repeated slowly.

He pointed up the slope, where the container rested under a bush. 'No need to get excited; I'm sure we can talk this over.'

'You for real?' Aggravated, Valerie extended her arm. the twelve bore still pointed at his head as he reached for a rucksack. 'Hands where I can see them.'

Bentley pulled a pack of cigarettes from a side pocket and held them up. 'Only want a fag. Let me go; you can have the stuff. I'll wander off and transfer a few bob into your bank... sort of a thank-you. What do you say?'

'All in all, I think I'd rather see you sitting in a Tehran jail.'

'Come on, you know they'll hang me.'

'Suits me.'

During a lapse in the one-sided negotiation, Rachid started to examine the container. 'Don't think it's been touched, but we need to get it out of here and into a secure facility.' He looked around for confirmation, but Valerie was busy pushing the shotgun into Bentley's face.

'Where's the precursor?'

Bentley threw a smaller container across. 'There you are, now can I be on my way?'

Instinctively, Valerie ducked. 'You stupid bastard!' she spluttered, 'What are you trying to do?'

'It's okay,' Rachid picked it up, 'they're both inert on their own. Got to be mixed.'

'I don't give a shit how safe it is!' Recovering her composure, she got to her feet. 'Right, come on.' She kicked the billycan over the fire and told Bentley to go a few yards back along the path. Then, realising they had a problem, said to Rachid, 'How the hell are we going to get that bloody thing back to the truck?' She turned again to Bentley, 'What did you use to get it up here?'

Valerie didn't hear anything, only sensed a movement. A shadow, then sudden pain in her wrist. The shotgun was ripped from her grasp as a second blow was brought down on her arm. Pins and needles rapidly replaced a momentary loss of feeling.

'Don't think we've met.' The newcomer held up the gun, 'Nice piece of kit,' he said, pointing it in the general direction of Valerie and Rachid.

It had not been possible to determine his height from the video at the residential home, but here Valerie reckoned him just short of six feet. He'd left a kind of designer stubble on his face, probably because shaving across the scarring would have been too troublesome. Healed gashes had repaired into little hillocks between the dishevelled beard. His arm looked almost shrivelled but, going by the pain in Valerie's wrist, was still fully operative. He looked up at the sun, down at his watch and then at Bentley.

'Can't leave you for a minute, can I? You know,' he said, motioning Valerie towards Rachid, 'I've had this prat under my command for the last couple of years, never been able to get him into the righteous way, as it were. Always sneaking off for a cigarette or swig of single malt. Not a good Muslim, are we, John? Always one step behind.' He gave him a good kick. 'You'll be going through the gates of Jannah with a bottle of scotch under your arm, whistling "Stairway to Heaven". You know what?' he pushed his face close to Bentley's, 'The great Prophet will kick you straight back down your bloody stairway.'

He waved the shotgun in Rachid's direction, 'You, help Bentley get these backpacks into the shed. And you, Missy, finish putting the fire out and clear it into the river.'

Valerie ventured to ask about the Sarin, although she could think of nothing likely to dissuade its use.

'Not worked anything out, have you? No idea what's going on. Clueless, aren't you? That's good,' he said, kicking at the stones that had surrounded the fire. 'You're a lot more intelligent than most of them down there,' he waved the shotgun in the general direction of the city, 'and if *you* can't work it out, then neither can they… Until it's too late, of course.'

The man still hadn't introduced himself when he told Bentley to put Valerie and Rachid into the blockhouse, along with their kit.

'I'm going up there.' He pointed his mobile up the steep escarpment, 'Should be a signal at the top.'

Valerie slumped into a corner and stared at the small window. 'What the hell are they up to?'

To her side, Rachid looked towards Bentley. 'Don't think there's much point in asking *him*.'

'No, it strikes me he's as much in the dark as we are. I reckon our friend up the hill works on a need-to-know basis.'

The hill behind went up to a couple of thousand feet or more, so it was about two hours before the man came back.

'All set.' Pulling off his boots, he emptied bits of stone. Then, turning to Valerie, said, 'Worked it out yet?' Valerie shook her head. 'Give up?'

Aggravated by the mindless game, she said nothing.

'Okay, let's start with what day it is, or more importantly, what day is tomorrow.' He pulled his boots on and laced them back up.

Valerie let her head flop back against the wall, 'Monday,' she said wearily.

'Very good.' His tone was flat as if his mind was elsewhere. 'But apart from being Monday, what is it?'

'Eid al-Ghadir,' said Rachid.

Valerie looked at him.

'It's to celebrate Mohammad telling his followers that Ali will be his successor,' he explained. 'Four days of public holiday.'

The man nodded, 'And where will everyone be?'

Rachid started to rise, but the man motioned with his pistol to stay

165

seated. 'On holiday with their families.'

'And where will all the armed forces be?' he asked.

'Out looking for that,' said Valerie, pointing to the Sarin, before adding, 'Why did you only ask for ten million? Seems such a small amount.'

'Helps with the assumption that the people behind it were unhinged, not connected to reality. That way, we get the maximum number of forces looking for the bomb, frightened anything might happen. But there's another reason.'

Stood by the doorway, Bentley was looking more and more frustrated. 'What the fuck is this all about?'

The man smiled, 'Some people. But *you* know, don't you, Valerie?'

'The other reason's about the money?'

The man gave a slight movement of the head and smiled, 'And there's the winner of tonight's prize. We don't want a large amount of money leaving the country, and then having a problem getting it back.'

'You can't be serious? You can't have enough people in place,' said Valerie, catching on before Rachid or Bentley.

'Pity you're not on our side.' He nodded across to Bentley, 'Sharper than this pillock.'

Valerie expelled a grunt. 'Thought your women were only fit for cooking and producing kids.'

Bentley sent a boot into a nearby rucksack. 'Will someone tell me what the fuck's going on!?'

His commander looked at Valerie with a slight smile, 'Would you like to tell him?'

'I'll try. Now, let's see if I've got this right. Well, for a start, John, I'm afraid you've been a decoy. All this running around with a bomb was just to put everyone off the scent.'

'What!?' he screeched, 'A bloody decoy? I've been running all over North Africa just for the benefit of these two fucking Muppets?'

'You'd better look up the definition of a Muppet,' chuckled the commander. 'Think you'll find it applies more to you than them. Sorry about the interruption, Valerie, please carry on.'

'Yes,' she said slowly, 'the rest is not so easy. Your friend over here... sorry, I don't think we've been introduced.'

'No, we haven't.' As if addressing a board meeting, the polite smile did not leave the commander's lips. 'Please continue with your hypothesis.'

Slightly aggravated, Valerie carried on. 'You want as many people out of the capital as possible... and any left, to have their thoughts elsewhere.'

He nodded.

'Now, all this chasing around....' She thought for a moment, 'It's bloody genius. The most important people in the country, clerical leaders, senior ranks of the armed forces, will all be at some headquarters in the

166

capital.'

'All will be quiet... well, relatively quiet.'

'There's no way you can get away with it unless....' Valerie's eyes widened with the realisation, 'Oh my good grief, you've got people at the radio and TV stations.'

Rachid seemed to be following but said, 'What's that got to do with it? The media outlets?'

Valerie's reply was slow and deliberate. 'Control what's being said, and you've got the situation in the palm of your hand.' She looked from Rachid to Bentley, to the commander. 'And tell them from a trusted source. Block social media, of course, and tell everyone not to listen. Anything contrary to what is being said on state TV and radio is Western misinformation.'

'And the army,' said Rachid, 'is everywhere except where it needs to be.'

This time Valerie was not stopped as she got to her feet and stood in the doorway. 'They get back into the capital, and it's too late.'

The commander turned to Bentley, 'Mobiles into the river,' he tossed his across, 'including ours.' Valerie gritted her teeth as Bentley made the most of searching her.

'Bloody pervert,' she whispered in his ear. The clenched fist sent a dull thud into her brain as pain momentarily flashed down her neck.

'Enough!' The commander held Bentley's hand back, preventing another blow. 'Do you know,' he said as they came face to face, 'I wouldn't give a single rial for your chances if you came up against her one-on-one.'

Bentley ripped his hand away, 'Bullshit.'

The phones, along with the weapons Valerie and Rachid had been carrying, went into the river. Seen only by Valerie, the shotgun bounced from a rock and landed on the other side of a thicket.

'We'll not need that.' Revealing how the bomb had been transported, the commander pointed to some canvas and short poles. 'We'll leave our surprise package locked up in here; it won't come to any harm.'

When they were ready to leave, Valerie asked to go to the toilet with no attempt to feminize it.

'No, you bloody pervert,' the commander turned to Bentley, 'you can't keep an eye on her.'

'This bush, okay?'

The commander gave a facial shrug, 'Sure.'

Out of sight, Valerie brushed the dirt from the shotgun and checked the chambers. Empty. She stuffed it into her rucksack. With the top cover tied down, it was short enough to be hidden.

# FOURTEEN

'The other side of this outcrop,' said the one in charge as they passed the parked Land Rover. 'We'll use our Landcruiser.'

'I need some things from the Land Rover.' It wasn't the first time she had used the excuse, and it probably wouldn't be the last.

With his regular monotony, Bentley once again jumped in. 'Such as?'

'I'm a woman, arsehole. When a woman asks for a few things, you don't ask why.'

The commander nodded and told Bentley to go with her.

Fumbling around in a pack behind the driver's seat, she produced some knickers and tampons. 'Okay? D'you want to search my frillies? Or maybe you want to try them on?' She took a kick at his shins before opening the front door. Bentley was about to retaliate but caught the commander looking across to them. 'You want a Coke, Rachid?'

Saying that he did, she searched under the seat, then threw one across. Another was pushed into the back compartment of her rucksack. Asking the commander if he wanted one, gave her a couple of seconds as Bentley looked over his shoulder. She scooped up a handful of shotgun cartridges and pushed them into her inside pocket.

'Thought you might want one.' She handed him a can, ripped the tag from another and took a sip. 'You want one?' Out of sight, she gave the can a quick shake and tossed it to Bentley, who pulled out the ring and got a face full of spray.

'No!' Once again, the commander put his arm out as Bentley drew back to hit her.

Bentley threw the can against a tree, sending up a fountain of froth. 'You starting to fancy her or something?'

'She's better company than you. Now, get that rucksack; we need to get out of here.'

***

There was little chance of reuniting gun and cartridges as she was bundled into the front seat.

After putting the rucksacks in the back, the commander slid behind the wheel and told Bentley to get into the rear seats with Rachid. 'Keep that revolver of yours handy. We don't want any heroics or anyone getting hurt.'

Turning the key, he blipped the accelerator, pushed the car into first, then glanced over at Valerie, 'Tell me about yourself.' He pulled hard on the wheel, taking the SUV back onto the road. 'What do you do when

169

you're not chasing us bad guys?'

'Oh, you know.' Any bond between the two of them, however, fabricated, could only be of benefit, 'Run-of-the-mill stuff, getting proof of infidelity in divorce cases. Only fell into this lot...' She nodded her head towards Rachid. 'My mistake. I was short of money, and along with a run-in with Customs and Excise, some unscrupulous bastard saw a chance to take advantage.' Before the language got worse, she stopped. 'Then,' she continued, 'someone screwed my arm up between my shoulder blades.'

'Do as we say or go to jail?'

'Oh yeah, I was under no illusion that if I didn't play, it was the bloody assises.'

They carried on for the next half hour as if they had just been introduced at a cocktail party.

'See it all from here,' he said, pulling off the road. Overlooking the capital, they were parked up to the side of some gently swaying Velvet Maple. 'Over there is the TV and radio station, and down towards that high crane is where the top brass will be.' He spoke as if a tourist guide indicating points of interest.

'How many?'

'Men?' He looked thoughtful, 'Enough.'

*How many was enough?* Valerie ran figures through her mind; hundred, two hundred, a thousand? It was futile. The only thing, the most important thing, was to get word to the brigadier. That's if he'd believe her. Or was it they would just sit here and watch the whole tragedy unfold before their eyes?

Lights came on in the early evening as Tehran began shutting down, preparing for the following holiday. The man by her side started the motor.

'Back tomorrow, we can watch everything from up here.'

\*\*\*

Behind a row of deserted shops, the city lights hardly disturbed the eerie scene. Backed up against a wall, the Landcruiser was unloaded in silence. A corridor to the side of a tall building led to a steel door. Rust was pushing the grey paint away from the battered metal. Through the door, a short passage ended in front of a flight of stairs. Valerie held on to the insecure bannister as she was bundled up the bare steps. Of the three doors at the top, Bentley opened the one to the left.

Chairs were occupied by half a dozen men, mostly hunched up to a map on a central table. Standing to the side, a little aloof from the others, a cleric was consulting papers with two army officers. A black Isis flag hung on the back wall. There was a casual glance in Valerie's direction before the low-tone discussions continued.

170

Rachid's grab at her elbow came at the same time the ayatollah looked up. Whether it was being dressed alike in the brigadier's office or because she hadn't paid that much attention, it didn't matter. She recognised him now.

Telling them to keep quiet, Bentley pushed them up against the wall.

'Guess this is the naughty step,' Valerie said through the corner of her mouth.

'I said—' Bentley raised his hand, only to have it knocked away by the nameless one.

'You're here under sufferance. Keep quiet and keep your hands to yourself.' Bentley scowled and took a coffee from a glass Kona.

A few words were exchanged between the cleric and one of the soldiers. The officer approached Valerie and Rachid. With gestures, he took them out. Valerie's request for her rucksack was ignored.

Back down the stairs, they were pushed into the only room that seemed to have a secure door. A key was turned, then silence. High on the wall, a small grid let in enough light to see a lamp hanging from the ceiling.

'Switch must be by the door,' she said, feeling along the wall. The brass fitting crackled as the bulb came to life. They were in some kind of workshop; a vice was attached to a sturdy but small table. One or two screwdrivers, a chisel and several files hung from a rack above.

'The cleric,' said Rachid.

'It's okay; I'm way ahead. I presume he's number four, five, six?'

'Yeah, somewhere around there.'

'And he's well known?'

'Of course, makes a lot of TV appearances. Don't much like the idea of him being part of this mess.'

'Much trusted and admired?'

'Absolutely.'

'Well,' said Valerie, 'as soon as they take control of the TV station, he goes on air and appeals for calm in this difficult time. Discredits those above and....'

'A hole in one.' Rachid kicked at a couple of bricks lying on the floor. 'Pity there's no more tools.'

The door opened, and Bentley threw in their rucksacks.

'Pillows,' he laughed. 'And I removed the shooter. So, your plans have hit the buffers.'

As he left, Valerie looked at her watch. 'How long before they're asleep, do you think?'

'Why, what difference does that make to us getting out?'

'We'll give it till two.' She took a foot to her rucksack and, pushing it to the wall, sat down. 'Where will the brigadier be?'

'Hold on,' said Rachid, giving the room a querying look, 'we're locked

171

up, in case you hadn't noticed.'

Tired, Valerie had fallen asleep.

'Two o'clock.' Rachid gave her shoulder a gentle shake, 'Time to get us out of here,' he said with little conviction.

Valerie blinked, the half-blur being apparent mostly when she woke. 'Okay.' She rubbed at her eyes and gave her head a shake.

'You alright, Valerie?'

'Sure, sure. Give me a hand with this bench.'

Pushing and pulling, they got the table up against the door, the vice against the lock. Valerie took the cartridges from her pocket and dropped them on the table.

'By the almighty, when did you get those?'

'When Bentley wasn't keeping his eye on me.'

She took a tissue from her pocket and started opening the cartridges. The shot she put on the table. The propellant, from all but one, she carefully piled on the small square of paper. She took the smallest screwdriver from the wall, prised the wadding from two shells, and then stuffed it into the lock. Careful not to let it fall from the other side, she pushed in more and more of the wadding, then tapped it into a solid mass. The nitro she made into small parcels, and these followed the wadding. Keeping the whole package in place, a small piece of tissue was put in last. She took the last live cartridge and made it secure in the vice just a millimetre or two from the lock.

'The propellant from that cartridge fires into the lock and the packed explosive goes off like a mini-bomb... Well, that's the theory.'

Rachid stood back, 'Time for the practice?'

Valerie put the rucksacks up against the vice and lock, leaving a small gap in the centre. 'Should help with any blowback.' She placed the screwdriver up against the cartridge's percussion indent. 'Okay.' She pulled the flap at the top of one of the rucksacks and placed it over her hand. 'Thump the handle with one of those bricks. A good thump.'

The strike and double explosion rebounded from the walls. The pain in Valerie's hand followed. 'Shit!' She threw the rucksacks to one side, shaking her wrist.

'Let me see.' Rachid took hold of her hand, only to have it snatched away.

'Later. Help me pull this table away; we've got a minute at most.'

The door was still stuck but gave way to frantic pulling from them both.

'Out, out! Anywhere, just get out!'

Rachid stumbled as Valerie pushed him through the doorway. 'Out, get out!' she screamed. In the dim light, she pushed him across the parking area. They ran down the opposite alleyway. 'This way!' She pulled him into an adjacent street, then across a square.

'How do you know which way?' panted Rachid.

'I don't.'

She turned up a slight incline and across the main road, then across a deserted strip of tarmac, around a park and into a dark side street. 'But if I don't know where we're going, then neither do they.'

She pulled him over a wall and leaned back, gathering her breath. After a minute, she looked around the side. Nothing.

Coughing, Rachid steadied his breathing, trying to speak.

'What is it?' asked Valerie as he took in a good gulp of air.

'We need to get in touch with the Brigadier, stop this thing before it gets started.' Under his breath, he stifled a laugh.

'What's so funny?'

'Nothing, nothing. It's just that I don't know how to contact the Brigadier, even if we had a phone. The only time I ever meet him is by going in through the front door.'

'Straight forward,' said Valerie, 'get a taxi round to headquarters. There's sure to be overnight security on duty. The hardest part will be finding a taxi; come on.'

Recognising Rachid, the guard saluted and held a hand towards the stairway. Rachid said a few words in Persian. The guard frowned and then rummaged around his pocket for the taxi driver's fare.

'Think he must be getting used to you having no money.'

In the brigadier's office, Rachid pulled drawers from filing cabinets, flicking through contents.

Valerie pushed around the few things on the desk. 'I wouldn't know if I'd found what we're looking for or not,' she said. 'Someone in this building must have his contact details, middle of the night or not.'

Rachid joined her behind the desk, emptying the contents of one drawer on the top.

'What's that?' Valerie took a leather notebook from beneath a few sheets of A4. Rachid thumbed through.

'Brigadier's number isn't here.'

'Don't see why it should be,' said Valerie, 'not in his own office.'

'We're wasting our time. There's only one place to go.'

***

On the army base, a girl answered Rachid's furious banging. He said something and pushed her back through the open doorway. Quickly scanning around the empty bedroom, he then said something else. She yawned and pointed down the corridor.

'Dear God.' Rachid led the way out and across a grassed area. 'Everyone's been moved.'

173

Another complex, and another door, Rachid was once again making a noise. A stranger pointed to the next room as Rachid repeated his query. With all the commotion, the door was already open.

Valerie followed the conversation as they swapped to English. The lieutenant didn't dispute what he was told as he quickly dressed; the only indication of a response to what he heard was the colour draining from his face.

As soon as Rashid had finished, the lieutenant had a sergeant assembling personnel in the canteen. The meeting lasted minutes.

'The guys here will get others that they know they can trust, then we'll be ready. We're also sending a detachment to guard the Sarin.'

'With strict instructions not to touch it,' Valerie emphasised.

Rachid confirmed that no one would go near it.

'TV and radio station first,' she said, 'we've got to have control of the news.'

The lieutenant held a hand in front of Valerie, 'You can't come.'

'Damn bloody right I can! I've chased these bastards to your front door; there's no way I'm stopping now.

'I know, we owe you a debt that never can be repaid, but you still cannot come. Only a handful of the men know you, trust you. The rest...' he shrugged his shoulders. 'We have clerics, officers that would not accept it. I would be proud to have you by my side, but....'

'It's true,' said Rachid, 'and you know it.'

The argument continued until, knowing further protest was futile, she fell silent.

'You can hear what is happening with this.' The lieutenant gave her a communication radio.

'Not unless your men learn to speak English in the next ten minutes, I won't.' For the first time since the lieutenant had been told about the terrorists, he smiled. 'Rachid will keep you up-to-date.'

'I see we got the Land Rover back,' she said as the keys were dropped into her hand.

\*\*\*

Valerie hung the walkie-talkie from the rear-view mirror, propped a mobile on top of the instrument binnacle, then leaned back, resting her knees on the steering wheel. The commanding view was as before, overlooking the media station and the central headquarters a few hundred yards away. At that moment, it housed the most important and influential people in Iran.

There was very little evidence of any fighting from the hilltop. Only gunfire and the occasional muffled explosion, coming over the radio, indicated what was happening. And the lieutenant was right; all the shouting, and what she presumed were commands and instructions, were in Persian. She'd have been a hindrance; adding to the casualties.

In the middle of what must have been heavy fighting amongst the shouting, now and again, Rachid found time to hold down the communication button.

'We're in… not too many… everyone is okay,' and so on.

'Like a regular reporter,' she said quietly.

In less than an hour, Rachid relayed that the clerics and senior commanders were safe. Minutes later, she was told that the all-important news media was securely in their hands. An update to the population was on the air, 'Probably before most are out of bed,' he added with a thoughtful chuckle.

When asked about injuries, Rachid declined to answer, saying that he would bring her up-to-date later.

With the adrenalin subsiding, she began craving a cigarette. The worry about her eye had been pushed away; it now came back. Blurred vision, and even risk to her sight, had to be addressed, and soon. A flight home, if not today, then tomorrow.

'Thought I might find you here.' The door swung open, and a pistol was thrust into her face. Behind, someone got into a rear seat.

'For Christ's sake,' she said, recovering her wits. 'Next time you're in my sights...'

'Yeah, yeah,' said Bentley, 'next time.' He slid in next to her, the gun levelled at her head. 'But for the moment, drive.'

'Where to? London? It's all up. You might as well give yourself up, and plead for mercy. By the way, who's your friend in the back?'

'Just drive.'

The communicator crackled. Bentley ripped it from the mirror and threw it into the night.

Valerie tapped a finger on the fuel gauge, 'Where are we going? There's less than fifty miles in the tank.'

'There's an all-night station on the outskirts.' He squirmed around in the seat and took a wad of notes from the person behind. 'You've spare cans in the back?' He looked over his shoulder. On the floor behind, two large cans were wedged up against the rear seat. 'Any more?' With no reply, he brought the butt of the pistol down onto her thigh.

Shouting in pain she spat the words out. 'Bastard! I think so… maybe.' She rubbed at her leg. 'How in Christ's name do you think you're going to get away? Twelve hours and the Revolutionary Guard will be after you. And I wouldn't fancy your chances against one of them, let alone a whole bloody brigade.'

He gripped the money as they pulled into the petrol station, telling her

to get out and look relaxed. 'Run, speak, or do anything else stupid....'
Bentley held the gun in his pocket but kept it pointed at Valerie. She
glanced to the back. Dressed in an open shirt, a bearded man took no
notice, his eyes fixed ahead. He took a baseball cap from a pocket and
pulled it down over his face.

Being on the edge of town, there was a possibility of it being self-
service. There could be a chance to mix a little sand with the petrol. A
handful would be enough. Valerie swore under her breath as a boy ran out
and removed the hose from the pump. He said something in Persian.
Bentley replied, nodding to the spare cans inside. He gripped Valerie's
arm, causing her to yelp as he dug fingertips into her bicep.

The man in the back remained silent as she got back behind the wheel.

'Which way?' She looked up and down the road, letting the Land Rover
idle in neutral. All energy spent Bentley signalled to the left with a shake
of the pistol. Valerie guessed he'd been awake for the last twenty-four
hours, and kept one eye on the pistol, ready to pull it from his grip.

'South?' she said as the sign for Qom and Kashan appeared.

He nodded; In grim determination, he fixed his eyes on the road.

'You'd be better off without me, you know. My description will be out
with yours.' She glanced to her side. He swayed from side to side, but he
was getting a second wind, his eyes refused to close.

'You could be useful.' His voice was beginning to slur, 'I might need a
hostage to get a boat.'

'I think,' she said, looking in the rear-view mirror, 'that the Iranians
think like the Brits as far as hostages are concerned. No negotiations, full-
stop. You should have taken a French captive in the middle of Africa, far
better chance. The frogs would have given you money *and* a helicopter...
probably kissed you goodbye.'

He reached across and threw the back of his hand across her face.

'Keep your stupid thoughts to yourself,' he said, seemingly refreshed.

Stroking a sore cheek, she moved her jaw from side to side. 'Okay,
okay. But I need to know where I'm driving.' She glanced in the mirror.
The man's head was slumped forward, his breathing slow and regular.

Even on the busiest of days, the main Iranian roads were free of
significant traffic. They made good time, only stopping to pay tolls before
skirting around Qom. Irrigation fields, decorating each side of the road,
were broken by the occasional supermarket or industrial estate. Valerie
began to wonder why Land Rover had such a poor reputation; the journey
was uneventful. That is until they entered Kashan when a scraping came
from a rear wheel.

Bentley guided her to a garage set back from a small complex of flats.
'Probably just a brake pad.'

Stretching, Valerie eased herself from the driver's seat. 'You seem to know your way around.'

Bentley shook the rear passenger awake, then pushed Valerie beneath a half-open roller door and into a workshop. The man followed; he was the cleric from the previous night.

There was little fuss made about the arrival: a wave from someone hunched over an open engine bay; a smile from an obese man leaving a wide landing and coming down a set of wooden stairs. Pushing Valerie to one side, the three exchanged handshakes. Rolls of fat hung from the fat man's chin and bulged over the back of a dirty collar. His eyes were small, pig-like. Finished with the greetings, he let them roam over Valerie's breasts.

'You can stay a few days; let the dust settle. Maybe I could get to know your friend a little better.' He stroked stubby fingers under Valerie's chin.

'In your dreams, pervert.' She took a swing at his shins but missed, falling to one knee as his nimble skip to one side took her by surprise.

'What is it, you Brits say? Oh yes, spirited little thing, isn't she? But I can wait.'

'You leave her in one piece.' The statement came from between gritted teeth. 'I might need her later... and you,' he turned to Valerie, 'behave your bloody self, that temper of yours is going to get you into a shit load of trouble one day.'

'*What do you mean, one day*?' she said to herself.

'Day after tomorrow,' said the overweight man after making a phone call. 'There'll be a boat; it'll take you off the beach at Mollu, then across the Gulf.'

'What, run the Strait of Hurmuz?'

The cleric said something. Bentley's reply was sharp. Valerie guessed the holy man was being told to make his own arrangements.

He grabbed the fat man's arm, 'I'll likely be stopped as not. You're not on. I go from somewhere on the south coast. And no extra,' he added, letting his grip relax.

'Okay, no problem, but getting across to Sudan and the DRC will cost more; they won't do that for free.'

'Listen, you bloody parasite, you've had every last cent of mine. Halfway is no fucking good.'

With bulging flesh hanging from arms and belly, the shrug from the fat man was grotesque. 'You overestimate me, my friend; I'm just a travel agent. I set everything up and get presented with a bill. That bill I hand onto you, with a little on top for me, of course. Can't run a business for the love of it.'

The cleric was getting flustered, chipping in when he had the chance. Between the three of them, Valerie was pushed up the steps and into an office.

Tapestries hung from walls that needed paint, worn chairs showed an odd spring. On a side table, a neat line of coffee cups sat to the side of a De'Longhi. On the other side, an illicit bottle of Jack Daniels. The two men now sat either side of a table, the Imam left out of any negotiations.

Bentley got up and emptied two inches of bourbon into a cup. 'Whatever it takes, you'll get paid.'

'Oh, dear.' The fat man seemed tired of explaining the theory of his basic monetary system. 'How do I know I'll get paid? You could be dead half an hour after going out that door.' He turned to look at Valerie, 'On the other hand, you could leave the little lady with me... kind of a deposit. What do you say? Five thousand dollars, and you get her back.'

'What, after you've been through her? Wouldn't know what I'd end up catching.' He thought for a moment. 'I'll sell her to you.'

The pig-eyed man scratched the stubble on his chin, then, like a farmer inspecting a prize animal, he pulled Valerie to her feet and ran a hand over her breasts, then thighs. She grabbed his hand and, pulling it out straight, had him cry in pain as he fell to his knees.

'Touch me, and you'll have to finish the job.' Giving his arm an upward jerk, she brought it close to breaking point. 'If you don't, I'll find you.'

Bentley took hold of her hair pulling her away. Like a piglet, the fat man gave out a squeal as his bicep twisted. He got to his feet, holding his upper arm.

'I'll kill the bitch now!' Shoving Valerie into a corner, Bentley held him away.

'You'll do nothing until we've completed negotiations. All the money you've had from me, plus her. Then you can do what you want.' Bentley held out a hand to shake on the deal.

'Okay, okay.' Still holding his arm, he opened the door and shouted. A large, fit, well-built man came in. The cleric started talking again, looking at each man in turn. His collar ripped as Bentley took hold and shoved him into a corner, giving out what Valerie assumed were words the Imam hadn't come across all that often. The man who had, so recently, wielded enormous power was lost and frightened.

Valerie was taken away and locked in a room.

*** 

In the corner of the yard, the Land Rover had been hidden beneath a tarpaulin. Fitted to the chassis before leaving the army base, a tracker ticked out a steady rhythm. Had it been found, a close examination would have told little. The signal could have been relayed to a satellite, trackable over thousands of square miles, or a system localised to a few city blocks.

***

178

Valerie managed to separate herself from reality and, lying on a reasonably clean bed, closed her eyes. She was tired, but the sleep she fell into was fitful. Hideous visions of the naked fat man swam into her brain. Rolls of flab, more hideous than any reality, came and went. Mixed in with what was fast becoming a nightmare, she saw Albert, then Rachid. A score of gunfire-like background music pulsed around. All accompanied by a blurring vision.

The shake on her shoulder was gentle, the hand across her mouth firm. Quick clearing of her eyes relayed an impossible picture to her brain. She tried to scream, but the hand on her mouth would let nothing escape.

'Shh.' The voice was as gentle as the shake on her shoulder had been, 'Scream, and we're both dead.'

Wide-eyed, Valerie slowly nodded. The hand was released from her mouth.

'How come you're alive? And more to the point—'

'Rescuing you?' He sat on the bed, 'I'll explain later. But for now, we need to get out. Agreed?'

'Agreed. But?' She said no more. Getting clear was the most important thing, and if her guardian angel had once been her enemy… 'Do I get to know your name?'

The man raised his badly scarred arm and thoughtfully rubbed at the matching disfigurement on the side of his face. 'Navid.'

Pushing a pistol into her hand, he pulled her to her feet.

'How did you know?' She checked the magazine of the Glock forty-three, then slammed it back into the handle.

'Guessed, maybe?'

'Who the hell are you?'

'Come on, there's a dozen or more villains around this place; we don't have time to swap niceties.'

As footsteps came from the end of the passageway, he told her to put the gun in a pocket as he grabbed her wrist. 'Pretend to be frightened,' he hissed.

'Pretend!'

Two men came around the corner from the staircase, jerking her arm, Navid made her stumble. He said something in Persian; the two men stood to one side.

From the open landing, the fat man was blocking the bottom of the stairway.

'Where are you taking her?'

'To the Land Rover.' Reaching the bottom, Valerie obligingly yelped as Navid yanked her along, 'There might be some explosives we can use.'

The fat man persisted with his questioning, 'Why in Allah's name do you want her with you?'

'Because—' Navid broke off as he stood in front of the fat man then sank his fist into the bulging belly; he brought the pistol butt up under his chin in one smooth but sudden movement.

Three more men burst from the back door; guns drawn. Navid dropped the first and Valerie the second. When Navid's gun jammed, he ducked behind a truck.

Sprawling on the floor, the fat man recovered and grabbed Valerie; falling to one side she dropped the Glock. Although still with an injured arm, the fat man used his weight, striking Valerie across the face and wedging her against a workbench. He hit her again as, at first, she vainly searched the benchtop with a free hand for some sort of weapon. A hammer slipped from her grip, but she managed to grab something cold and smooth. She struck him across the head several times. The can of builder's foam split, sending its contents into his hair. Valerie twisted the container as he put a hand to the resulting gash, filling his mouth with the deadly contents.

Coughing and spluttering, he released his grip. Globs of foam fell down his chest, but not enough to clear his airway. The rapidly expanding foam reached down his throat; an involuntary intake of breath took it into his lungs. He turned red, then grey. Two small streams of the setting bubbles dribbled from his nostrils as he fell to the floor. Like some absurd animal, limbs wildly flayed around as life was extinguished.

Recovering, Valerie picked up the pistol. The last of the insurgents raised his weapon at Navid but got no further. The look of surprise on his face as the bullet struck his chest was only matched by the relief on Navid's.

Squeezing beneath the roller doorway, Navid's inquiry about the Land Rover keys met with a head shake.

Down a side road, they tried one car door after another. 'We need to get out of here. Their tentacles,' he nodded over his shoulder towards the garage, 'are bloody everywhere. Don't know who we can trust.' A door opened, but it only brought an obscenity from Navid's lips. 'Bloody modern cars. We need something I can hot-wire.'

Around the corner, a white Opel Ascona from the early seventies yielded to an inquisitive tug.

'Have a look in the boot,' he said, going through the glove compartment. 'We need a piece of wire.' He swore again as all he pulled out were empty crisp packets and a black banana.

Valerie looked under the boot lid. 'How long?'

'Anything, only needs an inch or two.'

Wrapping her hand around a red cable disappearing into the rear light cluster, she gave a sharp pull.

'Okay?' Navid was sitting in the driver's seat as she handed the wire over.

He twisted around and underneath the steering wheel. A few seconds and the warning lights lit up the instrument panel. A few more seconds and the engine started.

'Where to, Madam?' he asked as Valerie got into the passenger seat.

'More important than where to... who the bloody hell are you?!'

The gearbox complained as Navid shifted it through third. 'Think the synchro's gone,' he said.

'You come in, grab hold, and we leave, all guns blazing... and I'm supposed to trust you?'

'Well, you're still alive, aren't you?'

'I suppose, but I could be on my way to another cell and held for ransom for all I know. Although,' she added quietly, 'you're going to be out of luck if you think anyone will fork out for my return.'

'No, I'm on your side.'

'What, a bloody terrorist? You can't think I'm going to swallow that one?'

'I'll drive you into Tehran and drop you at the front door of the Brigadier if you want. Or you can help me.'

'The Brigadier, you know the Brigadier?'

'You can ask all the questions you want... when we've found the bloody Sarin.'

A cold finger ran down Valerie's spine, but this time with relief. 'The Sarin? It's okay, safe, under guard.'

Navid glanced in the rear-view mirror but said nothing. Clear of the town, he pulled off the road. 'Sorry, but it's not.' He took a half bottle of Johnny Walker from an inside pocket and passed it across.

'Thanks.' Valerie took a good swig, coughing on the sharp sting at the back of her throat. 'I needed that.'

'Cigarette?'

Seriously tempted, she thought for a moment, then shook her head. Navid took a pack of Chesterfields from an inside pocket and flicked one out. Smoke filled the car.

'What do you mean, the Sarin's not safe? We've got it; it's safe; a platoon of soldiers are guarding it.'

'Sorry,' again he drew deeply on the cigarette, 'but your soldiers are guarding a box of sand.'

Waiting for an explanation, Valerie said nothing.

'I infiltrated Isis a while back and worked my way up to a kind of districted commander. Please don't ask anymore; I have enough trouble straightening it with my conscience as it is. Let's just say that when it's all put on the scales, the good outweighs the bad... hopefully. Anyway, I got to Smithy a while back, persuaded him as to which was the right path to follow.'

'Jesus, that's why the idiot was so mixed up,' said Valerie slowly. 'I think I know where this is going, but-'

'Correct.' Navid gave the cigarette another hard pull. 'To be on the safe side, I gave him the harmless box. They had a second truck before dumping it later on. Smithy hid it in that. When he took his turn on guard, he buried the real thing and replaced it with the sand. I suppose he wanted to make double sure, the stupid sod... smashed up the controls and got himself killed for his trouble.'

'I hate to ask, but do we know where it is?'

Navid shook his head, 'We don't, but there is someone who does, only he doesn't know he knows... if you get what I mean.'

'I dread to ask who.'

'Yeah, that's right. The only person to have been with Smithy on the overnight stops is Bentley. The Sarin is at one of those stops. And no, before you ask, the vehicle that he torched was not the one they used, it was before that, so it's no good sifting through the ashes for the sat-nav or tracker.'

'So, if Bentley finds out that it's at one of the stops from when they had the two trucks, he just gets a spade and works his way from one to the other. Jesus, he could make a bloody fortune.'

'Or worse.'

Navid drove back onto the highway.

'So, we need him alive… Christ, we're back to the beginning.'

# FIFTEEN

Disregarding the carnage he was leaving, Bentley pulled the tarpaulin from the Land Rover. He checked the fuel, then piled every spare can of diesel he could lay his hands on into the back. More guns and ammunition went onto the back seat. Backing out, his eyes darted around; panic setting in.

\*\*\*

'He's taking a boat across to Somalia.'

Navid shook his head, 'Not in one go. The boat will do it in jumps, Oman first. But where from is the problem.'

'Back in the workshop... I can't remember where it was, but he said he wouldn't go from there because it meant running the Strait of Hormuz.' Navid banged the side of the steering wheel with his fist.

'That means the south coast and nursing this car even further.'

'No good looking at me, I'm skint. What about you?'

'Enough for fuel, but not enough to buy something reliable, if that's what you're getting at.'

Valerie pulled at his arm as they approached a service station.

'Get some plugs, oil, oil filter. If this car's taking us south, it needs all the help it can get.'

\*\*\*

Navid sat on a mound of sand, chewing on a sandwich. 'Let me know if you want a hand.'

'It's okay.' She broke a box spanner from its plastic wrapping and started to remove the plugs. 'Got something far older than this at home.' Checking the gap and threading the new ones in, she then crawled underneath. 'That sump spanner.' Lying on her back, she held out a hand. 'Thanks.' Along with her hand, the spanner disappeared beneath the Opel.

'Gordon bloody Bennett!' She rubbed dirty knuckles on a rag. 'Okay, muscles, get this engine drained; I can't shift it.'

As Navid drained the oil, Valerie replaced the oil filter. 'Dear God,' she said, shaking sludge from the choked housing, 'this hasn't been changed since it rolled out the bloody factory.' Throwing the bagged rubbish into the boot, she told Navid she had half a mind to charge the owner for a service, 'When he gets it back, of course.'

'That sounds better,' said Navid as he blipped the accelerator a couple of times.

'Adjusted the distributor while I was in there.'

Pointing the Opel south, Navid re-joined Highway seventy-one. 'Not just a pretty face, then.'

He kept to a steady hundred kilometres an hour, all the time watching the instruments.

After dozing for a while, Valerie was awoken by a change in the road surface.

'Sooner or later, we're going to have to flip a coin, decide which port to go to,' Navid said.

'Not as bad as that. My bet... he'll go to the first quiet place past the Straits.'

She ripped the tag from a Pepsi, passed it across, and then wrapped a piece of flatbread around a chunk of goat's cheese.

'It's going well,' she said, biting at a corner, 'the car, I mean.'

Navid looked in the rear-view mirror, 'Burning a little oil.'

'Serious?' Turning around, Valerie watched the occasional wisp of smoke curl across the carriageway.

'Should be okay, I've knocked the speed back a bit, but we can stop and top the oil up in a minute.'

A small amount of oil brought the level back to normal, while a check of the radiator confirmed it was not leaking.

'German engineering.' Valerie dropped the bonnet, 'It's dead, but it won't lie down.'

*\*\*\**

Through a combination of Valerie's soft words and Navid's light foot, the Opel cruised into the first small village east of Bander-e-Jask.

They drove down to the shore between the mass of deltas and scrub vegetation over makeshift crossings and rock-reinforced tracks. Two brightly coloured boats were drawn up on the coarse sand. A nearby shack was deserted.

Valerie jumped out and started to walk towards the small breaking waves, surprised when each step sank several inches.

'Keep away from where the river enters the sea.' Navid pointed a hundred yards along the beach, 'It's very soft, much softer than here.'

Valerie made her way back to the car, where the ground was locked together by tough, short grass.

Navid opened the passenger side. 'Back to the village.'

The few houses formed little more than a hamlet, but there were people. Valerie stayed with the car, checking the oil and water, letting Navid go and make enquiries.

After a while, he made his way back circumnavigating the potholes and a sleeping dog. 'He's picked up a Land Rover.'

Wiping the dipstick on a rag, Valerie looked about. 'Have the population around here got nothing better to do than watch strangers go by?'

'Don't suppose they have.' He got back in and told Valerie to carry on along the road, 'Highlight of their day.'

'And we're the second,' she muttered.

The next stop was the same but came with extra information: a boat went out on long fishing trips at the next village.

'Very forthcoming.' Third gear gave out an extra growl as Valerie shifted through the box.

'Not much else to do, they jump at the chance of a chat. And mind that gearbox, or we'll end up walking.'

Valerie nursed the sickening Opel up an incline to a crossroads. The village was mainly to the right, the beach a few hundred feet down a winding track. Noticing the temperature gauge moving into the red, she pulled over and got out. 'This looks more promising.'

A dozen or more boats were drawn up. A harbour, of sorts, contained larger craft. In plain sight, a familiar vehicle was parked.

Simultaneously, while telling Navid the Land Rover belonged to the army, she noticed three or four armed men, then more. In all, she counted twenty-five, more or less. 'Not the best of odds.'

Navid looked at the pistol, 'No, not the best.'

The light faded around seven. Leaving the car, they made their way to the beach.

'You call it, Navid.' She said no more as she concentrated on keeping her footing on the uneven slope.

'Find him first.' Half crouching, he led the way to the only building on the harbourside. 'I can't see much point in splitting up; we've no communication, no backup.'

Valerie pressed her back against the wall, 'Pity they're not westerners.' In the half-light, she could just make out Navid's quizzical frown. 'They'd be half-cut by now.'

A shrill whistle accompanied a flash of lights up on the main road. They both stopped as a window opened, and a head appeared.

'Police?' Valerie's voice was hushed as she strained to see into the darkness. 'A crash? Or have they just come across the Opel?'

'No idea.' As the window closed, Navid started moving again. 'Come on, we need to get Bentley... that's if he hasn't gone already.'

Nailed to the door, dirty sacking covered a broken glass panel. Tentatively, Navid drew a corner to one side.

He let it slide back and turned to Valerie. 'Two on the right, one at a desk, three to the left. All armed, but the guns are slung over their shoulders. I'll cover the ones on the right and the guy at the desk; you cover the three on the left... They're close to each other; there won't be a problem.'

Valerie's answer was all but inaudible. 'Thanks.'

'On three. One... two... three.'

Navid swung the door open and levelled his pistol. Valerie followed and pointed at the group of three. No problem, just as Navid had predicted. He pulled the slide on his automatic and spoke quietly in Persian. It had the desired effect, or at least as far as Valerie could tell, it had. Weapons clattered to the floor as they raised their hands. The one at the desk got up and moved back. A little more Persian and Navid had them corralled in a corner.

Watching the captives, Valerie kicked the AK-47s into a heap. 'Has he left?'

'We'll have a couple of those.' Navid pointed a toe towards the rifles, 'And no, Bentley's still around.'

When Valerie had picked out two of the rifles, Navid threw the rest from the window. A series of splashes confirmed they could not be used; at least for that night.

'Check around, see if there's anything we can tie them up with.' He spoke a little more Persian, and the men sat down, holding their hands on their heads.

She found handcuffs, not enough, but rope was also hanging from a hook on the wall.

Navid neither heard nor saw, but Valerie caught the movement in the corner of her eye. A man came in and pointed an AK at Navid. At the same time, Valerie came from his side and, putting a leg in front, pushed the man over. With her knee hard on his chest, landing on top, she kept the Glock trained on the men in the corner.

'Glad I brought you along.' Navid regained his composure and, dragging the gasping man to his feet, thrust him amongst his comrades.

Getting the men into a circle, all facing out, Navid handcuffed them arm to ankle.

Valerie stifled a laugh. 'Love to see them making a run for it.'

'Keys,' said Navid, 'any keys around that might fit the cuffs, throw them out the window.'

Navid squatted in front of one of the men, selecting the one that looked most unsure of himself. He took out his pistol and, waving it under the man's nose, talked slowly and quietly. The answer was interrupted by one of the others pulling at the handcuffs and spitting out what Valerie assumed were threats between gritted teeth. The blow across his mouth from Navid had blood pouring from a broken lip. It also had the desired effect of shutting him up.

Finishing his conversation with the first, Navid patted the man's face, got up and tucked the pistol into his belt. 'According to our friend.' He nodded towards the man he'd been talking with.' Bentley goes tomorrow, first light. He's back up the hill, a place with a blue door.'

'Blue door?' Valerie threw a glance over her shoulder. 'There's half a dozen, at a guess.'

Navid checked the AK-47 and told Valerie it was next to a pharmacy. 'You know, luminous green cross?'

'How long before this lot create a commotion?' Valerie waved her Glock at the group of men, 'Get themselves noticed?'

Navid went back to the one he had been questioning and asked something else. 'Parcel tape in the cupboard, behind you.'

'Jesus, there's being cooperative, and there's being very cooperative. He must be scared stiff of you.' Throwing Navid one of two rolls, Valerie started covering mouths.

Before he began from the other side, Navid seemed to be making threats.

'Telling them to be good boys?'

'Something like that.'

Out on the harbour wall, the twilight had gone. Guiding them back up the hill, one or two lamps created yellow pools on the uneven street. As Navid had said, a pharmacy stood to one side of a squat building fronted with a blue door.

Valerie peered through a side window. 'Last time I burst in on a bunch of bad guys, I broke up a poker game.'

'Don't think it's poker,' said Navid, holding the AK to the side of his face.

'Well, it ain't a bridge party.' Valerie held her hand towards the door, 'Shall we?'

The door didn't yield to Navid's kick. He tried several more times as shouting came from inside. 'How many locks have they got on this bloody thing?!'

Valerie stood to Navid's side, then they both went at it with hunched shoulders. It gave, resulting in them both losing their balance. Bullets flew over the top as they fell to their knees. If it had been Valerie's call, the outcome would almost certainly have been different. Laying on his side, Navid coolly sprayed the two men crammed together in the narrow hallway.

Valerie realised she hadn't looked too carefully at the men around the table. 'Was Bentley among them?' Getting to his feet, Navid shook his head.

'Must be upstairs.'

'There's the small matter of the card players first.'

187

The corridor led off to a 'T'— one room to the left, one to the right. At Navid's command, they jumped, back-to-back, and let a shower of bullets fly in opposite directions. No one was there.

A short flight of stairs ran up to an extended mezzanine.

'No,' said Valerie, holding Navid back, 'that's a quick way to wind up dead.' She let the rest of the AK's clip off into the overhanging ceiling. As Navid kept the stairway covered, Valerie reversed the two magazines that had been bound together. She changed the rifle to a single shot and squeezed the trigger again, this time slowly.

Navid made his way up. As bullets flew past his shoulder, he let out two short bursts. 'No, Bentley,' he said, rolling over bodies with his boot.

A commotion outside had them running to a back door.

Again, Valerie followed as Navid led the way. 'The last place we want to get caught in,' she shouted.

'Shh.' Navid looked left and right as they ran into a back street.

'Shh? A bit too late for shh.'

'Keep bloody quiet,' he hissed, 'the bastards are everywhere.'

'You're right there,' came a voice as the bolt of an AK echoed behind them.

'Bloody Bentley.' Valerie dropped the rifle and raised her hands. At the same time, men came from in front, one of them ripping the rifle from Navid's grasp.

They were shoved at gunpoint back into the house. Stepping over bodies, they went into the room where the card game had been going on. Leaving just Bentley and one other, the rest of the men started clearing bodies.

Bentley flicked up a cigarette and put a match to it. 'So, Navid, playing both ends against the middle, are we?'

'Not really, but you wouldn't understand, so you just think what you want. It isn't going to make much difference.'

'Well, you're fucking right there. All that's to be decided is when you get blown away. You, lady, get to live a little longer... Hostage.'

Gunfire from outside brought shouting from the hallway. Bentley flung the back of his fist across Valerie's mouth, 'Who you brought with you?!' Grinding the cigarette into the floor, he lifted the AK, pointing it at Valerie's face, 'You fucking cow!'

She ducked, grabbing at his testicles as she went down. The grip was vice-like, making him drop the gun.

Taking Valerie's lead, Navid took the other by surprise. Ripping the weapon from his grasp, he thrust it several times into the man's astonished face. He was out cold.

Navid told Valerie to keep Bentley covered as he looked into the corridor.

'They're gone.' He pointed the rifle at Bentley, 'We need him alive,' then took the gun butt to the window. 'Don't want to be running out the front door; God knows what's happening out there. You go out; I'll shove this one after you.'

With Bentley between them, Valerie looked out onto the main road. 'Jesus, they've got white armbands; they're ours.'

Recognising Valerie, the lieutenant ran across the street. 'By the God above, thought you'd be dead.'

'Same thought crossed my mind once or twice.'

The lieutenant ushered them to one side. 'Explain later, for the moment, we need to keep you out of the line of fire. I brought some spares.' He handed them each a white armband. 'Can you keep an eye on him?' He pushed Bentley up against the wall. 'Best if you keep out of the fighting, don't want any accidents.'

Valerie was going to point out they now had the armbands but changed her mind. The lieutenant was right, and there was not much they could do to help. It all seemed to be going smoothly.

Navid took out a pack of cigarettes.

'What about me?' Bentley held out a hand. With both of them now relaxed and with nothing to lose, Bentley took a chance. He pushed the lit cigarette into the back of Valerie's hand and ran. He went down one alleyway, up a side street, across patios, and vanished.

Valerie flicked her injured hand. 'Shit! I don't fancy explaining that one to the lieutenant.'

Taking the rifles, they cautiously went out onto the main street. Two soldiers with armbands ran down the opposite side.

'Rachid!' Valerie screamed.

He ushered the other soldier to keep on down the road, took Valerie in his arms, and kissed her cheek.

Embarrassed, he jumped back. 'Sorry, I... er.'

'Don't be so bloody stupid.' She pulled him back into her arms, holding on tightly, she kissed him on the lips.

'When you two have finished,' Navid tapped Valerie on the shoulder, 'we still have a fight on our hands. Not to mention a search.'

'The Land Rover.' Kissing Rachid again, she let him go. 'He'll make for the Land Rover.'

'Tell your men we want him alive,' said Navid as they ran back towards the harbour, 'We've got to take him alive.'

Valerie slowed. Dropping the rifle, she held a hand to her side. 'What a time to get the bloody stitch. Go on, don't wait for me.' Doubled over, she rubbed at the pain.

The gunfire stopped. 'Presume we won,' she said, recovering her breath. The pain persisted as the Land Rover came up the road.

189

It screeched to a halt, and brandishing a sidearm, Bentley got out. 'In! Get in!'

She struggled as he tried to bundle her into the passenger seat. Bullets ricocheted from the road as men ran towards the truck. In the shadows, she could just make out Rachid shouting for the men to stop before they hit her.

Getting her in, holding her arm and trying to drive with one hand, Bentley put his foot to the floor. Valerie struggled free but received a fist in the jaw.

'Now sit still! There's nothing left to lose; I'll put a bullet in your brain if it comes down to it.'

The few street lights faded behind as they turned east. The gun in Bentley's hand followed Valerie as she leaned over the back of the seat.

'Pepsi. Thought there might be one left.'

'Jesus, you pick some fucking times to get a drink. What are you, an advert for the bleedin' company?'

She'd drunk most of the can when Bentley asked for a swig.

'I think there's another.' Again, she bent over into the rear and found one almost immediately, but waited a moment. The Land Rover jumped to one side as it hit another of the many potholes. Tumbling about, she vigorously shook the Pepsi.

Still sipping the remains of her drink, she handed the full one over. Holding the gun, steering wheel and can, Bentley was covered in a shower of aerated cola as he ripped the tab away.

Valerie grabbed at the pistol. 'Didn't think you'd fall for that again!'

Several times she managed to smash the pistol against his nose and teeth. Blows and Bentley's obscenities mixed as a screech came from one of the brakes. As smoke poured from the locked-up wheel, the Land Rover hit another hole. Trapped in a rut, the vehicle ran to the edge of the cliff.

Several pairs of headlights lit up the surroundings from behind as Bentley failed to keep the vehicle on the road. Without seatbelts, they tumbled around inside the terminally damaged vehicle as it rolled, end over end, towards the drop.

A can of fuel flew from behind, striking Valerie's shoulder as they came to rest on a ledge. For a moment, only the ticking of cooling metal broke the silence. The chasing vehicles lit up the scene as headlights were pointed at the Land Rover teetering on the edge.

Shaking her head, Valerie heard shouting from up the slope. As men gathered around, she felt a hand grab at her arm, then a blow through the window knocked it away.

'It's okay.' It was Rachid's voice.

The door was shut, buckled against the frame. Putting one foot on the wing, he pulled at the handle. It came off, uselessly taking a few fittings with it. Again, a hand grabbed at Valerie, this time at her throat.

'You bastard!' Rachid drew his automatic, sending two rounds in front of Valerie; one of them into Bentley's thigh.

She squirmed around, pushing her feet against the door. 'Think that slowed him down.'

Rachid grunted a smile. The door flew open and hung from its twisted hinges.

Pressing down with her hands, she tried to release herself. 'Foot's trapped.'

The Land Rover rocked as Rachid got in and felt down her leg towards her trapped boot.

'Touch me there, and you'll have to marry me.'

The Land Rover slid a couple of feet.

Valerie's foot was still jammed. She looked across where Bentley slumped over to one side was pushing a rag into his bleeding wound. Beyond, only the sheer drop was visible. The Land Rover slipped again. One of the men shouted something in Persian. Valerie understood neither the shout nor Rachid's terse reply.

She felt the balance of the vehicle change. 'Get out, Rachid!' She kicked him with her free foot, 'Get the fuck out, or we're both going over!'

From behind, one of the men tried to pull him away; only to receive a clenched fist and, Valerie presumed, more Persian profanities.

'Get out, Rachid,' Valerie pleaded while viciously pulling his hair away, 'both of us going over the edge is bloody stupid.'

The Land Rover rocked as, again, Rachid felt down her leg. He pulled his other hand in and felt for the laces. A short exhalation of breath and his fingers touched the neatly tied bow. The ends came away quickly. Then, reaching down, he unthreaded the lace and threw it over his shoulder.

'Looks like we're playing Cinderella again,' he said, easing her foot out.

A gunshot came from the cab.

The Land Rover door gave a departing blow, hitting Valerie and propelling both her and Rachid to the ground as it fell from the edge.

Faces surrounding her turned grey, then black, as she lost consciousness.

# SIXTEEN

Cloudy white shapes fluttered around in a warm breeze. Slowly Valerie turned her head. She felt peaceful. As an angel came to her side, music she didn't recognise filtered through. The angel brushed the hair from Valerie's forehead, then held her hand. She spoke, but nothing recognisable.

Why wasn't it English? For Christ's sake, the official language in heaven has got to be English. Another angel drifted in; this one she did understand. They must be changing shifts. She must have been assigned because she spoke the "official language". Curiously, neither had wings. Must be apprentices.

Then apprehension gripped, followed by fear. Dear God, how was she going to explain she was an atheist? Had they made a mistake, and she'd slipped through? Maybe they would never find out, lost in a myriad of floating souls. Say nothing.

From behind the angels, a tall figure, dressed in black, materialised. Slick black hair, a neatly trimmed beard, contrasted with pale skin. The fear returned, but this time accompanied by panic. This was an anti-room. He had come to take her to the underworld.

'No, I didn't understand.' She found it hard to speak; fear was gripping her throat. 'A God in heaven all seemed too far-fetched,' she said in a panic, 'it wasn't my fault. I'm sorry, don't take me away.'

As Lucifer leant forward, Valerie screamed, thrashing about.

His hand was calming as he patted her shoulder, his English perfect.

'It's all right, Miss Stone.' Curious he should address her as Miss Stone.

'Pardon?' Her heartbeat started to slow.

'You've had a bad time... but all's well now.' He tapped his temple, 'Optic nerve. You've had some work done not so long ago. After a blow? I noticed the scar under your hair. We did some scans.'

Still trying to take it in, Valerie nodded.

'They did a good job,' he continued. 'Have you had a little blurring to one side?'

Valerie nodded, 'Yes, but it seems to have gone.'

'That's normal. It might come and go but will be gone for good in a few weeks. There is an outside chance you may have a slight fuzziness to the extreme side, but nothing to worry about.'

Relieved, she fell back against the pillow.

'Got a friend to see you.' He stood to one side, and there was Navid. She almost flung herself from the bed, hanging on like a shipwrecked sailor to the last piece of floating timber.

Sitting on the bed, Navid patted her hand, 'What was that all about?'

She hung on for a few seconds. 'Nothing, I'll tell you sometime. What happened?'

'Later,' he said. 'You need more time; get back to normal.'

***

The next day, Navid was waiting at the end of the ward as Valerie stuffed her few things into a rucksack. She again pulled a baseball cap over the rapidly disappearing scar.

'Got you booked into a hotel on the edge of town.'

'Town? Where am I?'

'City,' he corrected himself, 'Tehran.'

'Where's Rachid?'

Navid went quiet for a moment, then said, 'He got hit by the door that got you. He's in hospital. Restricted visiting for now.'

'How is he?'

'He's okay, needs rest, only family allowed to see him.'

***

Outside the hotel, Navid and Valerie sat under a large sunshade. The desert rolled away from the raised veranda, the setting sun splashing red fingers across the dunes.

Valerie sipped at a mineral water, thick with lemon. 'Pity it's not Chablis.'

'We might be popular at the moment,' said Navid, 'but not *that* popular.'

'Bentley?'

Navid's reply was flat, devoid of emotion, 'Bottom of the Gulf of Oman, along with the Land Rover I presume; couldn't find his body.'

'Oh yeah, I remember. Bloody hell; the only reliable Land Rover ever made is at the bottom of the Gulf.' Valerie got up and looked out across the barren landscape. 'So, it's out there. The friggin' Sarin is still out there.'

'Yes, in the middle of thousands of square miles of sand.'

Navid cleared his throat. 'I did have a thought.'

'Oh yeah.'

'We couldn't find our friend's body. What if he's alive somewhere.'

'Go on.'

'Bit of a conundrum; isn't it?'

'In what way?'

'Well, he knows where it is; the Sarin that is.'

Unscrewing the bottle of water Valerie twigged what Navid was

194

thinking. 'It can only be in one of the places they stooped at; so he knows where it is, but he doesn't know that he knows. Scarry.'

Realising they were pursuing a ghost Valerie changed the subject. 'What were you doing in Isis?'

'Cover's gone, so I don't suppose it matters anymore. I was sending information back, anything that would help.'

'There was more than that; you weren't just stooging around.'

'Innocent people were in the middle of a filthy regime, and they couldn't help themselves or their kids, or... I managed to get some out, back to civilisation,' he said, pre-empting her question.

When asked who he worked for, Navid shook his head.

Valerie smiled. 'You need to get out, find life somewhere else. Find a woman, and have kids. It'll dim with the years.'

Navid managed a smile. 'The Caribbean... Always fancied The West Indies, surround myself with water instead of sand.'

'Do it, Navid, you've given enough... And of course, you could invite me over sometime.' She looked thoughtful, prodding at the ice in her drink. 'But I'll tell you one thing, you were good, bloody good... Frightened the hell out of me.'

\*\*\*

The following day, Valerie was woken by a gentle knock. Yawning, she pulled on a shift and opened the door.

'Sorry, Navid, been a bit tired lately.' Looking at her watch, she waved him in.

'It's Rachid; he's back in the land of the living.'

'We can see him?'

'Sure. I'll take you.'

The hospital was large, white and modern. Travelling in the lift, Navid explained that Rachid had attained some sort of hero status. 'Top floor, overlooking the city, every extra you can think of.'

The private room was similar to the one she had been in. A cooling breeze ruffled light, cotton curtains. No longer needed, medical equipment had been pushed to the side. The television was switched off; all was quiet except for the high notes that always seemed to escape from headphones.

'Beyoncé or The Who?' asked Valerie.

With a bit of difficulty, Rachid took the headphones off. 'Adele.'

Valerie sat on the side of the bed and looked into his eyes. Neither of them spoke. Unsaid words, needing no translation, passed from one to the other.

After a while, she took her hand from his and stroked his forehead. 'British music,' she said softly, 'and I should bloody well think so.' She

195

bent across, leaving the gentlest of kisses on his lips, before whispering, 'Thank you.'

Over the next hour, little about the past few weeks was discussed. While Navid and the nurse remained silent, Rachid and Valerie talked about his family and her family and continued their opinions on modern music.

'Sorry,' he said, putting the back of a fist to a yawn, 'body clock's all back to front. Need to get out and grab some exercise, return to normal.'

They carried on for a few more minutes until he surrendered to the unequal struggle, and fell asleep.

\*\*\*

The next morning Valerie was booked on the eleven o'clock flight to London.

On the way, she asked Navid to stop by the hospital. 'Just say goodbye to Rachid.'

'We've sedated him,' the nurse said, 'he kept threatening to go out for a run.' She smiled. 'I can wake him if you wish?'

Valerie shook her head, 'No, it's okay, keep him under. I've got a plane to catch, just wanted to come in one last time.'

By the bedside, the kiss on his forehead was soft, the whispered thank you, barely audible.

She removed her Rolex, fastened it on the young man's wrist and quietly left.